THE
STRANGER'S
WIFE

ANNA-LOU WEATHERLEY

Published by Bookouture in 2020

An imprint of Storyfire Ltd.
Carmelite House
50 Victoria Embankment
London EC4Y 0DZ

www.bookouture.com

ISBN: 978-1-83888-218-1
eBook ISBN: 978-1-83888-217-4

THE
STRANGER'S
WIFE

For CB, DC and L&F D

'Hell is empty and all the devils are here.'

— William Shakespeare

PROLOGUE

Beth

June 2018

Something is wrong. The house is silent; too silent. It's never quiet in Beth Lawler's house, not with a boisterous four-year-old running amok. Even when her daughter is taking an afternoon nap – a habit she must get her out of before she starts school – there's still always background noise of some sort; daytime TV, the radio station that Marta likes to listen – sometimes sing along – to or the low hum of white goods.

'Hel-looooo?' she calls out instinctively, throws her keys and handbag down on the console table in the hallway, kicks off her gym shoes, even though she hasn't been anywhere near the gym today.

'Marta? Hel-loooo…' She feels a trickle of something inside the pit of her stomach; it's not fear exactly, but it's somewhere approaching it. 'Marta?'

She calls out to her housekeeper again. Well, housekeeper-cum-nanny-cum-friend as it had turned out. The nanny part hadn't been in the original job description though; neither had the friend bit, but both of these things had transpired quite organically, something she was now extremely grateful for. Initially it had been Evan who had suggested they hire in some help.

'I want you to put all your focus on Lily,' he'd said. 'I don't want you to have to worry about stacking dishwashers and keeping the place clean and tidy. We can pay someone else to do all the menial, day-to-day stuff.' She was aware that usually this would be music to most women's ears, but secretly she had been disappointed. She had hoped to return to her job as a nurse six months after giving birth, maybe just part-time to begin with.

'You never need to go back to work, Beth,' he'd said when she had gone on maternity leave. 'Not now you're about to embark on the most important and rewarding job of all. Besides, it's not as if we need the money, is it?'

She had missed the sense of purpose her job had provided though, and her colleagues at the hospital, so having Marta on hand had turned out to be something of a godsend. Lily had been a tricky baby, plagued by colic and reflux, and she had spent the best part of the first year of her daughter's life in a cranky, sleep-deprived fug as a result. She didn't know how she would've coped without Marta back then and in truth feared she might not have coped at all. Now she was glad that Evan had insisted on an extra pair of hands because she had bonded with the kind and intelligent Norwegian girl who shared her dry sense of humour and happened to be blessed with the patience of a saint. She trusted Marta; trusted her with the things that were most precious to her. Including her secrets…

She calls Marta's name again but the cold, unsettling silence remains. The pushchair is in the hallway and Marta's Fiat 500 is still in the driveway. Odd. This is an indicator that something's definitely not right. She takes the stairs, two by two, calling out her name intermittently. She's not overly concerned at this point.

She moves along the landing towards the nursery. The door is shut and she opens it with an unfamiliar trepidation, the source of which she doesn't fully understand. The room is dark, the ridiculously expensive handmade unicorn appliqué curtains are drawn, daylight straining to filter through them. Creeping towards the cot bed on the balls of her feet, she peers into it and is relieved to see her daughter sleeping. Lily immediately stirs as if she senses her mother's presence, causing her to spring backwards. She studies her daughter's perfect face from a safe distance, her eyes closed, like two ticks on a page, her lashes dark like her own, curling upwards. Lily is undoubtedly a beautiful child – everyone says so – and this makes her feel proud, she supposes. She wants to touch her tiny face but is scared she'll wake her. The rush of love she feels watching her sleeping daughter soon dissipates into something else though; a terrible gnawing guilt that pulls at her lower intestines, tugging at her guts. Lily will forgive her, won't she? She's only four years old; she won't remember this time in her life. She'll understand when she is older, she tells herself in an attempt to appease her nagging conscience – and yet she can't shake the feeling that she's directly betraying her own daughter. *She's not a bad person, is she?*

She takes a breath, snaps herself out of her maudlin moment as her eye wanders to the baby monitor on the changing table next to the cot bed. It's not illuminated. It's not switched on. Now that *is* odd. Marta wouldn't leave Lily sleeping without turning the monitor on; it's a big house and they always switch it on in case Lily wakes up startled and they cannot hear her call out.

A sense of unease is gaining momentum inside of her, pushing past the guilt and up from her guts through to her diaphragm. She calls Marta's name again, loudly and more urgently this time. 'Marta! Marrr–ta! Where are you?' Nothing. Silence.

Leaving the nursery, she checks the bathroom as a matter of course, plus Marta's bedroom, but it's empty. She takes the stairs, her blonde hair swishing around her shoulders with her increasing momentum – and panic.

'Marta!' She pokes her head around the living-room door. It looks neat and tidy and smells freshly cleaned, but she's not there. She checks the downstairs cloakroom. No joy. Her initial perplexion has morphed into something more frantic now and she heads into the large, open-plan kitchen diner, the hub of her home. Her laptop is open on the oak table where she'd left it that morning. Marta's handbag – a colourful fabric hippie-type thing that she'd picked up in Camden Market – is still slung over the back of one of the kitchen chairs. She hasn't taken it. *She must be in.*

She notices that the sliding doors that lead out onto the landscaped garden are open – another oddity, given that it's chilly and drizzling outside, even though it's well into June. She scans the garden: nothing. She slides the door shut behind her, locks it. Beth shakes her head, confused, concerned. Even in the highly unlikely scenario that Marta has nipped to the shops and left Lily alone for five minutes, she certainly wouldn't have left the doors unlocked, let alone wide open. Were they open when she had left that morning, the doors? She doesn't recall. She doesn't think so. No. Definitely not, why would they be? Suddenly she feels cross. Marta would never be so irresponsible, would she? She trusted her friend with her child and her home. She trusted her with her life.

She tries to push back the nagging fear that something has happened. *Something horrible.* Maybe she's left a note. She checks the kitchen table for one, but there is nothing; no note. Marta knows Beth's schedule better than she does. And Marta knows where she has been today…

She stands still for a moment in a bid to gather her thoughts. Surely if there had been an emergency of some sort then Marta would've called her? Marta's handbag… her phone! She fishes around inside the bag for it but it's not there, nor her purse. She runs into the hallway, retrieves her own phone from her handbag and dials Marta's number.

'I'm sorry but the mobile number you have called is currently unavailable…'

Shit! She dials again and is greeted by the same parrot-fashion reply. *Shit, shit, shit.* Why is her phone off? Marta's phone is never off. In fact, she cannot recall a time since she's known her when she hasn't been able to get hold of her – not once.

Suddenly a chill comes over her, like a cold knife against the back of her neck. *Something has happened to Marta. Something awful.*

As Beth contemplates her next move, she remembers that she didn't check the master bedroom upstairs; her and Evan's room – well, hers really because she can't remember the last time they had shared a bed, not since Lily had been born anyway. Maybe Marta had gone to change the bedclothes and had lain down and fallen asleep. She knows it's highly unlikely, but her mind is desperately searching for some sort of rational explanation.

With a trickle of hope, she rushes upstairs and crashes through the bedroom door. The bed has been newly made and there's a basket of dried clothes on top of it, some of which have been discarded, as though she were in the middle of folding them and had simply abandoned them mid-task, but there's no sign of Marta herself. She hears Lily stirring in the bedroom next door and inwardly wills her to stay asleep – she needs to get her head around the situation; she needs to think. Frustrated, she returns downstairs and sits down at the kitchen table, tells herself to keep calm and that Marta will be back any minute. Maybe she just had to rush off somewhere, some kind of emergency, but that doesn't explain why her car is still in the driveway, or why she's left her handbag behind but taken her phone and purse.

Beth puts a hand to her chest to steady the thud of her heart against her ribs and tries to envisage her friend walking through the front door, apologising for scaring her in her strange yet endearing accent. But her instincts are aggressively chopping through her positive thoughts like a machete. Something is wrong, very wrong and she senses it like an animal senses danger. She'll make a cup of tea, no, coffee – it will sharpen her mind; help her to focus. She knows she should call the police but is fearful of what will happen if she does, if the police start sniffing around…

'*Oh God, Marta, where are you?*' She says the words aloud in desperation. '*Please don't do this to me.*' How long should she leave it before she dials 999? Another hour? A few? Should she wait until tomorrow? Will that look strange? After all, Marta's an adult, isn't she? Maybe she's just gone for a long walk and she'll be back soon, maybe… Beth knows she's trying to convince herself of this unlikely scenario so as not to involve the police. And she knows why. *Jesus Christ, what should she do?* She's fully aware that she has a moral duty to report her as missing but dreads what will inevitably come next. Perhaps it's for the best; perhaps it was all meant to come out this way and Marta going AWOL was the cosmos's way of telling her she needed to do it now, *today*.

She decides to check Marta's bedroom, see if she's taken anything. At first glance, nothing appears amiss. Marta's a neat freak and keeps her bedroom as tidy as she does the rest of the house. The bed is made, pillows plumped and Marta's small collection of beauty products remain neatly displayed on the dressing table. She opens the drawer, lightly fingers the contents – cotton pads, feminine products, some Norwegian face cream… She closes it, her eye noticing that the wardrobe door is slightly ajar. Inspecting the contents, she notes there's some empty hangers… and Marta's weekend holdall, a vibrant seventies-style carpetbag, is missing. Has she taken it? Perplexed, she thinks of calling up some of Marta's friends. She hardly has any family left – a brother she thinks, back in Norway – but she can't recall his name and certainly doesn't have his phone number. Perhaps she'll look him up on Facebook…

Returning back downstairs to the kitchen, she chews her lip as she stares out through the glass doors, trying desperately to get some clarity on her thoughts, only they're all jumbled up and overlapping, not one of them quite reaching fruition and… something in the garden suddenly catches Beth's eye, on the back lawn. At first she thinks it's maybe something the builders have left; they're having a swimming pool dug out at the moment and the garden is in a state of disarray, filled with equipment and tools.

She pushes her face closer to the glass and squints. Instinctively, she opens the sliding doors and goes outside. She strides across the lawn with urgency, still in her socks. It's drizzling heavily, the kind of rain that gets into your eyes and makes your hair frizzy. She feels her heartbeat increase as she moves, adrenalin giving her an almost unbearable lightness under her damp feet. She can feel her trachea tighten slightly; fear creeping in like tendrils around her neck. She recognises it instantly. It's Marta's favourite scarf – that yellow silky thing with an odd pattern on it that she often wears. Why is it in the garden, abandoned like this?

She bends down to pick it up. It feels damp between her fingers and she can no longer stave off the feeling of terror that is threatening to engulf her.

The drizzle has turned into rain now – heavier drops splash spitefully against her skin. 'Oh my God… *oh my God!* Marta!' she says, as she runs inside to get her phone.

CHAPTER ONE

Dan

October 2019

I can recall it clearly. It was my day off when the call came in. I remember because I'd been on the sofa trying to sleep and my phone had woken me with a start. It wasn't long after Rachel and our unborn baby had been killed in the motorcycle accident by that 'man' whose name I cannot bear to say. It had only been a few months – maybe six, maybe longer – but it still felt like just a few days had passed. I was in the grip of the first stages of grief and sleep, back then, was like a twilight zone I slipped in and out of. I've never had an unbroken night's sleep since she died – but at least I can manage a few hours straight now, which in my book means I'm winning. At least it'll stand me in good stead when Junior arrives. Fiona's only a couple of weeks off giving birth, or 'dropping' as she prefers to call it. It's not a term I'm particularly fond of. I've had nightmares about 'dropping' my imminent offspring already, but who am I to argue with a heavily pregnant woman – or any woman at all for that matter?

Anyway, back then I could never have imagined that I would be where I am now, about to become a father with a colleague-cum-friend-cum-lover who I managed to get in the club after a one-night stand. But as I of all people should know, life has its own agenda sometimes and takes you down a road you never planned to travel.

'MP, boss, Buckhurst Hill area, possible foul play.' DS Lucy Davis had been breathy on the phone, like she'd just run up some stairs, although I'd put it down to excitement at the time. Davis was – still is – brimming with enthusiasm for homicide. I like the fact she's not yet jaded by the horrors we human beings commit towards each other. I hope she never changes or begins to see the world as I do now.

'A Mrs Beth Lawler... she just called to say she returned home this morning and her 28-year-old nanny, Marta Larssen, is missing... left the little one asleep upstairs, alone apparently... back doors open.'

I'd rubbed the grit from eyes.

'No note?'

'Nope. Nothing. Left her bag, keys... car still in the driveway... just disappeared without a trace. Never done anything like it before apparently, says she's highly reliable, would never leave the child alone, not even for five minutes... Delaney's already there at the property.'

I'd groaned. It was all we needed. Davis knows I'm not Delaney's greatest fan – and why. His presence always seems to put me ill at ease, like he's always trying to get one over on me or trip me up.

'Brilliant.'

'Exactly,' Davis had said. 'So we need to get down there, gov, pronto.'

I'd already been sliding one arm into an unwashed shirt and trying to button it up one handed as she'd given me the address.

The first thing I remember about walking into the Lawlers' home was the tension. It felt oppressive somehow; the feeling had covered me like a blanket, made me feel cumbersome like I'd just eaten a big lunch. The high-pitched wails of a little girl crying had made it nigh on impossible for me to concentrate on what the woman in front of me was trying to say. Beth Lawler was trying to console her daughter, concern, maybe even fear etched on her face as she'd tried to calm her. I'm fascinated by how much children sense things. They're often a good indicator. Without the capacity of a full range of vocabulary, their feelings are transmitted through their primary instincts. We adults could learn a lot from them, and I remember that day Lily Lawler seemed particularly distressed.

'I'm sorry' – I'd looked at the woman in front of me apologetically and then at Davis, who was straining to listen over the din, 'but can we go somewhere quieter where we can talk?'

'I'm so sorry.' Beth Lawler had apologised once more. 'The terrible twos seemed to have gone into the terrible threes and fours…' I'd detected the strain in the woman's voice as she'd frantically tried to appease the girl.

'Tell me, Mrs Lawler – Beth, isn't it?'

She'd nodded, attempting to soothe her fractious daughter with a 'shhhh'.

'Tell me what happened from the beginning.'

CHAPTER TWO

Beth

June 2018

'Marta. Her name is Marta Larssen. She's from Norway. She's twenty-eight years old and—' Beth was trying to calm Lily. She'd been squirming and fussing, crying intermittently, and she couldn't concentrate on what the policeman was asking her. She can't concentrate on anything. All she can think about is that now that she's called the police, everything will have to come out. And she doesn't want it to come out, *not like this.* Beth feels the tension fizzing through her body and silently wills Lily to be quiet. *Please be quiet. Give me a chance to think!*

'Maybe I should take her into another room? Distract her a bit with some toys.' The policewoman smiles at her kindly, hand outstretched towards Lily. 'Then you can give Detective Riley as much info as possible, and we can find out what's happened to Marta, OK?'

'OK.' Her brain struggles to process what is happening; too many thoughts are rushing through it for her to gain purchase on a single one. 'I'm sorry,' she says, checking herself. 'Would you like to sit down? Can I get you something to drink? Tea or coffee? Juice? Water?'

'No. Thank you.'

The detective takes a seat at the table. 'So when was the last time you saw Marta?'

Beth swallows. Common sense commands her to tell the truth. Perhaps if she does then they will understand, but she can't bring herself to. Perhaps they'll find Marta before she needs to say anything at all. She prays that will be the case.

'I saw her this morning, before I left for the gym.' She knows this is a lie. *She is lying to the police.*

'What time was that?'

'About 11.35 a.m. I like to get there for midday and be finished by 1 p.m.'

'What's the name of the gym?' The detective nods and takes notes.

'The Source; it's the spa and gym down on Queens Road.'

'How long have you been a member?'

She pauses, wondering why he is asking. Is it relevant? She doesn't think so. She swallows back the nerves that dance in her throat, tells herself he's just doing his job. The other detective enters the kitchen then, the one who had arrived first, Martin somebody she thought he'd said his name was.

'Gone through the house, gov,' he says, shaking his head. 'Nothing.'

'Check the outsides, front and back,' the detective in charge replies. 'Sorry, Beth, carry on.'

'About five years ago. I joined not long after we moved in here.'

'We?'

'Yes. Me and my husband Evan. He's on his way home right now.'

She had called Evan, breathless, as soon as she'd hung up from the police. She had wanted to call *him* instead but somehow had the foresight not to.

'Marta has gone missing.'

'Missing? What do you mean, missing?'

'I mean she's… gone… disappeared, Evan. I came home to find the house empty; Lily was asleep in her bed… alone… Marta's car is here, and her bag, I think some of her belongings have gone… but… no note… no phone call, nothing! She's just vanished. I can't get her on the phone and the back doors were wide open…'
She had heard the panic escalate in her own voice as she relayed the situation to her husband on the other end of the line.

'OK… OK, calm down… are you sure she's not just popped to the shops or something? Gone for a walk… have you tried calling her?'

He hadn't been listening to her.

'Yes, I've tried calling her! Her phone is off. And her purse is missing too. But her keys are still in her handbag… She wouldn't just "pop to the shops" without them, would she? And she wouldn't leave Lily on her own – never. I'm scared to death that something's happened to her…'

'Her keys are still there?'

'Yes, they're still bloody here… but she isn't! She's gone!'

'Please calm down Beth,' he'd said wearily. 'There's going to be some kind of explanation for this, OK?'

'I've called the police.'

'The police?'

She'd had to stop herself from screaming down the phone at him.

'Yes! The police, Evan! They're on their way now.'

He had been silent on the line for a moment.

'You said, when you got back this morning, Marta was missing. Where had you been?'

'To the gym,' she'd replied, quickly adding, 'Like I always do on a Friday morning. Please come home. I want you to be here when the police come. I'm worried, Evan; I think something dreadful has happened to her.'

'It'll be nothing,' he'd said, 'but I'll leave now. I should be back within the hour, traffic depending, OK?'

'OK,' she'd said quietly.

'It's all going to be OK, Beth,' he'd said before hanging up.

'What time did you get home, Mrs Lawler?'

She feels the detective's eyes on her and the nerves in her throat tighten into panic. *It wasn't supposed to be like this, not like this.*

'Call me Beth, please,' she says, because that's what she's supposed to say, isn't it? She clears her throat, can hear Lily and the policewoman next door, playing with wooden building bricks, can see the other detective in the garden, searching. 'I got back around 1.15 p.m., 1.20 p.m., something like that. I called Marta's name when I came in, just expected to see her, like usual. But she didn't answer. I went to look for her, checked on Lily…'

'She was in bed asleep?'

'Yes. She still has an afternoon nap… I know she's probably a little old and I should phase it out but… but anyway, I kept on calling her name, but there was no answer and—'

'Can you remember what Marta was wearing this morning?'

Beth tries to think but she can't focus properly. She is silently freaking out.

'Jeans… grey skinny jeans and a white shirt or vest top maybe… she had a cardigan over the top. Mustard thing, long, and Converse trainers, white ones, although they were more grey – a bit grubby.' She feels a stab of grief as she describes Marta to the detective, suddenly wondering if she'll ever see Marta and her quirky dress sense again. The detective is scribbling furiously in his notebook.

'How tall is Marta? Do you have any recent photographs of her?'

'Gosh, let me think.' *Gosh.* She's never used that word before, not that she could ever recall. She feels self-conscious, like she is on the outside of herself looking in.

'She's tall; around five feet seven or eight, I'd say.'

The detective nods and looks up as the other detective enters the kitchen from the garden.

'No sign of anything, boss.'

He nods at him.

'Thanks, Martin.'

He's turned his attention back to her. 'Did you notice anything unusual when you returned home Mrs… sorry, Beth? Was anything amiss?'

'No,' she says quickly, too quickly maybe. Her paranoia is making her jumpy. 'Actually yes – yes there was. The baby monitor wasn't switched on. Marta always switches it on whenever Lily goes down for a nap. It's a big house and sometimes she gets frightened when she wakes up alone. I thought that was odd. She's really reliable like that, she wouldn't forget… and so I went downstairs, called out to her again, a few times. Her car was still in the driveway, still *is* in the driveway. Her handbag' – she points to it on the kitchen table – 'it's still here, with her keys in it. Her phone doesn't seem to be here although I rang a dozen times, but it's switched off. I think maybe she's taken some of her clothes but I really can't be sure… she didn't have many clothes…' Suddenly she feels like crying. 'I… I… checked all the rooms, checked the whole house a few times over.'

'So the baby monitor was off. Anything else struck you as unusual?'

The questioning is making her nervous. Do they suspect something bad has happened to Martha, just like she does?

'The back doors were open – wide open – but there's no reason for them to be. The builders aren't due back for a day or two so it can't have been them who left them open. Besides, they don't have keys, and I'm sure they weren't open when I left the house.'

'You're having some work done?'

'Yes, we're building a swimming pool. My husband's firm are doing it. He owns a construction company, Lawler and Co.

We hope to have it ready in time for the summer. Lily loves swimming…'

The detective nods and she notices his eyes, a greyish blue, similar in colour to *his*. She finds this momentarily reassuring.

Where the bloody hell was Evan?

'So the doors were open? Had anything been taken, anything stolen?'

'Nothing. I've checked the house.'

'Jewellery? Paintings, anything of value?'

'No. Nothing's been touched and the lock hasn't been smashed.'

'OK. So the doors were open, and you went outside?'

'Yes. I looked out onto the garden, couldn't see Marta, but then something on the lawn caught my eye so I went outside and found her scarf on the grass, just by the pond.'

She points to it on the table, realising that it now has her DNA all over it. She made to pick it up again to show him.

'No! Please don't touch it, Beth.'

She snatches her hand back in alarm.

'I'm sorry,' he apologises. 'Forensics are on their way and we need to make sure there's no contamination. We'll need to take all of Marta's personal belongings, her handbag, phone, maybe her toothbrush…'

'Her *toothbrush*?'

'Yes, for DNA purposes. We'll have to take her car too. And the scarf, obviously.'

Beth feels her adrenalin spike.

'I'm assuming Marta has a passport? Have you checked to see if it's missing?'

'I didn't think to; I wouldn't even know where to look. I'm sorry.'

He holds his hand up. 'No, no, please… this is just standard procedure, you understand? We need to try and establish if Marta left of her own volition or if… or if other factors were involved.'

Beth nods sagely. 'Other factors' doesn't sound good.

'Did she seem OK when you left for the gym this morning – what time was that again? Did she seem agitated, or upset?'

'No, not at all. She seemed her usual happy self.' Beth shrugs. 'Just normal Marta.'

He asks her again what time she had left for the gym. Is he trying to trip her up?

'I left around 11.30ish, or thereabouts. *Now she's been forced to lie twice.* Her eyes follow his pen as he writes in his notebook, her guts churning.

'Can you think of any reason why Marta would just suddenly up and leave, Beth? Did she have a boyfriend, any relationship or family problems? Did she have any issues with alcohol or drugs, any illnesses or debts that you know of? Could there have been an emergency that might have forced her to leave the house suddenly? Were the two of you close? Would she have confided in you if she had a problem?'

Questions. All these questions are making her head spin.

Before she can answer, Evan blusters into the kitchen – finally.

'I came as quickly as I could, darling,' he says, leaning in to kiss her cheek. She feels herself flinch. He never calls her 'darling'. She had hoped his presence might've made her feel a little better, the familiarity of him giving her a modicum of comfort, but it has the opposite effect. He introduces himself to the detectives, shakes both their hands.

'Evan Lawler, pleased to meet you.'

'Likewise, Mr Lawler,' the detective says.

'Tell me what's happened.' Evan throws his keys onto the table and stands behind her, squeezing her shoulders. She feels sick.

'Marta's missing. She's just vanished.' She can feel herself hyperventilating as she wills her husband to stop rubbing her shoulders, something else he never normally does. *Please don't touch me.*

'I'm sure there's an explanation, Detective,' Evan says in a measured tone. 'Marta's not the type to just up and leave without good reason.'

She can't believe he is so calm. Ignoring him, she turns back to the detective.

'To answer your questions, Detective, no, she's really not a big drinker, and certainly doesn't do drugs. Marta's a vegan; she's into all that clean living and eating stuff. She doesn't have a boyfriend and yes, she would've told me if she had one because we're very close.' Although as she says it, it suddenly strikes her that maybe, like her, Martha had secrets too.

'Yes, they're like best friends, aren't you, darling?' Evan interjects. 'Tell each other *everything*.'

He's called her 'darling' again.

'What I do know is that Marta would never leave Lily alone. I know she wouldn't. Something's happened to her, hasn't it?'

Beth thinks she might burst into tears, as the true realisation of the situation brutally crashes down on her. Suddenly she doesn't feel safe and everything has changed. 'Oh God, what's happened to her?'

'We don't know yet, Beth,' the detective says. 'Maybe nothing has happened to her, but if it has, we will find out what, OK?'

Beth nods silently as the tears finally trickled down her cheeks. She knows that's not all they'll find out, either.

CHAPTER THREE

Beth

June 2018

'I need to talk to you, Evan.'

The police officers and forensics finally leave some three hours later, for now anyway, but she knows they will be back – and that there will be more of them. Grown women don't just disappear, do they?

'What do you think has happened to her?' Evan is standing by the sliding doors, staring blankly out onto the garden. 'Do you think the police suspect foul play? What did you think of that detective? Wasn't sure of him myself… something about his demeanour…'

'I don't know,' she replies, wiping her eyes with a shaking hand. 'Oh God, Evan, I hope she'll turn up and nothing terrible has happened… not to Marta, not my lovely Marta…'

'Did you like him… that detective?' He's ignored what she had said about needing to talk.

She feels irritated by the question. What did it matter whether she did or didn't? Why was he even interested?

'Which one?'

'Riley, the one in charge.'

'Actually yes, I liked him; I thought he had kind eyes.' She pauses. 'Do *you* suspect foul play? Do you think something bad has happened? Because I do, Evan… I mean, we know Marta – she wouldn't just take off like that for no reason, leave everything behind and—'

'I thought you said she'd taken some clothes… that her phone was missing.'

'I did… she has… the back doors were wide open… none of it makes any sense. Do you think she's been abducted?'

'I don't know… maybe… no… oh, I don't know…'

He gives her the strangest look then, one he has never given her before – or not that she's ever noticed – and she can't decide if it is a good look or a bad look, but either way it unsettles her. She stares at him as though seeing him for the first time.

She tries to recall the actual first time she saw him, and how she'd felt in that moment; it had been almost seven years ago at the Lawler and Co. Christmas party. She had been temping there, a side job while she was studying to be a nurse. She'd only been with the firm for two weeks but had felt obliged to accept the invitation. She'd been twenty-six at the time and had been surprised to learn that he was ten years her senior – and that he was the boss. He'd made eyes at her all evening, much to the delight of her female co-workers, who'd egged her on with encouraging elbow jabs and chants of 'he's loaded!'

She'd kind of been taken with the idea of dating an older man back then, someone more mature that she could rely on; someone who would take care of her. Evan had been polite and charming, qualities she'd found old-fashioned and endearing. They had dated for quite a few months before anything intimate had taken place between them, leading her to wonder for a time if he didn't really fancy her and simply wanted a platonic friendship. She hadn't been able to work it out; most men couldn't wait to get her into bed, and she didn't know whether she'd felt flattered or offended by his lack of urgency. Their courtship had been romantic enough, though, even if it had lacked passion – and yet when she looks back she cannot recall one conversation they'd had during that time which had resonated with her.

Evan had ticked a lot of boxes she supposed; he was reasonably attractive, intelligent and ambitious, but he had never given her that 'boom, pow' kind of feeling, the one that feels like a swift punch to the stomach and gets your heart racing and adrenalin pumping and starts making you see the world in different colours.

Evan had offered her the stability she hadn't even known she was looking for. Beth had lost her father when she was twelve years old – quite a crucial time in a young woman's life, she supposed – and she wonders now if this was partly why she had been drawn to him. Evan had lost his own mother when he was just nine years old and had been brought up by nannies and sent to boarding school; his father had died only nine years later, leaving him orphaned at eighteen. Beth understood; her heart had broken when her dad had passed away and life had been difficult for her and Mum.

Evan was safe – and she had needed safe. She realises this all now, with hindsight. She knows it's largely the reason why she said yes when he had asked to marry her in Dubai, on a lavish holiday he had taken her on. They had only been together eighteen months when she'd walked down the aisle with him, but even then she had known, somewhere deep inside of her, that it had been a mistake, that something fundamental was missing. She'd just not been brave enough to admit it to herself, let alone to him. After all, he had wanted to give her everything – and pretty much had. *Except for what she really wanted.*

She had tried to convince herself that she was in love with him, and for a while she had succeeded; they had been happy, or certainly not unhappy. Only Beth had learned that lying to someone else was one thing, but lying to yourself was something different altogether.

'Do you think she might have gone back to Norway? Maybe there was some kind of family emergency…'

She shakes her head. 'Marta wouldn't just up and leave. She's too responsible. I know her; I know she wouldn't just do that without telling me – and she wouldn't leave Lily alone like that, I—'

'Yes, but do you, Beth? Do you *really* know her? I mean, *really*? Maybe she was keeping things from you, things you never knew about, things she didn't want you to know about…'

'What makes you say that?'

He pauses, looks directly at her. 'At the end of the day do any of us really *know* anyone?'

She blinks at him, a little dumbfounded. This is very profound for Evan. He is acting oddly, or perhaps it's just the whole situation. She feels a little odd herself too.

'I need a drink,' she says, getting up from the table.

'Sit down – I'll get it,' he says, opening the fridge. 'We've only got champagne in.'

'No, no… I couldn't! Champagne's for celebrating. It wouldn't feel right… not with Marta missing.'

'Come on, I think we both need it,' he says, popping the cork.

'Well, I'm not toasting to anything,' she says, the algorithms in her body going haywire. This is all wrong; it feels wrong.

'What if she *has* been abducted? What if she's been murdered, raped or God knows what else? She could be lying dead in a ditch somewhere right now and we're here drinking bloody champagne.'

He holds his glass up towards his lips. 'She's definitely not in a ditch.'

'How do you know?' she says. 'You watch those programmes on TV. There could be a prowler around… It could've been me… He could've taken Lily!' She takes a large swig of the champagne.

'Calm down – you're letting your imagination run riot. You know, I really think she'll turn up again, if not here then somewhere… and if it makes you feel better we'll install more security measures, get some more sensors, add a few more cameras.'

Cameras!

'God! Evan! We have CCTV! Front and back! If someone came into the house then they'll have been caught on camera, won't they? Did the police take the footage?' In her blind panic she has clean forgotten about the CCTV. They lived in a big house in a salubrious area; as targets for professional criminals they were CCTV'd up to the hilt.

Evan nods. 'Yes, they took it… I gave it to that detective – the other one, Delaney.'

She feels a sense of relief wash over her, or perhaps it's the alcohol hitting her empty stomach – only it's soon replaced by dread again. *The police will start digging. They will check her alibi and find out that she is lying. She has to tell him. She has no choice.* She throws back the remainder of her glass.

'Evan… there's something I need to talk to you about.'

He's turned to look out into the garden again, his back to her; he doesn't respond.

She waits for a moment, breathes deeply, takes another large gulp of the champagne.

'I'm sorry, Evan,' she says gently, 'but… I want a divorce.'

CHAPTER FOUR

Beth

June 2018

She says it quickly, like ripping a plaster off in a bid to lessen the pain. She's had these words bottle-necked at the back of her throat for what feels like a lifetime and finally saying them aloud brings instant, palpable relief, like the moment a rotten tooth is extracted.

He doesn't answer her, doesn't turn around. She waits nervously for a response, thinks about pouring herself another glass of champagne but wonders if that would appear callous. 'Evan, did you hear me? I said I—'

'I heard what you said, Beth.' His voice is a monotone, cold even, but then, Evan isn't one for public displays of emotion – or any emotion for that matter.

'Will you sit down, Evan?' she asks after a moment's silence. 'Please.'

He ignores her again and she exhales some of the adrenalin that is coursing through her like rapids.

'I… I want to explain… I want you to understand, or try to.' She really wishes he'd just sit down; the way he is standing – statue sill – is making her edgy. 'I haven't been happy, Evan.' She hears herself as a cliché, even though it is the truth. '*We* haven't been happy; not for a long time – we both know that, don't we?' She's rehearsed this moment over and over again in her mind for so long that she knows it verbatim, like an actor knows a script; only now her mind has gone whiteboard blank.

'I mean, there's this huge gulf between us; surely you've felt it yourself? We don't communicate with each other… we don't talk… we don't… well, we don't do anything together… do we?' His silence is making her babble, desperate to fill the empty space. She'd always been the fixer in the relationship, the one who addressed any problems, but she no longer possesses the energy, or passion, to make things better. 'Evan? Will you look at me?' She's pleading with him now. 'I've tried to talk to you about this before… about this distance between us.'

She had attempted to express her feelings to him a year or so before she'd fallen pregnant. Looking back, it was nothing short of a miracle they'd ever managed to conceive their daughter. Sex between them had been practically non-existent, despite her attempts to spice things up a bit by wearing nice underwear and suggesting 'date nights', but mostly there was always a reason or an excuse for him to avoid any intimacy. She'd felt hurt by his physical and emotional rejection of her; it had knocked her self-esteem. She was young and attractive and took care of her body – why didn't he want to make love to her?

'We haven't shared a bed since Lily was born,' she says. 'I know we don't really argue – in fact, sometimes I've *wanted* to argue with you, Evan, just to see something from you, some passion, some emotion… *anything*…' She looks over at him. He still has his back to her. 'Don't tell me you're happy with the way things are because I know you're not – neither of us is. We've been plodding along now for years, disconnected from each other – we're like strangers who live together, little more than housemates. You don't know what I think, or how I'm feeling; you never ask me about myself, or my opinion on anything, or what I want or what makes me happy. You don't even ask me how my day has been, or about Lily much. When we do talk it's about your job; we talk about construction, Evan! We don't even watch TV together or listen to music or—'

He turns round to face her finally.

'Have you finished, Beth?' he says, his voice still a monotone.

She blinks at him, a little stunned. She's always hated him speaking down to her, like she was a naughty child.

'Well, yes, I… no, actually I haven't… I'm not trying to make you out to be a bad person, Evan… I'm just… it's just that it's—'

'Is this to do with Marta's disappearance? Is that what's set you off, her going missing?'

Set her off? This is nothing to do with Marta's disappearance, and yet at the same time it somehow has everything to do with it. She has been putting this moment off again and again, and it had been Marta who'd encouraged her to pluck up the courage to tell the truth: '*Carpe diem*, Beth!' That's what she'd said. 'Life's not a dress rehearsal!' The shock of her disappearing has somehow brought her emotions to the fore, and, if she is honest with herself, she is scared she's going to be found out. She doesn't want him to hear it from the police.

'You certainly pick your moments, don't you?' he says dryly.

She drops her head. 'There is no good moment, Evan.' She feels like a bomb has detonated inside her, piercing her internal organs with sharp emotional debris.

'Have you or Lily ever gone without, Beth?'

She tucks her chin into her chest. 'No. Never, but—'

'How do you think we got all of this?' he says, gesturing around their state-of-the-art kitchen. His voice is calm and low, which only adds to her unease. 'Me: that's how…'

'Oh, Evan, it's not about the house, or the cars, or the holidays… it's not about money full stop. It's about you and me.

Us. And the fact that there is no "us".' She cannot believe that he is reducing everything to material possessions. Where are his emotions? Where are his feelings?

'You have a wonderful life, Beth.' He cuts her off. 'You have all you could ever want or need.'

Suddenly she feels annoyed. How does he know if her life is wonderful or not? How does he know what she wants or needs? He never asks her how she *really* feels; he's not interested.

'Materialistically perhaps, but I'm in a loveless, passionless marriage to a man who is more like my brother than lover, a man who spends his whole time either working – or playing golf or at that bloody lodge when he's not – and who practically ignores me day in and day out. We don't do anything together; we don't do anything as a family.'

She knows she's said too much, but his unemotional response has so far only served to highlight what she's trying to say. She really doesn't want things to turn nasty. Surely Evan felt as relieved as she did? One of them had to say it, didn't they? They couldn't carry on like this…

Evan's face has flushed slightly; it's the closest she's seen to him showing any kind of emotional response to what she's said.

'Oh, Evan… I don't want to hurt you… I've never wanted to hurt you, but you know it's been over between us for a long time.'

He stares at her, pauses for a moment.

'OK,' he says. 'If this is what you really want, Beth.' He sits down at the other end of the table directly opposite her and she thinks how much this gesture demonstrates everything she's said about the distance between them. OK? That's all he's got to say to her? *OK?*

'So,' he says after a painful and loaded silence, 'are you going to tell me his name?'

'Whose name?' She knows exactly who he means and he casts her a look that confirms it.

'You know whose name, Beth. The name of the man you're having an affair with. The man you've been having an affair with for goodness knows how long…'

She feels her sphincter muscle contract. Despite her unhappiness, she still has the good grace to feel ashamed. She had never planned for any of this to happen; she had never wanted it to be this way. An affair wasn't part of the script. She wasn't sure she could even call it an 'affair' because the word itself conjures up something sleazy, something deceitful and wrong, and it is none of those things. It hasn't been about sex, about scratching an itch or even about craving the attention she so desperately lacked in her marriage. It was about the love she didn't have with her husband and the love she has found with *him*.

Nick. *Nick*; *Nich-o-las, Nicky*… even saying his name fills her heart with a thousand possibilities. His entrance into her life had been so unexpected, the clichéd bolt from the blue. She had certainly not been looking for anything, or anyone – at least not consciously. But it had found her anyway; *he* had found her, and from that moment onwards everything had changed. She couldn't even really describe it to herself, the feeling of everything falling into place when she'd met him, a comfortable yet exhilarating ease that she had never before shared with a man – perhaps with anyone – it had been an 'ahh… so *this* is what they mean…' moment.

Beth was not a religious woman, nor especially spiritual, but she had truly believed that somehow the gods had been at play the day her and Nick's paths had crossed, that somehow they had been witnessing her daily desperation and had decided to navigate them towards each other, steering them closer every day until – boom! Pow! Perhaps that's what a soulmate really was, the feeling of coming home to yourself. What she did know was that since they had met she had felt like the best possible version of herself; she had felt energised again, her desires and dreams resurrected, like she was finally living instead of simply existing.

They had both tried to fight it, grappling with the overwhelming conflicting emotions, attempting to defy the gravity that was pulling them together like magnets – but the guilt was secondary to the strength of her euphoria, no matter how much she'd always despised dishonesty, looking down upon people who cheated on their spouses and thinking they were weak and shallow individuals. But now she realised it wasn't as black and white as that, and that sometimes good people found themselves in less than good situations.

'The heart wants what the heart wants,' that's what her mother used to say to her, with a resigned sigh, when she was younger. She had never fully understood what her mother meant at the time. But now she did. Now it all made perfectly beautiful sense.

Beth swallows deeply, reaches for the champagne bottle. She owes it to him to tell the truth. Everyone deserves the truth, don't they?

Evan hasn't taken his eyes off her, and she desperately wishes she could read his thoughts. Is he surprised? Is he upset? Hurt? Or is he secretly relieved? She genuinely cannot tell.

'I'm sorry, Evan,' she says. 'I never planned to meet anyone else. I never ever went looking for it, truly… it just happened.' She wants to reiterate how lonely and unhappy she's been for so long but knows this will simply come across as a feeble attempt at justifying her infidelity. She puts herself in his shoes, wonders what she would feel if their conversation was reversed. Would she feel angry? Betrayed? Hurt? She thinks she probably would, even though she doesn't love him.

'I see.' Evan sniffs, leans back into the chair. 'And this man… you love him? You're *in* love with him?' He asks the question like a maths teacher might ask a pupil a particularly challenging algebra equation.

'Yes. I am. I'm sorry, Evan; please forgive me. But we're both to blame for…' She stops herself short, doesn't want to sound like she's trying to make him responsible for her actions. She knows she'll just have to wear it. 'I know I shouldn't have done this; I know it was wrong, but I don't want to live a lie, and I don't want you to, either. You deserve honesty; we both deserve to be happy – everyone does, don't they?'

His poker face remains unchanged.

'How long?' he says eventually. She wonders if his lack of emotion is the quiet before the storm. Surely he feels *something*?

'Around six months,' she says softly, waiting for the questions to come – where did they meet; how often did they meet? What does he do for a living? When did things turn physical between them?

Only they don't come, and he simply looks at her and says: 'So when are you leaving?'

He gets up from the table, places his champagne flute inside the dishwasher. Beth watches him in a confused mix of shock, surprise, fear and relief all rolled into one quivering mess. It wasn't the question she was expecting him to ask her. Had she expected him to fight for their marriage, beg her to stay? Had she thought he might shout at her, call her names, get angry with her, see some tears even? She doesn't know, but she isn't prepared for such calm indifference, like she's handing in her notice to the boss of a large corporation who can't even remember her name.

Ironically part of her feels hurt and angry by his reaction, but it only serves as affirmation that she's doing the right thing.

'I… I don't know exactly… I… I wanted to talk to you first obviously.'

He has his back to her again and she stares at it, dumbfounded.

'I suppose you had to come clean really,' he says. 'Giving the police a false alibi about where you were this morning… you could get into trouble for that, Beth.'

'How do you know it was false?' The rush of adrenalin pumping through her veins is making her feel light-headed.

'Just a guess.' He turns round, gives her a thin smile.

She's momentarily lost for words.

'I want us to be as amicable as possible for Lily's sake,' she says. 'I want us to try and work things out as fairly and kindly as we can, Evan.'

He nods. 'Fairly. Yes. What would you say is fair, Beth?'

'Um… well… I don't know… I mean, as far as Lily is concerned… I won't stop you having access or anything, of course not…' She's tripping over her words. 'I was thinking weekends and holidays… whatever you like. We'll share responsibility for her; she'll always have a mummy and a daddy. You'll probably get to spend more quality time with her now…' She doesn't mean this to sound the way it does and inwardly winces. Evan is being so calm – too calm – and she doesn't want to say anything that might light the touchpaper.

'And you'll want maintenance, I assume, plus half of everything? The house, cars, my pension?'

Beth hadn't really intended this conversation to get to the stage of agreeing finances. All she knew was that she had to leave their unhappy marriage – the rest she assumed could be discussed in due course, dealt with by solicitors.

'I don't know… I… I thought we could talk about that later. I…'

Nick has asked her and Lily to come and stay with him while things were finalised between her and Evan and she's agreed. It was this part she dreads telling him the most. She knows how it will look – not just to Evan, but also to everyone. She'll be the most heartless harlot in Buckhurst Hill.

'I'm… we're going to stay with Nick, for a while anyway, until things are resolved.'

'Resolved… yes…' He nods and she's not sure if it's a facetious nod or one of acquiescence – either way it's unsettling.

'She's only four years old, Evan. I want her to grow up loving both her parents, knowing us both, knowing that we both love her. It's best we do this now, while she's young enough not to remember, not to be damaged by it.'

'Whatever you think is best, Beth,' he says coldly. 'I'll speak to my solicitor in the morning – get the ball rolling.'

His reaction has completely blindsided her. Is he humouring her? She wonders that perhaps he isn't taking her seriously, that he doesn't believe that she will really leave.

'Right then. OK. Well… thank you for being so understanding, Evan,' she says awkwardly. 'You know, I just want to be happy at the end of the day… I want Lily to be happy, and I want you to be happy too, Evan – I really do.'

He looks through her, like she isn't even there, like the past seven years of their lives had never taken place.

'I'm sorry you've been so unhappy, Beth,' he says in his measured tone. 'I've only ever wanted you to be happy, to *make* you happy.'

She swallows back the lump that's lodged in her oesophagus. She wants to scream at him. To ask him how, how has he tried to make her happy? By throwing money at her? By giving her cars and Pandora jewellery for birthdays and Christmas? If he'd known her, if he'd ever spent time with her, he'd know that she doesn't even like Pandora jewellery. But she figures there's no point trying to explain.

'I'm sorry too, Evan,' she says, her voice cracking like the embers on a bonfire.

He makes to leave the kitchen then mutters something as he walks past her. She can't quite make out what he's said, but she's sure it was something like, 'You will be, Beth…'

CHAPTER FIVE

Cath

April 2019

'Cath, Catherine… can you hear me? You need to push now, OK? I'm going to ask you to push in three and I want you to squeeze my hand… OK? Catherine… Catherine, can you hear me, love? One…'

The first midwife, the Irish one with the round smiley face, is leaning over her, her large bosom almost touching her dry lips. Simultaneously, the other midwife, Carol she said her name was, with the comparatively thin and pointy face, is dabbing her forehead with a damp towel. Bizarrely they remind her of a female version of Laurel and Hardy.

She can smell the sweat mixed with cheap body spray on the larger midwife's clothes as she bends in closer to her – vanilla, she thinks. The smell reminds her of her sister's house; it's a small comfort.

She tries to say something but can't answer through the pain; the noise in the room sounds like it's coming from someone else, only she realises it's coming from her, noises she didn't know her body could make, strange low growls followed by high-pitched piercing screams that sound disjointed and alien. She has never experienced pain as intense as this – not physically, anyway. It was never like this with Kai – at least she doesn't remember it being that way – and she wonders if this is somehow her punishment – punishment for all the mistakes and bad choices she's made.

The midwife offers her the gas and air again, some pethidine, but she refuses. No drugs. She wants to feel every second of this pain, every agonising moment, so that she never forgets, accepts it as her due for letting her baby down, for not protecting him like a mother should. She didn't deserve to be his mother, or a mother at all.

She can feel the sadness and pity coming off the two midwives in waves, like sonar, as they go about their professional duty. The registrar, an Asian man with spectacles, had broken the news to her with a kindness that had felt scripted and false when she had arrived in A&E that night. The beating had been the worst he'd ever given her; injuries she couldn't hide or blame on a fall. Her eyes were black, her lip split open, a cracked rib and three of her fingers shattered, sustained when she had tried to protect herself – and her unborn baby. The attack had been frenzied, violence and aggression on a level most people couldn't comprehend, the sort you watch through one eye framed between your fingers during a particularly gruesome film and don't imagine ever happens in real life.

She'd told them she'd been in a car accident and they seemed to have believed her; her injuries correlated, so it wasn't too much of a stretch of the imagination. She'd come to them broken and smashed, clutching her swollen stomach containing her baby, a baby who at thirty-eight weeks was ready for the world. She had instinctively known that something was very wrong. He had squirmed and wriggled during the attack; she had felt him turn inside her, felt the pull of his tiny body as it had tried to remove himself from harm's way. Then afterwards there was nothing, no movement at all, just a strange stillness inside. She had known then, as she lay there, unable to move, that he was gone.

'We'll need to check the baby's heartbeat, sweetheart, OK?' the midwife had said as she had lain her broken body down onto the bed. 'Then we can clean you up and get you X-rayed and all of that. We just need to check everything's OK with the little one first.'

It hurt to speak; it hurt to blink. So she had nodded through the numbness, a familiar feeling she had experienced whenever he had beaten her before, like somehow her body had shut down in self-preservation; like playing dead. She hadn't been surprised when the midwife had been unable to find a heartbeat. She had watched the woman's face slip into badly disguised concern, like a dark curtain had fallen across it, shutting out the light. She had told her not to panic, not to worry, and that she was leaving the room for a moment to get her colleague. Cath had nodded again, the shock paralysing her trachea, making her mute. Her ears were ringing from the blows he'd rained down upon her and she had wiped some congealed blood from one of them. Her earring was missing; it had been ripped out during the assault. She thought about how they were her favourite pair.

The midwife had returned quickly with another in tow who had duly attempted to find what she already knew was no longer there. They couldn't disguise the crestfallen expression on their faces this time, the clandestine concerned glances shared between them.

'We can't find the heartbeat, my darling,' one of them had said eventually, the Irish one, she thinks – Hardy. 'We need to wait for the registrar; he's performing a C-section – he'll be about twenty minutes.' She had held her hand, the one that wasn't broken, and had stroked it gently, squeezed it intermittently. Cath had wanted to scream but was frightened that if she started then she wouldn't stop; the silent screams inside her head were loud enough.

She could feel him crowning, the need to push. It was strange, she thought, how nature kicked into action, her body knowing it had this job to do, even though she knew there would only be loss and pain and devastation at the end of it.

Her baby had died inside her, a perfectly healthy baby boy. A child that despite her circumstances had given her hope, a sense of purpose to carry on, a reason to live another day. And now part of her had died too and she would never again be the same as she was before this moment – she was grieving for two people, her baby and herself.

Like so many abused women, Cath didn't know how she had ended up where she now found herself. She had pretty much been a normal girl from a normal family. She had grown up on the outskirts of Bristol with her mum and sister – her father had deserted them not long after she'd been born – and while they had been hard up, they had been happy. She'd met Saul while she'd still been at school. The clichéd tall, dark and handsome older boy with a car and reputation for being a 'bit of a lad'. Saul had been nice back then; he really had, hadn't he?

He'd pursued her relentlessly, despite the fact that at twenty, he was five years her senior. She could never forget how she'd felt about him back then, like he was God or something. All the girls loved Saul Bennett; he was the catch of the estate they lived on, handsome and full of cheeky, boyish charm. 'There's nothing more dangerous than a boy with charm,' her nan had said to her once and she'd never forgotten it. Not least because she had been so right.

Saul had said Cath was the best-looking girl he'd ever laid eyes on, 'like an angel from heaven', and that he'd known the moment he'd seen her sitting on a park bench with her friends one afternoon after school that she was 'the one', even if she had been wearing school uniform.

She'd been pregnant at sixteen. Her mum had gone absolutely spare. But Saul had stood by her, and her mum had supported her, and when Kai came along she had never been happier. They'd been given a council flat and she couldn't wait to turn it into their haven, a home for her two special boys. Cath thought about her sixteen-year-old self then, how naïve she had been, filled with hope and thoughts of a happy ever after. She wasn't the smartest girl on the block, not academically, and all she'd really wanted was a little family of her own and to be happy. Despite being extremely pretty, she knew she wasn't destined for a life of luxury – she just wanted the simple things. That wasn't too much to ask, was it?

Saul had stuck around after Kai had come along, got himself labouring jobs here and there, and he'd doted on their gorgeous boy – for a while at least. His own dad hadn't been around much for him as a boy either, and he'd sworn he wouldn't follow in his father's footsteps. But gradually things had changed; Saul changed, but it had been insidious, so much so that she hadn't really noticed his mood swings at first.

It's incredible how people make excuses for the ones they love. She'd put his rages and flare-ups down to stress at having to provide for them all; she'd attributed his jealous and possessive behaviour to his passionate love for her; and eventually she put his violent outbursts down to both. Saul was her first love and the only man she had – has – ever known; she had no benchmark to compare. She'd simply believed that his behaviour was normal – that this was what a relationship was.

She knows now of course, sixteen years on, that what you accept will continue, and it will get worse – much, much worse. But she had been conditioned to acceptance, knowing no different, and by the time she did know different, it had been too late; she had been trapped in a diabolical cycle of emotional torment, conditioned and controlled and completely dependent, unable to break free from the prison he'd created for her, one where, in spite of the abuse, she felt paradoxically safe.

He had, over the course of their sixteen years 'together' left her and returned so many times that she had lost count, and sometimes, the fear of him leaving was worse than him returning and the abuse that came with it, such was her dependency and addiction to the cycle. Because Cath had believed, regardless of the emotional, sexual and physical abuse she had suffered at Saul's hand, despite the drink and the drugs and the blatant cheating and lying, that he loved her – and moreover, that she loved him, because that was love to Cath, back then, anyway.

'One more push, love… Come on now, you can do this… Come on, Cath, love, just one more…' The pain as her baby moves through her pelvis and into the world feels like dying and being reborn herself. The sweat on her skin feels cold and wet and she watches, crying, as though through a smeared windowpane, as the midwife takes him away.

'You'll be able to hold him soon,' the pointy-faced midwife – Laurel – says gently. She can't speak through the crushing ache inside her chest, like a cage has erected itself around her heart and in doing so has shut off every other part of her. She wonders if she will ever be able to speak again. And if she does, what she might say.

It feels like hours before they return with him. He's perfectly wrapped in one of those cotton cellular receiving blankets, blankets synonymous with newborn babies. She feels a strange sense of calm as she holds him to her, inspecting his perfectly formed features like any new mother would. She touches his skin with the tips of her good fingers. It feels cool but not cold, and his tiny lips are still pink, though she can see the colour fading from them fast. She wipes away the tears that have splashed down onto his chubby cheeks from her eyes.

'He weighed 8lbs 4oz,' the round-faced midwife – Hardy – says. 'A very good weight.' It was, wasn't it? A healthy weight for what was a healthy boy. She inspects his head, a lovely apple shape with the lightest peachy-blonde fuzz, and she lowers her head to smell him, to breathe him in. He smells new and innocent; the scent of pure unadulterated love. She wishes she could bottle it and wear it every day to remind her and be forever close to him.

The midwives are saying something about pictures, photographs, taking hand and foot prints, but she's too absorbed in him to hear them exactly – she just wants to look at him for a while longer, memorise every inch of his tiny body, the smallest consolation for the lifetime she has lost, for the privilege of watching him grow.

His eyes are closed and she wishes she could look into them so he could see how much she loves him.

'Cody.' She whispers his name as she kisses him, feels that rush of oxytocin and her milk let-down reflex. She'd planned to call him Cody all along, although she'd never told Saul this because he'd not wanted another boy.

'This world doesn't need another dick in it,' he'd said. 'It already has enough.'

And so she'd lied and said she didn't know the sex, even though she had found out at her sixteen-week scan. She'd been over the moon about her little boy. 'I'm sorry, Cody, my beautiful boy, my angel… Mummy's sorry. Mummy loves you… I love you and I'm sorry.'

Her voice is scratchy, barely audible. The midwives are crying, she thinks, and she wishes more than anything that she could hear her son crying too.

CHAPTER SIX

Dan

October 2019

'I'd say, simply on preliminary visual inspection, by the extent of the decomposition, that he's probably been dead around four days.' Vic Leyton, my favourite pathologist and one whose company I strangely enjoy in spite of the eternally grim circumstances in which we always meet, is standing by the bed to the left, looking down onto the cadaver that's lying on it and doing that thing I hate when people are pondering something: tapping her bottom lip. 'You see, Detective Riley, the first stage of human decomposition is called autolysis…' She glances at me briefly, knowing full well I haven't a clue what she's talking about. 'It's otherwise known as self-digestion.'

I pull a face.

'And it begins immediately after death as the body has no way of retaining oxygen or eliminating waste. So,' she continues, amused by my discomfort, 'all that carbon dioxide must go somewhere, so it internalises, causing membranes in the cells to rupture and release enzymes that begin to eat them from the inside out.'

I wince from beneath my hand, which is covering my mouth and nose in a futile bid to prevent the stench from entering my respiratory system.

'So effectively he's begun to digest himself?' I say, queasily, grateful that I hadn't had time for breakfast when the call came in early this morning.

'It's a marvel really, isn't it?' Vic muses, her bespectacled eyes scrutinising the bloated corpse on the bed. 'The human body really does take care of itself, even in death.'

'I'm sure our partner here is relieved about that, Vic,' I say, unable to prevent myself from retching.

She shoots me an amused look. 'An involuntary reaction, Detective.'

She smiles brightly, making me wonder if she's had her teeth whitened. In all the years we've been acquainted, I've never ever seen Ms Leyton outside of her whites and part of me is fascinated to know how she scrubs up. Maybe I have a crush on her, or maybe it's more of an intrigue about what type of woman she really is when you strip away all the gore and grizzlies.

'The gag reflex, that's because of the gases. All those leaking enzymes produce many of them, the bacteria contain sulphur – which is what you can smell now – and which is why the poor chap's almost doubled in size and has all this foam coming from his mouth and nose.'

She's doing this deliberately, I think, as I take reluctant, tentative steps towards the bed.

'You know, Dan, you really ought to know this by now; you've worked on homicide long enough… and as for that squeamish streak, well, what are you going to be like when your child comes into the world? It can't be long now, can it?'

I'm caught a little off-guard by the question. Vic Leyton has never asked me anything personal before.

'No… about six weeks, or thereabouts,' I say from behind my hand. 'Fiona has a feeling she'll be overdue.'

Vic is still scrutinising our stiff on the bed. 'Well, a mother's intuition is rarely wrong, Detective Riley.'

'And I'll be fine at the birth,' I say, which we both know is a lie. 'I'll have a light lunch that day.'

Truth be told, Fiona and I have yet to discuss her birth plan or whether she even wants me there or not, which is cutting things a bit fine, I realise. But then I suppose it's not exactly your average situation. We haven't even discussed what will happen after the birth. All I know is that currently, she's staying in my apartment with Leo, her five-year-old son, whose real father has long since disappeared and whose batteries never seem to wear flat, while her apartment is being redecorated.

I didn't think it would be good for a heavily pregnant woman to be around all those paint fumes, so I invited them to live with me until it's finished. It's been strange, I suppose, not to mention a bit of a squeeze for the three, soon-to-be-four of us, as I'd always envisaged it to be Rachel and I and our baby who'd fill the place with clutter and noise and the sound of children.

'Life is what happens when you're busy making other plans, Danny Boy,' as my dad somewhat irritatingly likes to remind me. I know it wasn't supposed to be like this, but it is. I'm about to become a father and I'm neither mentally prepared nor emotionally ready for it. Who is? Anyway, I like to think I'm quite hip and new age, having a baby with a friend. At least I think that's what she is; I'm still not sure what exactly it is we actually are. For now though, I'm doing what I think is the right thing and taking care of the mother of my child, giving her the odd foot rub, ordering in takeout and teaching Leo how not to play *FIFA* on the Xbox; he's beaten me every single time. And he's five.

'He was shot in the head, not point blank, but pretty close, I'd say,' Vic continues. 'The entry wound went in just ever so slightly to the right, just above the eye and through the front cortex of the brain, exiting just below the right ear, towards the base of the neck. Single bullet, killed him instantly.'

'No sign of the weapon?'

'Nope… not so far, boss,' Davis says. 'Or the shells…'

'Organise a fingertip search,' I say, 'inside and out. Shut the whole area down and seal everything off. We need to find the weapon. Oh, and keep the press out if you can, for now anyway.'

'Gov.' Davis nods, punching numbers into her phone already.

'Ballistics will be able to tell you what type of gun was used,' Vic continues. 'There's no defence wounds to the arms or body, by the looks of things – no abrasions, cuts or bruises. Doesn't look like there was a struggle.'

'He was in bed when it happened? The body hasn't been moved?'

Vic shakes her head.

'Doesn't appear to have been, so I would say no, and judging by the blood-splatter pattern on the headboard, I'd say yes, he was in bed when he was shot.'

Forensics has arrived and begins to fill up the room like giant marshmallows in my peripheral vision.

'Do we know who he is, Davis?'

Carrie Mitchell – my newest and tenacious team member – has arrived on the scene now and answers the question for me. 'Morning, boss.'

'Ah, DC Mitchell.' I acknowledge her with a nod. 'What have you got for me?'

'His name is Evan Lawler, forty-five. His resident address is number 6 Cheney Gardens. It's in the Buckhurst Hill area.'

'So what's he doing here?' I glance around the pristine studio. It's one of those hotel apartment-type things favoured by rich overseas businessmen in a posh high-rise in North London, all very plush and urban with its floor-to-ceiling windows and chrome appliances. It's the sort of thing I might have once dreamed of owning when I was single and in my twenties and wanted to impress women.

'Well, he owns it, apparently. The woman on reception confirmed his identity, said he was here on and off quite regularly, nights… weekends… some evenings…'

'What else?'

'He's a businessman – well, was. Construction. Owned a company called Lawler and Co. Construction. Had some big contracts… Baylis and Harding are looking into it now.'

This fills me with confidence. Sarah Baylis and Mark Harding, two of my most trustworthy and experienced DCs, are a dynamic duo and have naturally gravitated towards each other over the years. Whatever they've got going on between them professionally, it works and they get results.

'Who found him?'

'Maintenance man, John Riley – no relation I'm assuming, gov?' Davis chips in. 'He's out in the lobby. Says some of the residents began complaining about the…' She looks like she's about to throw up. 'The smell.'

'No shit,' I say between tightly closed lips.

I stare down at the corpse on the bed. It's swollen and bloated, naked save from a pair of boxer shorts that I assume were once white but have now taken on a similar colour to Davis's face. It's an ugly sight; not one I would recommend, but as I look at him, something in the back of my mind is niggling me, smashing against my memory like a trapped fly against a window. I watch as Mitchell stares at the corpse on the bed, unable to completely disguise the shock and repulsion on her face. I suddenly realise it's probably the first dead body she's seen since being on homicide – maybe ever – and I'm impressed by the fact she hasn't thrown up because the stench is indescribable.

'Your first?' I ask her and she nods, covering her mouth with her hand.

I lightly touch her elbow in solidarity. You never forget your first. Mine was an old lady who'd been strangled in her armchair by, it turned out, her own grandson, no less. The look on her face, one of sad realisation and horror, will haunt me forever.

'Welcome to homicide, Mitchell,' I say. 'Go and get a drink of water.'

I let forensics go about their business as I scan the small but elegant studio again. It looks untouched, very much like a hotel room. His clothes are in a neat pile on the floor next to the bed. There's a phone on the sleek black bedside ledge. There's also a wedding ring. Interesting.

'We'll need the phone, Davis,' I say, distracted by that fly that's buzzing inside my head. Something… there's something familiar about this scene that I can't put my finger on and the cogs in my brain are turning so fast I'm sure there's smoke coming out of my ears.

'I'll know more when he's on the slab and we've done a full autopsy,' Vic says, turning to me and catching my expression.

'Something wrong, Detective?' she says, and I think it's funny, and in a strange way touching, that I've known her long enough for her to be able to read me so closely.

'Yes,' I reply. 'But I'm not sure what – yet.'

She takes her glasses off and wipes them against her scrubs. I think it's the first time I've ever seen her without them and I get a little thrill from it.

'John Riley's on his way up, boss,' Davis says, wiping her face with a tissue. You really can't describe the smell in the room, but suffice to say, no one wants to be here longer than they need be.

'Whoever shot him was standing at the end of the bed,' Vic says. 'It looks like an execution-style killing to me.'

I smile at her; nod my gratitude.

'I'll be the judge of that, Ms Leyton,' I say before leaving the room.

CHAPTER SEVEN

Dan

October 2019

John Riley, no relation I'd hasten to add, looks as you would expect any man to look who has just discovered a bloated, rotting corpse on his watch.

'He was a lovely fella,' he says, shaking his balding head while simultaneously rubbing his brow, like he's trying to erase the gruesome image from his mind – and failing. 'He was only in his forties… Nice fella,' he says again.

'When did you last see Mr Lawler, John?' Davis has seemingly recovered now that she's a safe distance from the scent of a putrefying corpse. She's probably already started thinking about what to have for lunch.

'Oh… blimey… I dunno… few days ago… maybe four or five. He owned this apartment… lovely view from up there,' he adds. Not anymore, I think. 'He had something to do with this whole building, you know, the architecture. That's the game he was in – architecture and construction.'

'How well did you know him, gov… sorry, Mr Riley?' Davis is winding me up deliberately. I chalk it up.

'Oh not well, like, just in passing. We had the odd chat here and there. Like I said, friendly, down to earth… not like some of the ponces you get here,' he says with some degree of bitterness.

I'm half listening to Davis as she questions my namesake but my mind is going off course. The name… Lawler… it rings a bell but frustratingly I just can't quite remember… It's like having an itch that's just out of reach.

'When you last saw Mr Lawler, was he with anyone? Did he arrive here alone?'

The man's reaction immediately brings me out of my thousand-yard stare and into the present.

'I think so… I'm not entirely sure… He may have arrived alone and been joined by someone later.' He looks down at the floor a little awkwardly. 'Look, I'm not a man to judge… he was going through a divorce, you know… nasty business it was. We talked about it a bit. The wife left him for another bloke, a right wrong 'un apparently an' all. Messed around with the little kiddie, or so it was said. Like I said, nasty business…'

Davis says nothing and I'm proud of her for not probing. Keep quiet and people will fill the gaps, that's what I've always told her.

'Last I saw him he was alone… but there was a few times… well, a few times when I saw him with, well, you know, *women*.'

'Women?'

'Yeah, you know…?' He clears his throat.

'Prostitutes, you mean?' Davis cuts to the chase. 'What makes you say that, Mr Riley?'

'Oh, I dunno. I might be wrong. There were a couple of times I saw different girls; done up like dogs' dinners with that vacant look in their eyes…' He stops himself. 'Not that I'd know what a prostitute looks like – never had to pay for it, meself.'

Davis wisely refrains from giving me the look I know she wants to.

'Would you be able to identify any of these girls, Mr Riley, if you saw them again?'

'Jesus.' He blows air through his lips. 'I couldn't rightly say. I see a lot of people come and go, you understand?'

'Of course,' Davis says, bolstering his obvious need for self-importance.

'There was this one girl I do remember though.'

'Oh?'

'Yeah. Funny little things she was; sort of all mismatched… think that's why she sticks out in my mind. She wasn't like the others… weird clobber, scarves and long cardigans, bit of a hippie type – used to be one meself back in the day, if you can believe it… I spoke to her once.'

'Did she give you a name?'

'I didn't ask. But I think I said, "Have a nice evening," or something like that… and I remember noticing that she had an accent.' He scratches that balding head of his again.

'Could you identify the accent?'

'Well, I asked her where she was from because I couldn't place it – the accent – and she says she was from Norway, that she was Norwegian.'

Bingo! I slap my own head suddenly, causing Davis and Mr Riley to look at me. The girl who went missing from the address in Buckhurst Hill, the nanny… Marta Larssen! That was her name! Beth and Evan *Lawler*… I glance at Davis wide-eyed but the penny obviously hasn't dropped.

If I remember rightly, Delaney had been assigned to take over before downgrading it to an MP. I'd never felt comfortable about that case right from the off, despite there being no evidence to suspect foul play. Sometimes people just want to disappear – Lord knows I've wanted to a few times in my life too. But I'd still felt there was something off about the whole thing; those instincts of mine… forensics had found zero though and the CCTV had come back kosher apparently, so it was decided there was nothing to see here and then we'd been put on the

Cedar Close murder and forgotten about Marta. Just another nobody lost in the ether.

'Thank you, Mr Riley,' I say, as I begin to close down the conversation. 'You've been incredibly helpful.' Although I don't know why I'm thanking him, because now I have a bad feeling that I might've gone from having one murder to solve to two.

CHAPTER EIGHT

Dan

October 2019

'So, DS Davis, your initial thoughts?' I say as we step inside the lift, away from the crime scene and that godawful stench of decaying flesh, although I can still smell it on my clothes – and this shirt was clean on this morning; Fiona – who has just left her reporter role at the *Gazette* to take maternity leave – has been washing them, which is something I've not been used to in a while. I can't say I don't like it, having a woman around to look after me – and vice versa, of course, even if I suspect she's only doing it out of sheer boredom. Fiona's a bit like me in that she needs things to do to occupy her time and mind. She's already rearranged my bookcase and CDs into alphabetical order and colour coordinated my exceptionally unremarkable wardrobe. 'I couldn't help it, Dan,' she said. 'It's the journalist in me and I have to do *something.*'

'Well, Harding and Baylis have confirmed that Mr Riley was right – he was in the midst of a bitter divorce with his estranged wife, Beth Lawler. Apparently, they were at loggerheads over the daughter, Lily, currently almost six years old. Apparently, Evan Lawler had temporarily been awarded sole custody of the girl and Beth Lawler had been "out to ruin him as a result".'

I pull a face in the lift mirror.

'Seems odd. Why would he be awarded temporary custody? It's usually the mother who gets the kids.'

'Well, it transpires that there had been allegations made against the boyfriend, Beth Lawler's lover…' Davis checks her notebook. 'No name on that yet, gov.'

'What kind of allegations?'

'Abuse – sexual apparently. Social services got involved and the child was taken from the mother's care while it was being investigated. They're running checks now, gov. And the team are trying to get background from social services too.'

'OK…' My mind is on fire. 'Where is she now, the daughter?'

'Back living at the home address.'

I shake my head.

'Oh, and this will please you, boss! Apparently, Woods is familiar with the deceased.'

I roll my eyes. 'Ah, Detective Chief Inspector Woods. Jesus Christ, that's all we need.'

'Thought you'd be pleased.' She smirks. 'They were Freemason friends, apparently.'

'I didn't realise Woods was a Freemason – or had any friends,' I say dryly, not liking the sound of this one iota. It's never been a secret that we rub each other up the wrong way, but there's always been an unspoken and reluctant mutual respect between us, and deep down, I have always believed he was decent.

Davis laughs. 'Lawler was quite a successful businessman by all accounts, had some pretty big – and lucrative – contracts. I doubt you make it to his level without pissing a few people off.'

'Where there's money there's murder, Davis,' I say, although this is beginning to look like a melting pot of motives already: a messy divorce, an accused lover, a custody tug of war and a well-off businessman with a penchant for prostitutes. 'Does the name Lawler ring any bells to you?'

She shoots me a perplexed look from the mirror. 'Are you suffering from short-term memory loss, gov?'

I roll my eyes again. 'Well, I *know* it's the name of the stiff upstairs, Davis, but does it sound familiar to you, like you've heard it somewhere before?'

She shrugs, adjusts her fringe in her reflection, but it falls back in front of her eyes and she exhales, giving up. 'Should it?'

'Yes, Davis, it should,' I say, putting her on the spot.

She pauses. Lucy Davis is ambitious and eager to please and doesn't like to think she's missed a trick.

'Give me a clue?'

'Missing person… about eighteen months ago, just before the Cedar Close case… getting any warmer?'

She pouts, shakes her head and I can almost hear the cogs of her brain turning as the lift judders to the ground floor.

'Oh hang on… Yes! The housekeeper! The missing nanny in Buckhurst Hill!'

'We'll make a detective out of you yet, Davis,' I say, teasing her.

'Beth and Evan Lawler!' She looks excited now and I think what a paradox our profession is; one minute you're staring at a bloated, rotting corpse trying to hold in your breakfast, and just a few minutes later, you're fist-pumping the air with a wide grin on your face.

'Exactamondo,' I say, knowing what a naff expression this is – one my dad would use – but saying it anyway.

'The wife, Beth… she made the call, came home to find her gone and the child was alone, upstairs… am I right?'

I nod. 'Gold star for you, Davis. And my namesake up there said something about seeing the deceased with a Norwegian girl, did he not?'

'Among others,' Davis quips. 'Oh my God! So you think there's a connection between Marta's disappearance and Evan Lawler's death?'

'We'll need to speak to Mr Riley again, find out when it was he saw this Norwegian girl, see if we can get a positive ID, but if I was a betting man – which I'm not – I'd say it was beginning to look that way.' And my instincts are singing in agreement.

'Maybe Lawler and the housekeeper were having an affair and the wife got wind of it, felt betrayed, got rid of them both?'

'Maybe,' I say, reserving my judgement. 'I'll let you know more after we've met her.'

'And when are we going to do that, gov?' Davis says, eyes aflame. I can see she's itching to get cracking. I am too, despite my concerns. I've a feeling that this one is going to be as tangled as a barber's hairbrush.

'Now, Davis,' I say. 'Right now.'

CHAPTER NINE

Beth

August 2018

'Faster! Faster, Nicky, faster!' He is pushing her on the swing, head thrown back in the moment of abandon. And Beth is smiling as she watches: her Lily and her Nicky, having the time of their lives, playing at the fun park together. He swings her daughter out of the seat and into his arms, does a little twirl.

'Here you go! Whoa!' he says. He looks a little dishevelled from the ride, his hair sticking up at funny angles, and in that moment she has never loved him more.

'Whoa! Such a brave girl!' he says, squeezing her leg. Lily holds her arms out to him. 'I thought my head was going to spin completely off my shoulders and roll across the grass like a football.'

She giggles at him, a childish helium sound. 'Spin me round, Nicky. Spin me fast!' And she screams in high-pitched laughter as he does what she asks. Beth watches her daughter interacting with the man she adores, the man she knows she wants to grow old with, and thinks her heart might explode, scattering the theme park with love-shaped confetti.

'Do you know, Mr Wainwright, I've never felt happier in my whole life.' She kisses the side of his face as her daughter vies for his attention at the same time.

'You're so good with her... I'm so lucky.'

He raises his eyebrows in a comedic fashion as if to affirm the statement. 'Hey, I'm the lucky one. I mean, look at me: the two most beautiful girls on the planet on each arm… plus a bag of candy floss… what more could a man want?'

It's her turn to raise her eyebrows at him. 'I have a few suggestions,' she says provocatively.

'Ummm, can't wait to hear them.' He gives her a lingering kiss on the lips, just long enough to tip into something sensual.

Beth has never felt contentment like this, the feeling of everything being just as it should. As well as everything else, he is a complete natural with her daughter, doting on her – on them both.

'How are my two favourite girls?' he'd say whenever he walked through the door at night. It had become a race between them as to which one could get to him first and throw their arms around him. She'd never seen so much affection from her daughter before.

Perhaps Lily had noticed the change in her mother, how she had smiled and laughed much more in a few months than she had done in the little girl's lifetime.

'Children want their parents to be happy as much as their parents want them to be,' Nicky had wisely said. 'And once everything's sorted out, we'll buy a place of our own, the three of us – a home. And we'll do it up and make it our palace, with a magical garden and a bedroom for a princess!'

'Can I have unicorns?' Lily looked up at him wide-eyed.

'You can have unicorns and rainbows and glitter and fluffy cushions and…'

Lily had gasped and squealed, putting her small hands over her mouth. 'And a horsie too?'

Nick had given Beth a sideways glance. 'A horsie! *A horsie!*' He'd tickled her, lifting her up off the ground. 'Well… we'll see, eh? See if we can't talk Mummy round.'

That week Beth had appointed a solicitor in a bid to get the ball rolling with divorce proceedings. She wanted things to move quickly and amicably and had made that clear to her brief. Her solicitor, Dwaine Simpson – a friend of the family – had looked at her like she wasn't of this earth when she'd said she wanted a clean break.

'Your husband is a very wealthy man, Beth,' he'd said, the sound of a cash register kerching-ing in his ears. But she was adamant that she wasn't interested in going after Lawler & Co. Construction, mindful of appearing like the avarice-filled ex out to rinse her well-off husband. She had been the one who had left after all. Her half of the Buckhurst Hill property would be more than enough.

Anyway, she'd be back to work at the local hospital in a few weeks, so she'd be earning her own money again, something she feels good about. She knows they need money to survive – everyone did – but it was not her god. And right now she has never felt richer.

This time she'll be doing things for the right reasons, and Lily will grow up knowing that she is loved by both of her parents, well looked after and cared for. They can respectively offer her stable homes and unconditional love. Just as long as she and Evan remain amicable and willing to put their daughter's needs first then she can't see any of it being too much of a problem. After all, other people manage it, don't they?

So far Evan has been his usual aloof but courteous self during Lily's handovers. There have been no real dramas, except for one.

'Are you still sure this is what you want, Beth?' he'd asked her during the last pick-up, moving a little closer towards her on the doorstep. 'We could always just forget this ever happened and go back to how we were.'

She'd tried not to show contempt for the question. *How they were*? Was he serious? There never really was a 'they'. Did he think that maybe she'd 'return to her senses' and come home?

'I'm sorry, Evan. Please don't make me go through it all again. I want us to stay amicable for Lily's sake, for our daughter. I mean, you're spending more time with her now than you ever did when we were together. That's a good thing, right?'

He'd stood, slightly forlorn-looking on her doorstep, and she'd felt those guilty pangs again. 'Look, you know this isn't just about Nick…'

'Isn't it?' he'd replied, but she'd detected no malice in his voice, not then anyway.

Beth had shifted on her feet awkwardly, wondering how to broach the subject with him.

'Actually, we're buying a place together… Nick and I… and Lily, obviously. It won't be far from ours… from the house. You won't have to travel far to see Lily.'

She'd waited for him to say something but he'd remained silent for a long moment.

'OK, Beth,' he'd said eventually as Lily had skipped to the front door with her new Peppa Pig rucksack.

'Look what Nicky bought me, Daddy!' she'd squealed, delighted to show him her new prized possession that she'd taken to bed with her every night. 'A Peppa Pig bag!'

Beth had never been able to read her husband; he was a closed book emotionally. With Evan, it had always been difficult to know what he was feeling; his face never gave anything away. She'd always put it down to him being reserved by nature, even shy, but in that moment, she could've sworn she'd seen hate flash up in his eyes.

'Get in the car, darling,' he'd said, unlocking the Range Rover with a click. 'Daddy will be there in a moment.'

Beth had smiled as Lily had done what she was told. 'We took her to a theme park this week… she had a wonderful time. Look, in case you're worried, I want you to know that she gets on well with Nick. She's been good as gold… I've explained to her as best

I can that me and her daddy still care about each other but that we're not going to live together anymore, and that we both love her and that now she will get to spend more time with you and—'

'Oh for God's sake just shut the fuck up, Beth!' Evan had roared at her, surprising her so much that she'd actually physically taken a step backwards in the doorway.

His outburst had stunned her into complete silence and she'd blinked at him, shocked.

'I'll bring her back here by 5 p.m. And remember these words I'm about to say, Beth,' he'd said slowly, turning back and pointing a finger towards her. 'You started all of this – you!'

CHAPTER TEN

Cath

May 2019

'Cath… CATH!' His voice is loud in her ear, startling her out of her sweaty slumber.

'What? What do you want, Saul?' she says in a rasping voice. She can hardly lift her head she feels so ill. Her temperature is high and she's boiling one minute and shivering the next. With a bit of luck, she thinks she might die. 'I'm not well, Saul. I need a doctor…'

The pains in her lower abdomen have gone from sporadic to permanent in the space of a few days; a crippling, debilitating pain that feels as if she's dragging her uterus behind her. It's been almost eight weeks and still the blood won't stop, day upon day, a claret-coloured reminder every time she uses the bathroom. *Your son died. You let him kill your son.* The police had visited her while she'd been recovering in hospital, wanted to know about the 'hit and run' car accident she'd been involved in. Saul had remained by her bedside the whole time, the doting, concerned and grieving partner, stroking her hands and face with a tenderness that almost came across as genuine. Perhaps somewhere deep down in the tiny part of his soul that was left, it was.

'I'm sorry, Cath,' he'd cried in her ear before the police had arrived, his alcoholic breath making her feel nauseous. 'Please… please forgive me, baby. I didn't mean… I didn't mean for this to happen. I lost control… I need help, Cath. Don't let them lock me up, please… please, Cath. You're the only person who can help me. You know how much I love you. I love you, Cath, and I'm sorry I hurt you, I'm sorry about…' He'd wiped the mucus from his nose onto his dirty sleeve and looked into her eyes. 'You're my girl, Cath. You've always been my girl, and I'll always be your man… We belong together, baby; you know we do – thick and thin, remember? I'll get help, I promise. It's the drugs, Cath, they've got me all messed up… I need you so much…' He'd rested his head onto her chest and she'd winced in pain. 'We'll have another baby – I promise you I'll make it up to you, just please don't let them lock me away.'

Cath had looked into his pleading eyes and for a moment she had thought she'd seen a tiny flicker of the Saul she had once known a long time ago, that cheeky Jack the Lad who could charm the birds from the trees, one who had promised to love her forever and take care of her. But the light that had once burned so brightly in those eyes had gradually diminished, like ever-decreasing circles, until there was nothing left but pinpricks of darkness. This time Cath *knew* there was no going back. Saul Bennett was lost, gone forever, and in his place was a monster, one that had taken him over and swallowed him whole. This time she could not forgive him. He'd killed their son, and in doing so he had killed off that small part of hope within her. Now she would grieve him too.

Cath had fobbed the police off as best she could, watching as they had exchanged disbelieving glances with one another as she'd told them her tall hit-and-run story. 'You don't have to cover for him you know, Cath?' the policewoman had whispered to her before they had left. 'Not this time, not after this.' But Cath had remained adamant. She knew the truth would land her in a women's refuge again, and possibly Saul in prison, though this was not guaranteed. Even if it was, he'd be released within a few months and she'd be back to square one again. It wouldn't be justice for what he'd done. She'd just have to find her own justice somehow.

'I need money, Cath. Where's your purse?'

She doesn't want him to go through her bag. She doesn't want him near anything of hers. She doesn't want him near her at all. His promises of getting help and the remorse he'd shown at the hospital had been even shorter-lived than her lowest expectations, like a dud sparkler on bonfire night.

'I haven't got any money,' she manages to croak. 'I need a doctor.'

He ignores her, goes searching for her bag, angrily throwing things aside in his desperation.

'Yes, you fucking have. I know you have. You get your Universal Credit on Wednesday, every four weeks. I need it.'

She doesn't need to ask what for.

'We need that to pay the rent and bills and buy food, Saul. I need medicine… Please, Saul, call a doctor – I'm not well.'

'Tell me where your purse is, Cath, and then I'll get you one, OK.'

She groans, attempts to roll over but the pain is too much and stops her halfway. Her insides feel like they are burning.

'What's the matter with you anyway?' he snaps.

What's the matter with her? How can he even ask her that, *how*? She wants to show her incredulity but doesn't have the energy. She's gone past the point of being able to feel anything at all.

'I think I might have an infection.' She's delirious, like she's teetering on the edge of a cliff, a hair's breadth away from falling over it.

Saul is still scrabbling around the tiny, untidy bedsit, throwing clothes and shoes and miscellaneous objects around him in a bid to locate the money. He needs it to buy a fix.

'An infection? Ear infection, tooth infection… what?'

She can feel rage join the burning sensation inside of her. She wishes he were dead. She wishes *she* were dead. Anything to take away the pain she feels inside her body and her heart.

'Please, Saul… I need a doctor. You promised me… you swore to me… no more drugs, Saul… look at what they've done to you… to me… to us…'

He makes a sudden move towards her on the bed, grabs her sweat-matted hair, yanking her upwards. 'Just give me your purse, for fuck's sake, Cath!'

She is too weak to fight, physically and mentally. She'd given up fighting long ago.

'We had a son, Saul, remember? The baby boy you killed inside me. Our *child,* Saul; your own flesh and blood. You haven't even asked about him, not one thing. What he looked like, if he had hair… what he smelled like… You don't care. You murdered your own son, Saul and you don't care…' She's crying now, tears she knows are fruitless and a waste of energy. They mix in with the sweat on her face. He releases her roughly and she slumps back onto the sweat-sodden pillow. He turns away from her, not able to look at her.

'They told me I can never have another child. That my insides were too damaged so I'll never conceive again.'

He pretends he hasn't heard her; he's still searching for her handbag, a pathetic wretch of a human being, *sub-human.*

'The bag, Cath.' He speaks softly but she senses his aggression is not far away.

'It's in the bathroom, hanging up behind the door underneath the towel,' she says resignedly. There is no point. He will find it eventually and she just wants him to leave, to let her rest and grieve and cry and be alone. She cannot withstand another beating, another attack on her weak and fragile body, and if she hadn't acquiesced she knows it will come, ill or not.

He rushes into the tiny bathroom, grabs her bag, rifling through it desperately until he finds her purse.

'I'll come back with medicine for you, OK, baby? Some Chinese food – your favourite, yeah?' He kisses the top of her sweat-drenched head. 'It's going to be OK, Cath. We'll get through this, like we always do.' He touches her face with the back of his hand tenderly before slamming the door behind him.

Cath exhales in relief. He's gone, for a while at least. At least she can rest now. She winces as she rolls onto her back, exhausted and in pain. She glances around the bedsit they share, a tiny dark and damp-ridden room with a kitchenette and a postage-stamp-sized bathroom, one precarious step away from being on the streets. She knows that if she stays, that's where she will end up.

Cath casts her mind back many years ago to the council flat she had been given when Kai was born. It had been very modest – two bedrooms, a bathroom, kitchen and living room, even a little balcony where she'd kept two chairs and Kai's push bike, but compared to this, it had been Buckingham Palace. They'd been thrown out eventually, though she can't recall exactly why now; it could've been any number of reasons: drugs, antisocial behaviour, noise, non-payment of rent. They'd lived in numerous places after that: at her mum's place, at his mum's place, a friend's caravan for a while, a place above a shop where they were eventually evicted again…

It had always been the same old story, time and time again. Saul would promise to clean up his act, would show himself willing, for a few weeks at least, lulling her into a false sense of security, making her believe that he really did love her, that he really meant it this time. It was a cycle that had kept her trapped on a diabolical merry-go-round, a prisoner of her own hope. Eventually she had learned to expect the abuse, to manage it, because it had become part of her life.

But Kai had suffered. They'd taken him away eventually, the social services, put him in foster care when he was just ten years old. It had destroyed her, even though Cath had known that it was the right thing for him. Kai was seventeen years old now. He'd joined the army and was based down in Plymouth. She'd written to him so many times that she'd lost count. He'd only ever replied to one of her letters in which he'd told Cath that unless she became free of his dad, he could never again have anything to do with her. He'd told her that he loved her, and that he'd tried not to blame her. But she knew he did – how could he not? She'd failed him. She'd failed Cody. She'd failed herself.

'If you ever try and escape me, Cath, I *will* find you. I'll make it my life's mission to hunt you down…' It was a mantra she had heard so many times that she had no doubt he meant it, every word.

But things were different now; after what he'd done to her and their unborn son…

There is a knock on the door and Cath groans. Surely he's not back already? She'd hoped he'd be gone all night, holed up in some junkies' filthy living room with a bunch of like-minded zombies.

The knocking is louder and Cath knows she must answer it otherwise he will kick it down. She struggles to pull herself up and out of bed, shuffling like an old lady towards the door.

'Good grief, will you look at the state of yous!'

It's her neighbour, the old Irish woman, Neve, from across the hall. She speaks to her sometimes, although Cath tries to keep herself to herself. Saul doesn't like her talking to people. He doesn't much like her talking at all. She leaves the door open, turns to make the few steps back to her bed. She needs to lie down before she falls down.

Neve follows her inside, closes the door behind her.

'Jesus Lord above,' she says underneath her breath as she surveys the state of the tiny room, tutting. 'I came to see how you were bearing up, lass,' she says in her strong accent. 'I heard about the bairn… about the wee one… You don't look well, girl… let me get you some water.'

Cath says nothing, neither accepting nor rejecting the woman's offer.

She fills a glass from the tap in the tiny kitchenette and brings it to the bed.

'Drink this… and take some of these,' she says, producing a packet of pills. 'Painkillers. Though by the looks of yous, you need to see a doctor.'

Cath takes them willingly, swallows them back in silence. Her neighbour watches her sadly for a moment; she can feel the pity coming off her in waves.

'Listen, Cath, love. This can't go on. You know, you'll end up dead, don't you, if you let this carry on…'

Cath doesn't understand. Even after everything, somehow she is held responsible. It was never 'unless HE is stopped, then this will carry on'. The onus is always upon her. Don't they realise that she doesn't have the strength? That she lives in a cage of constant fear and that simply putting one foot in front of the other most days takes all the energy and strength she only just possesses?

'He's killed the bairn; you'll be next, Catherine, you know that? You look half dead as it is already…' She shakes her head, tutting some more. 'Can nobody help you? Yer mother, family… the police?'

Cath has been to the police on numerous occasions over the years. She's called them, the neighbours have called them, her mother has called them. And they would come out, and they would do their thing, and they might arrest him and they might not. Saul had never once been prosecuted, largely because she'd always drop the charges for fear of retaliation. 'If I end up in prison because of you, Cath, when I come out, I'll kill you. I'll kill you, your mother and sister and our boy. I'll do them all first, so you know that I've done it, and I'll come for you last…'

Perhaps it sounds fantastical to outsiders looking in, just idle threats from a crazed junkie. But Cath has absolutely no doubt in her mind that Saul is completely capable of acting out those threats. She believes him. She knows she is an addict almost as much as Saul is; she's been groomed and condition, brainwashed and controlled, managed down so that she is no longer autonomous, no longer Catherine Patterson; she is Saul Bennett's zombie.

'No one can help me, Neve.' Cath starts to cry again and Neve strokes her hair and makes soothing noises in a bid to calm her.

'You listen to me now, love – listen to an old lady who's been around the block more times that you've had hot meals. You're young, Catherine, young and a pretty lass. You've got a brain in that head of yours. This time you have to find the strength inside of you to leave and don't look back. You think you can't get out of the situation, but believe me, my girl, you can, if you dig deep – if you dig really, really deep.'

Cath starts wailing as the image of Cody's angelic face flashes up inside her mind.

'You need to get angry, girl; you need to realise now that enough is enough. You're young enough to start again, to put all of this behind you, and go on to be happy. You have the chance to do that, Catherine.'

How can she ever put all of this behind her? It isn't possible. She's lost everything; her children, her family, her home, her friends, any chance of a career, her dignity and self-esteem; she can't even have children anymore, such was the damage he'd done. She has nothing left to live for.

'You think that it's impossible but it isn't,' Neve continues. 'You've got to fight, Catherine – fight for your life, for your kids, for yourself.'

Neve's breath smells of alcohol as she moves a little closer and she realises that Cath can probably smell it as she says, 'It's too late for me now; I'm an old girl. I just want to live out my remaining days in peace with my telly and my whiskey and my books. I've ended up here because I never fought hard enough to battle my demons, but if I had my time again… Life is precious, Catherine. It's a gift from God and it's your gift, no one else's – don't give up your gift for him, for anyone, especially those you know don't deserve it.

'Listen to me, love,' she says, producing a small hip flask from the pocket of her cardigan and taking a small swig. 'It'll take the edge off.' She offers it to Cath and she accepts. It tastes harsh on the back of her throat and she gasps a little. 'Hasn't that bastard robbed you of enough already? Kai gone and now this wee one… your family estranged because they can't bear to see this happening to you, helpless…'

Neve is still stroking her hair and it feels nice, a gentle human touch that makes her feel like she wants to drift off to sleep – and never wake up.

'I have a friend in London, an old pal of mine from back in the day, Ivy. She's more me sister's mate actually, but she's as good as gold, so she is. She has a house. I'll ask if you can go there, stay for a bit, disappear. You think he'll come after you, but that waste of space can hardly make it up the stairwell he's so out of his box. He hasn't got the brains.'

Cath moans a little, caught somewhere in the vortex of a thousand emotions and pain, the kindness of a virtual stranger almost undoing her completely. Kindness has become alien to her now; it makes her feel uncomfortable.

'I'll see what I can set up. I'll write to her. She doesn't have a phone, one of these technophobics, so she is. Can't say I blame her meself. The world still existed without all these contraptions; it still managed to turn…'

Cath feels a sharp stab in her lower abdomen and yells out as Neve tuts her sadness again and strokes her hair some more.

'There there, lovie… once this is over, you must promise yourself that you'll do something, really do something this time, something to help yourself. If you can't do it for you, do it for that wee boy who should be here now, next to his mother.'

Cath wails; she can't bear it.

'Because I'm telling you something for nothing, if you can't or won't or don't, then you'll die here, in this filthy hovel. He will kill you, you know that – he will kill you eventually…'

Cath can feel the burning sensation inside of her again, the pain and hatred rising like a tsunami wave about to crash and destroy everything in its path.

'I feel like I'm already dead,' she manages to say before passing out.

CHAPTER ELEVEN

Dan

October 2019

After we attend the hospital where Beth Lawler works – or worked very briefly up until a couple of weeks ago, as it turned out – we head over to the address in Buckhurst Hill, hoping she'll be home.

'Why do you think she left her job after such a short time?' Davis asks. 'That head nurse said she was shocked when she handed her notice in out of the blue. Said she loved being a nurse, was good at it.'

'There could be a million reasons, Davis,' I say, not wanting to speculate at this stage. But she's right; a change in behaviour and circumstance is always a potential red flag right before someone gets murdered.

'Nice drum – I remember it,' Davis says, as we roll into the gated driveway of Cheney Gardens, tyres making a satisfying crunch on the white gravel below. I look up at the house. It's undeniably big with an impressive façade, but there's something soulless about it too, like it's never seen love and laughter.

'Not my chai latte,' I remark.

Davis sniggers. 'You're just well jel, boss, as they say round these parts. He built it apparently, Evan Lawler, a few years back. Acquired the land, designed it himself and got his construction company to erect it. Makes it all sound so easy…' She sighs. 'Anyway, it's a bit seventies for my taste.'

'You weren't even a thought in the seventies, Davis.' I give her a sideways glance accompanied by an eyebrow raise. 'Well, seventies or not, I wouldn't say no right now. You can't swing a cat at mine with me, Fiona and Leo. If we're all in the kitchen at the same time, you can't actually open the fridge door without someone getting injured.'

Davis laughs. 'And soon there'll be one more…'

I roll my eyes comically, but the mention of Junior's almost imminent arrival gives me a little pang of excitement tinged with acute anxiety. God knows how we'll all fit into my little gaff, but we'll manage. That's what people say, isn't it, in the face of adversity: 'We'll manage.'

Judging by the size of number 6 Cheney Gardens, I'd say the Lawlers had 'managed' pretty well. I feel a little depressed as I think of Woods and his association with Evan Lawler. I imagine he's going to be breathing down my neck on this one, even more so than usual.

'So,' Davis says, 'turns out that apparently, not long before he was shot in the head, the Lawlers attempted something of a reconciliation – they got back together.' She raises an eyebrow.

'I thought they were in the throes of a nasty divorce? That it was all very acrimonious.'

'They were.' She shrugs. 'Maybe they were giving it another go.'

Questions begin bubbling up inside my brain. 'Guess we're about to find out.'

'Beth Lawler?' Davis asks the attractive-looking blonde woman who answers the front door almost immediately. Beth Lawler is petite and femininely dressed in a flowery sundress with puff sleeves. She looks almost painfully young, which I suppose at thirty-four she is, relatively speaking, but there's freshness to her face that somehow makes her seem younger. She's not one of those high-maintenance-looking Essex women, all hair, nails and teeth, but you can tell she looks after herself.

'Yes?' she says, not overly concerned. 'Can I help you?'

'I'm Detective Riley and this is DS Davis. Can we come in?'

'Of course,' she says, mildly perplexed. 'Is everything OK?' She leads us through the oak-floored hallway and into the large open-plan kitchen. I'm reassured by how much I remember of the place from the time we were here before, to investigate Marta Larssen's disappearance: a clock on the wall and an umbrella stand in the hallway. I rely heavily upon my memory in this job; you have to, really. The best detectives I've ever known have all had photographic memories. I suppose it's all in the detail.

'Do you remember us, Mrs Lawler?' I ask her as she enters the kitchen and scrapes some chairs away from the large table. There's a laptop open on it and she snaps the lid shut.

She looks at me, glances at Davis, her puzzled expression remaining.

'Should I?' She pauses. 'Oh, hang on… were you here for Marta? When Marta went missing?' Her eyes widen. 'You were the two detectives who came to see me… us?'

'That's right.' I smile gently. 'Can we sit down?'

'Yes… yes of course, please. I've just made some fresh coffee. Can I get you both some?'

'No, thank you,' Davis and I say almost in unison. This is something that happens when you work as closely together as we do.

'So do you have some news on Marta?' she asks eagerly. 'I still think about her, every day. I miss her. I've never got over how she just vanished like that, and I never heard from her again…'

'I'm afraid we've got some bad news, Mrs Lawler.'

She sits down quickly, like she's playing musical chairs and someone has just taken the needle off the record.

'Oh God—' She puts her hands over her mouth. 'Don't tell me something's happened to her, to Marta?'

'I'm afraid we're not here about Marta,' Davis says in her softest voice, the one she reserves for moments like this. 'We're here about your husband, Evan.'

'Evan?' She stands as suddenly as she had sat down, goes towards the coffee machine and begins to prepare herself a cup. 'Is he in some sort of trouble? Is he OK?'

Davis and I exchange looks across the table. I get the sense that Beth Lawler doesn't want me to see her face.

'I think it would be better if you sit down, Beth,' Davis says. And it would be, at least for us to be able to gauge her reaction.

I take a breath, preparing myself for the least favourite part of my job – telling people their loved one is dead, murdered. Sadly, I've chalked up quite some practice on my time in homicide, and of course, I've also been on the receiving end, yet still I find myself tripping over my words and feeling emotional; usually anyway, but on this occasion I get a different sensation. Relief? I can't be sure.

'Your husband has been found dead, Beth,' I announce. 'He's been murdered. I'm so sorry.'

She's silent for a moment, no immediate reaction. In my regrettably plentiful experience this appears to be quite common. Most people fall into one of two categories when you drop such a bombshell: those who clam up in shock and go silent as they take the words in and those who go into full-on hysterics. There doesn't seem to be much in between – and both are perfectly normal.

I study her as she absorbs my words. Her hands are folded in front of her, in her lap, and they appear to be shaking slightly. Her head is dropped, and yet there's something in her body language…

'Dead?'

'Yes,' Davis says. 'We're very sorry.'

'How?'

'He was shot in the head,' I answer succinctly. 'He was found at an address in Islington, at an apartment he owned in

The Mulberries. It's estimated he's been dead for at least a couple of days, maybe more.'

She covers her hand with her mouth and I can see her fingers visibly shaking now, but her eyes are looking down at her lap.

'Evan is dead.' She says this more as a statement than a question. There's no incredulity in her voice. 'Oh God…'

The body and its expressions give so much away – tiny silent clues if you look hard enough – and I'm looking very hard indeed. But in my experience, it's always in the eyes. The eyes tell you the most. I think of Rachel's eyes then, a cobalt blue with hints of violet and dark indigo flecks if you studied them – and I did, often. No one I've ever met before or since has the same colour eyes as Rachel had. They were as unique as she was. I miss looking into them, seeing my own stupid reflection grinning back at me. I miss the things I saw in them: love and comfort and kindness and mischief – a future.

Beth Lawler reminds me of Rachel, not so much in the features but something subtler; the way she carries herself maybe, or perhaps it's the flowery sundress. She's the age Rach was when she died too, and it brings it home to me, looking at Beth Lawler, just how young she was, and all the life we've already missed – and will go on to. Time stands still for no man. But I wish it did.

Leo, Fiona's boy, who's taken over my flat with his impressive collection of WWE figures and Xboxes, asked me a question the other day: 'If you were a superhero and could have only one power, what would it be?' I'd really had to stop and think about my answer; it needed careful consideration after all. I think I'd said something like 'the power of invisibility' which Leo had nodded at in satisfactory agreement, but now I think about it, I wish I'd said 'the ability to change time, to stop it in its tracks, to be able to reverse it…'

'An apartment? What apartment? Evan lived here… we lived here…'

'Well,' Davis answers her, 'according to records, your husband owned a penthouse studio in The Mulberries. We believe he had some hand in designing them?'

'Yes, he did. Ages ago though, even before I knew him, I think.'

'You weren't aware that your husband owned this property, Mrs Lawler?'

'No, no I wasn't. I had no idea…' Her voice sounds weak and monotonous, like a thought has kidnapped her and run off with her mind.

'Mrs Lawler – Beth,' I say. 'We need to ask you some questions. You understand this, yes? We have to ask you certain questions that will help us with our enquiries. Is that OK? We'll also need to search your property, look through your husband's things, maybe take some items away for forensic examination.'

She snaps back to reality and I note that her eyes are red and she appears visibly upset although she isn't crying.

'Who on earth would want to shoot Evan?'

'That's what we're hoping you can help us with, Beth,' Davis says.

'When did you last see your husband?' I ask.

She shakes her head, as if she's ridding herself of unwanted debris inside of it.

'Oh God… what day is it now? Tuesday?'

I nod. 'The seventeenth.'

'Let me think, well… Thursday last week, or was it Friday? God, I can't remember… no, it was Thursday. I go to the gym on Fridays, and I didn't go that day.'

Davis gets her notebook out.

'Your husband hasn't been home since Thursday? Were you not concerned about his whereabouts?' I make sure to ask the question in the least accusatory tone I can muster. I don't want her to clam up.

'No,' she says, 'Evan goes away all the time – always has done since I've known him. He often takes trips away, work trips, sometimes golfing trips too, with his friends from the Freemasons' lodge.'

'When you saw him last, did he say where he was going, if he was going away somewhere on business? What time did you see him on Friday?'

'Thursday,' she corrects me. She's sharp and alert; the news seemingly hasn't muddled her brain like it does the majority of people who've just learned their spouse has been murdered.

'Um… I don't know, in the morning sometime… he was dressed for work, shirt and tie… We had a bit of breakfast together, I took our daughter to school and he was just leaving by the time I came back.'

'He didn't mention anything about where he was going, what he was doing?'

'Well, he was working on a large project in Slough. He'd been contracted to design and build social housing… he said he might be away for a few days.'

'So he did mention he would be going away?'

'I think so, yes. But like I said, Evan was away all the time. It was just the norm, you know? If he didn't come home then I knew he was away on business somewhere.'

'You didn't keep in contact while he was away? Phone calls, texts?'

She shakes her head. 'Not often. My husband was an incredibly busy man. I never wanted to bother him while he was working, unless it was an emergency, like that time with Marta,' she adds.

'I see. So you took your daughter to school and came home? Then what did you do?'

The corners of her mouth turn outwards as she attempts to recall. Her hands are still tightly clasped in her lap.

'Well, I was just here. I did a little bit of admin on my PC, sent a few emails, that sort of thing. I pottered around a bit, did a little housework. Actually, I remember now I had to wait in for some deliveries, Ocado – my groceries – and a dress I had ordered. Then I went to pick my daughter up around 3.30 p.m.

and we came back here. The school's only up the road – the little one on the corner, Bickley Road.'

Davis is scribbling furiously.

'You're a nurse, that's right, isn't it? I remember you telling me the first time we met.'

'Yes. I am.'

'You were working up at the General, weren't you?'

'Yes. I went back to work part-time for a little while.'

'But you left recently, quite suddenly according to the head nurse. Why was that?'

She lowers her eyes and her small shoulders visibly drop.

'It's not been the easiest of times, Detective,' she says, and this time she makes eye contact with me and I see it all right there in them; raw, undiluted anguish and pain, as though her pupils are projectors, playing out her emotions on a blank wall.

'I suppose I should tell you everything,' she says, although I think we both somehow know that this won't be true. 'It'll all come out anyway.'

I can feel my heart rate increase from beneath my shirt.

'Actually…' I smile at her. 'If you don't mind, I think I will have that coffee after all.'

CHAPTER TWELVE

Beth

October 2019

Beth is grateful for having her back to the detectives as she makes the coffee. She'd been expecting them, although she hadn't been expecting the same pair who had come here the time Marta had disappeared. *Disappeared.* Beth feels sick to her stomach as she looks out across the garden through the window. Poor, lovely, young Marta…

She knows she is going to need all the strength she has inside of her to get through this next hour or so, and that everything she says – every word she utters – is crucially important and must be carefully considered down to every syllable. But the truth is, she's just so tired, so mentally and physically exhausted, that part of her wants to give up, give in, tell the truth, the whole truth and nothing but the truth, *so help me God*. But she can't, not now. She must draw strength from somewhere within herself, from everything that's happened, dig as deep as she can. She has no faith in the law, not anymore. That only worked for people with money and status and power. Who got to decide what was right or wrong anyway, what could be atoned and what couldn't? Justice didn't exist for normal people like her or Cath or Nicky. Sometimes you had to find your own justice.

The arrival of the two detectives, the same ones who had come to investigate Marta's sudden disappearance, has triggered the memory of that day; the day she told Evan she wanted to leave him. She wonders now what would've happened if that conversation had never taken place, or perhaps more poignantly, what *wouldn't* have happened.

What a difference a day makes. This thought runs through her mind, gathering momentum. How a day can change your entire life's trajectory; how it can alter your life irrevocably, and in turn the lives of everyone around you. In those 1,440 minutes, or 86,400 seconds, the life you once knew could disappear forever, and you could disappear with it.

Beth realises now more than ever that life is little more than a series of choices and decisions. She asks herself the question why some people seem to make the right ones and others can't seem to stop making the wrong ones. Is it simply down to luck and timing, intellect, chance or a culmination of all of them? Or is it something more complex than that? We are all just guessing in the dark really, so how come it works out well for some and not for others? Are choices instinctive or are they predetermined? Has it all really just been mapped out for everyone already? Intelligent people make bad choices just as much as ignorant people make good ones. Wisdom and age only seem to play a part to an extent. What makes someone meet their soulmate at thirteen and die in their arms at ninety-three, and yet another never meet theirs at all? Does one right choice lead you onto the path of all good choices and vice versa? All she knows for certain now, with these two detectives standing in front of her, is that she, and everything that has happened, is the sum of her own choices.

'Last year, Evan and I separated,' she explains. 'I had an affair.'

She brings the coffees to the table, looks the detective in his blue eyes. She remembers when she'd first met him how they'd reminded her of Nicky's and feels a sharp stabbing pain through her heart. Perhaps if she'd asked to see him, this Detective Riley character, maybe he would have listened to her, maybe he would have helped her… but she doesn't think so really – no one could've helped her.

'We know about the affair, Beth,' the female detective says. 'We're not here to judge you.'

She manages a smile that she hopes mimics gratitude. But she knows that it's exactly why they're here.

'Our marriage had been in trouble for a few years… Evan was always working away, you know, I was a bored housewife at home and well, I just got a bit lonely, I suppose… it wasn't anything really.' She dismisses it; she dismisses *him* because she has to. She knows Nick would understand.

'But you left your husband didn't you, for this man? What was his name, Beth?'

'Nick,' she says. 'Nicholas Wainwright.' The female detective scribbles it down.

She takes a sip of her coffee, but it's like swallowing fire. 'Briefly, yes. We lived together for a while, but it didn't work out.'

'We know there was some kind of custody battle going on, regarding your daughter?' Detective Riley speaks this time and she tries not to look into those eyes of his, but she can't help herself. It's as if he's silently willing her to.

'Yes, well, kind of. Lily was with me, with us, Nick and I, for a while but then… well, some allegations were made and so she was put into Evan's custody, temporarily, while it was looked into.'

'That must've been difficult for you?' the female says and it sounds patronising and she wants to scream at her, 'You have no fucking idea!' but she doesn't. It's not her fault; she's simply doing her job.

'Yes. It was a trying time. I didn't believe the allegations… not at first.'

'What were the allegations, Beth?'

She swallows a little bile that's collected at the back of her throat. She doesn't want to say the words; she's frightened they'll stick, or that she'll suddenly come undone and start screaming like a banshee.

'Sexual abuse…' She can hear her own voice shaking as she says it. 'Evan claimed that Lily had told him, and a teacher at school, that Nicky…' She closes her eyes for a second, the words illicit. 'That Nick had touched her inappropriately.'

She watches the exchange between the two detectives in a bid to try to gauge what they're thinking. Mud sticks, doesn't it, once that evil seed of doubt is planted?

'I dismissed it as ludicrous at first. I thought that maybe Evan had been poisoning Lily's mind, getting her to say things, or that she was saying it for attention because her mummy and daddy had split up and… well, I just didn't believe it; Nick was a decent man, very decent. And he adored Lily. But then they found those images on his laptop and…' Beth starts to cry; though it's really not for the reasons she imagines the detectives think it is.

'So he was arrested for having indecent images of children on his computer?'

'Yes, but not for any assault on Lily. She retracted her statement in the end, anyway, said she'd said it because she wanted her mummy and daddy back together. Nick was released on bail and a court case was scheduled a few months down the line.'

'And you supported him – were still supporting him at this stage?'

Beth reminds herself to breathe. 'He said they'd been planted on his computer… I didn't know what to think.' She shakes her head. 'I thought I knew him… I was in denial, I suppose.'

'And Lily, she was living with Evan still at this time?'

'Yes. He was awarded temporary custody of her and they were living here, in this house, the family home.'

Detective Riley nods at her to continue.

'Things were strained between us – Evan and myself obviously, and with Nick being accused too – and then my mum died suddenly. She had a heart attack; she was only fifty-six years old.'

Beth notes the look of genuine sympathy in the detective's eyes, or perhaps it's something deeper than that.

'I was inconsolable. I was… I was very close to my mum. It was just me and her growing up. She brought me up alone, you see; my dad died when I was twelve.'

'I'm so sorry, Beth,' the detective says, sliding his hand across the table towards her. She doesn't want to take it; she really will come undone if she does.

'I think it was the strain.' She wipes her eyes with her thumb and forefinger, rubs the mascara residue into her fingertips. 'She was devastated about Lily, about all of it. She adored her and couldn't bear the idea of her being hurt or damaged in any way.'

'Of course,' the detective says.

'So when did you reconcile with Evan? How long ago was that?'

'A couple of months before Nick's trial was due. I realised I'd been in denial, messed things up, made some mistakes. I wanted us to be a family again, for Lily to be with her mummy and her daddy. So I called off the solicitors, stopped all the nonsense…'

'And Evan was agreeable?'

'He never wanted us to break up in the first place. He was very happy that I'd come to the decision I had and came home.'

Beth shakes away the tears that are now falling from her cheeks. She needs to remind herself why they're here and keep to the script. *Evan is dead, shot dead.* 'I just can't believe any of this has happened. First my mum, then Nick and now Evan too…'

'Nick?' Old blue eyes is on it straight away.

'Yes,' Beth says. Her stabbing pains have returned and she only hopes she can disguise them. 'Didn't I say? He's dead too.'

CHAPTER THIRTEEN

Beth

August 2018

Beth watches Lily playing in the garden with the other little girls and smiles as she shrieks and laughs and sings along to the cheesy pop music. Her daughter is a vivacious and confident girl for her age, and the other girls seem to look up to her and follow her lead. Beth isn't entirely sure where, or who, she gets her pluckiness from. She had been quite a reserved child herself and only really came into her own when she reached her twenties. Plus she'd never really needed to court the limelight; somehow she had always managed to find herself in it quite naturally. She has no idea what kind of a child Evan was; he rarely spoke of that time, or either one of his parents. Sometimes she wondered if he'd ever even been one.

It's Amber's birthday party and the girl's mum, Lorraine, has gone to town with the decorations and the spread of party food, which she has assured her is 'more or less completely vegan'. Vegan party food for six year olds! Beth hated all those overtly PC mums. It was mostly for appearance and so fake. She'd seen Lorraine coming out of the McDonald's drive-through at least twice in the past month.

She looks over at a group of mums gathered by the trestle table, enjoying a glass of wine – organic probably – and chatting to each other. She thinks about going over to join them, but they're huddled tightly together, like a coven, and she feels awkward.

Amber's dad, Brian, is busy trying to inflate the paddling pool and she looks over at him, feeling like a spare part.

'They said it was going to be warm.' He smiles at her as he catches her eye. 'But I didn't realise just how warm it would be, otherwise I would've set this up earlier. You never know with the weather, do you? Hit and miss. Lorraine is furious with herself that she didn't ask all the children to bring their swim gear now.'

'Oh, I know,' Beth agrees. 'They didn't predict a heatwave, did they? Not that I'm complaining. Anyway, the kids will love it – they'll just strip down to their underwear and jump in.'

'Good idea,' he says. 'Will you be joining them?' He flashes her a cheeky smile and she laughs it off but feels mildly paranoid and a little offended by the comment. She knows what he's thinking; she left her husband for her lover, must be a bit of a slut, must be up for it, bit of a goer. She wishes she hadn't worn this sundress now – the straps are thin and it's quite low-cut.

Feeling eyes upon her, Beth looks over and sees that the other mums are staring in her direction. One of them turns back round and they all start to laugh. Now she's really paranoid. Are they talking about her? Laughing at her? She doesn't really know them very well; only to say hello to during drop-off and collection times. She hasn't really made friends with any of them because she's had so much else going on – the divorce, moving, Nicky… Besides, she wants to keep herself to herself, doesn't want everyone knowing her private business.

'That's some bruise on your little girl,' Brian says. 'How did she get that? Looks nasty.'

'She fell over,' Beth says, adding, 'poor thing.' But in actual fact, she has no idea how Lily got such a bad bruise on her thigh. She'd returned home from an overnight stay at Evan's and it had been there.

'What happened, darling?' Beth had enquired. 'How did you get a boo boo?'

But Lily hadn't really given her an answer, not a definitive one anyway.

'I tripped over when I was in Daddy's garden,' she'd initially said but later had changed the story to falling off a swing. Beth had iced it. It looked swollen and she could see angry shades of purple forming underneath the skin.

'That's going to be a big girl's bruise,' Beth had said and thought no more about it, though she'd made a mental note to ask Evan about it. He'd not mentioned anything about Lily falling over.

Beth looks over at the gaggle of women again and her awkwardness spills over into annoyance – who were they to look down on her and judge her? They knew nothing about her life. Fuelled by two glasses of Prosecco and slight indignation, she heads over towards them. Maybe she'll really give them something to talk about!

'Hi,' she says, breaking the circle. 'Beautiful day, isn't it?'

The women stop chatting immediately.

'Oh hi, Beth, isn't it?' A small woman with short brown hair smiles at her. 'You're Lily's mum, aren't you?'

'That's right,' she says.

The woman nods. 'I'm Linda. Yes, it's gorgeous, isn't it? Lovely party. So lucky to be born in the summer – both mine were winter babies.'

'Well, I'm a February girl myself, so I understand completely. I was always jealous of my friends with summer birthdays. They got to wear all the pretty dresses while I was wrapped up in hats and scarves on mine.'

'Made up for it today though,' another of the mums says sweetly, looking her up and down. 'I love your dress. It suits you.'

'Thanks.' Beth smiles at her although she knows it was a backhanded compliment and feels like throwing the woman's organic wine all over her nasty face.

'How are things with you? How's Lily coping with everything?' another of the mums chips in. Beth doesn't recognise her though; never seen her at the school before – or perhaps she's just not noticed her. 'Evan says she's taken it all quite hard.'

A bolt of adrenalin hits Beth's stomach, putting her on high alert.

'Coping with what?' She manages a small smile.

'The break-up,' the stranger says, cocking her head to one side in a bid to mimic sympathy. 'Evan said she's been very upset, that she's struggling with your new— Can't be easy for her, poor love, for any of you really.'

Beth is so taken aback by the woman's directness that she feels momentarily paralysed. How dare she! What had Evan been saying to them? What had he told them? She doesn't want to have to explain herself to this woman, to any of them. The small brunette, Linda, looks like she wants the ground to swallow her up and shifts awkwardly on her feet.

'Well, that's news to me,' Beth replies as graciously as possible. 'Lily has been fine. Evan and I have explained things to her and… she gets on very well with my… with Nick and…' Beth stops herself. Why is she justifying herself to this spiteful gossip? She can feel her face burning with anger.

'Evan thinks she might need some counselling about it all… I mean, divorce is such a big thing for them to deal with, well, for anyone really, but you don't know what's going on in their little minds at this age, do you?' She gives her another sickly smile. 'Can't be easy can it, all that adjustment. Evan said she keeps wetting the bed and—'

'I didn't realise you knew Evan so well,' Beth interrupts her. The other mums have wisely stood back and begun a conversation among themselves, leaving just the three of them: Beth, Linda and this woman whose name she doesn't know, standing awkwardly in a triangle.

The woman laughs, pretends to be embarrassed. 'Oh, I don't, not really, and certainly not like that!' Her loud laugh rings out across the garden like gunfire. 'You've nothing to worry about there.'

Beth can feel her irritation spilling over and wills herself to hold it together.

'Not that you are, I'm sure, not with a handsome new toy boy in tow.'

Toy boy? Nick was eighteen months her junior, for Christ's sake.

'I see Evan up at the school occasionally, and we took the girls horse riding together last week. My Imogen is a budding equestrian.'

Yes, and her mother is a complete bitch. Horse riding? Together? What the hell? This was news to her.

Lily had loved horses ever since she could remember. Beth had been promising to take her riding just as soon as she was big enough, but it seemed Evan had beaten her to it. This mildly aggrieves her. Evan has never done a thing with Lily since she'd been born. He's never even taken her to the park or pushed her on a swing. But now that she's left him it seems he is suddenly Father of the Year. Or is it something else? One-upmanship? Perhaps she's being unfair. She's always wanted him to take more of an interest in their daughter, any interest in fact, but hearing about this rankles. Evan has not told her he was taking their daughter horse riding, certainly not with this dreadful woman, and moreover, Lily hasn't mentioned it to her either. She feels confused, upset and angry. Annoyingly, this must show on her expression because the woman says with an over-exaggerated and somewhat self-satisfying gasp, 'Oh! Didn't Lily tell you?'

'Yes,' Beth lies. 'She did mention it.'

She can tell the woman doesn't believe her. She's never been a good liar. 'We all had such a lovely time. Lily's a natural rider, you know. Took to it like a duck to water she did. Even when she fell off, she just got right back up again and straight back in the saddle.'

Fell off? Beth feels like screaming. Well, she supposes that would explain Lily's nasty-looking bruise. But why hasn't she said anything? Why has she lied? Why hasn't Evan mentioned any of this?

'She's always loved horses,' Beth says feeling chocked. She'd wanted to see her daughter on a horse for the first time, and somehow this horrible woman has been given this privilege instead. She feels angry with Evan.

'We had a little picnic afterwards. Such a shame…' the woman says, her voice trailing off.

'What is?' Beth wants this conversation to end but can't help but be sucked into it, which she's pretty sure is the woman's sole intention.

'About you and your husband. He's such a lovely fellow, really lovely. He adores Lily and you too you know… He said you were the love of his life and that he's heartbroken that you went off… when you broke up.'

'I'm just going to top myself up,' Linda interjects breezily before quickly backing away. 'Can I do the honours for anyone else?' She's gone before either of them can answer.

'Did he really?' Beth cannot keep the sarcasm from her reply. Now that they're alone the gloves are off and she wants to tell this interfering old cow the truth. How her 'lovely' husband had as good as ignored her for the past decade and hadn't so much as taken Lily to the toilet, let alone horse riding. She wants to tell her how cold and unemotional Evan is, how he's a workaholic with zero interest in her or their marriage and… but she knows she will only look like she's trying to justify her affair and doesn't want to give the woman this satisfaction. 'Guess you learn something new every day,' Beth says. She wants to leave.

'Well, he said he's devastated about you wanting a divorce. Personally, I think he's taken it quite well. I know my husband would kill me if I went off with another man and moved our daughter in with him. He'd see me dead first.' There's that gunfire laugh again. 'But Craig has a terrible possessive streak. Goes berserk even if another man looks in my direction.'

Beth feigns laughter of her own.

'Well, I'm sure he doesn't have much to worry about in that department,' she says sweetly. 'It was nice meeting you…?'

'Miranda,' the woman says, her jaw dropping slightly as she realises what Beth had meant a few seconds after she walks away.

'I think Evan is up to something.' Beth says as she lies in Nick's arms that night in bed.

'Oh? What makes you say that, babe? Has he said something?'

She nuzzles into his armpit. He smells of soap and the outdoors.

'At the party today, Lily's friend's birthday… I think he's been saying things to some of the mums about me.'

He pulls her in even closer to him, throws his thigh over hers, locking her in tightly to him.

'Like what?'

'Well, he took Lily horse riding with another mum… *Miranda.*' She says her name in a silly voice.

'Really? What, and never mentioned it?'

'No. Neither of them said a word about it. I had to learn about it from this awful smug woman who seems to think the sun shines out of Evan's backside. You should've seen the way they were looking at me, Nick. Like I'm a slut. I felt so self-conscious, it was horrible. She referred to you as my "toy boy"!'

Nick laughs. 'You're kidding me?' He nuzzles his face into the back of her neck. 'Mmm, my sexy little cougar!'

'I'm serious! It's not funny,' she says, laughing. 'God only knows what Evan's been saying about me, about us.'

He squeezes her waist with a strong arm. His strength feels reassuring somehow.

'They're just jealous, babe – you know what some women are like. Who cares what they think? Let them gossip, nothing better to do with their time. Evan can say what he likes. He should've appreciated you while he had you – you and Lily.'

His words are making her feel a little better and she feels a little of the tension release in her shoulders.

'Don't worry about Evan, OK? What can he do or say? Soon you'll be divorced and won't have to have very much to do with him, only when it comes to Lily, and the courts will sort all that out, consent orders and contact and all of that. We'll be yesterday's news in a few weeks.'

'You're right,' she says, kissing his fingers, which are interlocked with her own. 'But I can't help wondering why Lily didn't mention the horse riding. You know how much she loves horses and what an occasion it would've been for her. Why didn't she tell me?'

Nick blows air from his lips. 'Maybe he told her not to, babe.'

'Yes, but why?'

He exhales again. 'Who knows? Maybe she just forgot to mention it… Don't worry about it, darling. It's good that he's doing things with her, isn't it?'

He rolls onto his side to face her, their noses almost touching and she nods in agreement.

'Yes, it is but…'

'With a bit of luck the divorce will be plain sailing and now that I've just secured another big contract…'

'Another one! You didn't tell me!' She playfully pinches the end of his nose.

'Yes… you are currently looking at the new contractor for Wilmington's Preparatory School and College!'

Beth sits up. 'Oh my God, Nicky! That's amazing! Why didn't you say anything earlier, letting me bang on about those silly women?'

He laughs. 'Are you proud of your boy?' he says with a grin. 'It's a huge contract, Beth; we won't need to worry about finances. We'll be sitting pretty.'

'I'm soooo proud of you, Nick.' Beth feels emotional, like she wants to cry. 'The gods are watching over us, I swear it.'

'Well, in the infamous words of the late Roy Scheider, "We're going to need a bigger boat!" I'm going to need to take on more permanent staff, recruit more contractors. I went to see some office space today… nothing fancy, just a little cabin-type place where I can do all the admin, maybe hire a secretary…'

She kisses him. 'Just make sure she's not younger or more beautiful than me.' Beth laughs.

'Impossible,' he says. 'Well, the latter at least. *My sexy little cougar!*'

'Oi!' She slaps his backside playfully.

Nick had started his gardening business on his own, just a one-man show, and over the years he had nurtured it like one of his plants and now it was finally blooming.

'I love you so much,' she says, thoughts of Evan and that horrible woman disappearing from her mind.

'I love you too, you gorgeous creature,' he says, tickling her side and making her squeal. 'This contract means we can get our own place sooner than I'd hoped. We might not even need your share of Buckhurst Hill first. And hopefully there'll be enough left over for our wedding – once you get your decree nisi, anyway.'

Beth gasps. 'Are you serious?' Her face aches through smiling.

'Deadly,' he says, pulling a mock serious face. 'I want to marry the love of my life. I don't want to waste time; we've both done enough of that. I want you to be my wife, Bethany Ann.'

She feels tearful as she squeezes his strong body against her own. 'I want to spend the rest of my life with you, making you happy.'

'You already make me happy,' he says, his hands beginning to feel the contours of her naked curves beneath the sheets. Beth feels warm with happy feelings as they begin to make love, but somewhere, in the back of her mind, buried beneath her euphoria, a tiny cloud is forming, an Evan-shaped cloud.

'And don't worry about Evan,' Nick says, as if sensing her thoughts. 'He can't touch us, I promise.'

CHAPTER FOURTEEN

Dan

October 2019

The incident room is always an intense place to be at the start of any murder enquiry, these first forty-eight hours being the most crucial, and the atmosphere is filled with tension and expectation as I enter it. It still gives me a buzz though, even after my ten years on the squad. I imagine soldiers experience a similar feeling when they're about to go into battle.

'Right, folks, listen up,' I address the team. 'As you know, Evan Lawler's body was found this morning at an address in Islington.' I point to the photograph of his bloated, greying corpse on the whiteboard and feel a little queasy as I'm reminded of the smell. 'It's estimated that he's been deceased for around five days, which means we're looking at TOD as last Thursday, probably somewhere between 12 and 4 p.m. Preliminaries from path say he was most likely shot at close range, probably with a Glock 9 mm although we will have more on that as soon as ballistics deliver. Nothing came back from the fingertip search, no sign of the weapon or the shells at the scene and no obvious witness as yet. We're waiting on full forensics – fingerprints, DNA, anything left at the scene – but I have a nasty suspicion we're not going to get much back from them and that whoever assassinated our Mr Lawler did it professionally and precisely.'

I take a breath, a swig of lukewarm coffee and it hits my empty stomach almost instantly.

'So…' I look around at their eager faces. 'At this point in time we don't have any evidence – so evidence is what we need to get, but Beth Lawler, Evan Lawler's wife, is currently our number-one person of interest. Evan and Beth separated sometime in June last year. She was having a relationship with another man, Nicholas Wainwright, and they had embarked upon a pretty acrimonious divorce by all accounts…'

Mitchell raises her hand. 'Gov, I've run some checks on the boyfriend, Wainwright. Turns out he died a few months ago in a freak accident. Well, I say freak, what actually happened was that he'd been drinking in a pub up near Buckhurst Hill when he allegedly got into some kind of altercation with some local men. He'd been arrested some months earlier for having child pornography on his computer and released on bail. It was also alleged that he'd been abusing the daughter, the Lawlers' little girl, Lily, five years old and social services had put the child in Evan's care, temporarily anyway, and… well, it transpires that Nicholas Wainwright lost his business as a result of the accusations made against him – he'd not long started a big gardening contract at Wilmington College.

'Wainwright had a fight outside a pub, The Punch & Judy; he was drunk, falling-down drunk according to witnesses. The fight was broken up and Wainwright left, only he fell over making his way home and hit his head on the pavement, knocked himself out. He was taken to Epsom General but died some hours later of an aneurysm. He vehemently protested his innocence regarding the accusations and the charges for the indecent images of children. Beth Lawler also gave a statement at the time protesting

Wainwright's innocence and claiming it was a malicious set-up on Evan Lawler's part. Delaney took it.'

'Delaney?' I look over at him and he shrugs.

'Nothing in it, gov. Sticks and stones. From what I could gather, Beth Lawler didn't want to believe that her boyfriend was a nonce. They were in the midst of a custody battle, just a lot of mud-slinging, nothing to substantiate her claims whatsoever.'

'Right.' I nod at him by way of thanks. 'But get me the transcript of that interview, yeah, Martin? I'd like to have a look at it.'

'Boss,' he replies. That's twice he's referred to me in the subordinate in as many sentences, which is not like Delaney at all. I know it pains him to refer to me as either.

'Apparently,' Mitchell continues, chewing the end of her biro, 'the little girl ended up retracting her original statement, saying she'd never been abused by Wainwright at all and had made it all up for attention because she wanted her mummy and daddy back together again. I've got all the reports from SS, boss, plus copies of statements from Beth Lawler and Wainwright.' Mitchell holds them up like a trophy and places them down on my desk. I nod my thanks, even though I'm about to brutally burst her tenacious bubble.

'Thank you, Mitchell, that's good police work; only we already know this as we've just come from Cheney Gardens – from seeing Mrs Lawler to give her the good news about her husband.'

Mitchell tries not to look too deflated but is a little shy of succeeding. Davis shoots me a look that reads 'meanie' as she takes over.

'Beth Lawler claims that a few months ago, following Wainwright's death, she and Evan reconciled and she returned to the family home.'

'Seems a little strange, doing a complete U-turn like that,' Harding says.

'I'm inclined to agree with you at this stage,' I say. 'Beth Lawler is someone we need to look very closely at indeed. She has very clear revenge motive and stood to gain from her husband's death financially. It could be that the reconciliation between them was a placebo on her part, faked to take a bit of the heat from her after she killed him, or had him killed. This was an execution-style murder. Quick in and out, get the job done and leave no trace. No grizzly gore, nothing too over the top. Beth Lawler's life was pretty much in ruins after she left her husband. She lost her home, her daughter, her mother – who died of a sudden heart attack in amongst all the conflict and drama – and then of course, Wainwright, all in the space of a few months. Until she agreed upon a reconciliation, Evan's lawyers were geared up to annihilate her in court, and he certainly had the means to do so. I'd say if anyone harboured any hatred for Mr Lawler it was Mrs Lawler herself.'

'Plus,' Harding pipes up, 'it transpires that Evan Lawler never changed his will, or his life insurance of, wait for it, £2.5 million.'

Whistles echo around the room, punctuating the tension. 'And as they were still married, Beth will inherit everything: Lawler's estate, his business, the house, the kid, the cars, the holiday home, the whole enchilada, boss.'

'Which is why she's our number-one priority, people,' I say. 'But we've also got to dig a little deeper into Lawler's private life. He was a very successful man, wealthy, and the business he was in – construction – may well have forced him to accrue a few enemies. Lawler may have come across as a decent family man, albeit with marriage troubles, but we can't afford to judge a book by its cover at this stage. So let's start digging, OK? Apparently, he liked the company of high-end escort girls, so we need to speak to the agencies he used, and the girls. Baylis, I will leave that task in your capable hands.'

'Right you are, boss.'

'We need CCTV, running up to and on the day of the murder; check to see who went in and out of The Mulberries building. I also want CCTV from the marital home address in Buckhurst Hill. Beth Lawler has already given us that. She claims to have an alibi for Thursday last week; says she was home all day, waited in for shopping and deliveries. This needs corroborating, so cross-reference everything very carefully and check with the neighbours too. We'll get a search warrant if we need one to go through the home, see what that throws up, if anything. And Mitchell—'

'Yes, boss?' She looks up, seemingly having made a full recovery from my little rain on her parade earlier.

'Seeing as though you've been so proactive already, I want you to get as much information as you can on a missing-person file, someone by the name of Marta Larssen. She was the Lawlers' housekeeper, a Norwegian girl in her late twenties. Davis and I looked into it initially about eighteen months ago but it was downgraded to MP when it turned out her passport and some clothes were also missing, no sign of foul play. Find out where MP are on it, or where they got, and if it's gone cold I want it reopened.'

'I'll do that, boss,' Delaney says. 'I worked with them on it. I was the first at the scene as well.'

Bingo! Delaney has bitten. I'd tasked Mitchell with it deliberately in a bid to see how or if he'd react.

'Yes, so I recall,' I say. 'So what did you make of it at the time? Did you sense anything off about the whole thing?'

Delaney gives a nonchalant shrug. 'Not really, boss. We did all the necessaries… checked the whole place over. Nothing from forensics, nothing amiss. MP drew a blank.'

'You think Marta Larssen's disappearance is connected to Evan's murder, boss?' Mitchell asks.

'Could be no more than coincidence, Mitchell. But if it isn't… we could have a double murder on our hands. Oh, and Woods knows the deceased, people,' I say, addressing the rest of the squad. 'This means that he's going to be keeping a close eye on us. And when I say "us" what I really mean is "me". They played golf together on a couple of occasions, both Freemasons and all that "you scratch my back and I'll scratch yours" business.'

There are groans from the gang and I note that Delaney looks over towards Woods' office.

'I know, I know. Let's get this one cleaned up quickly, shall we? Starting with corroborating Beth Lawler's whereabouts on the day of the shooting, and in the run- up to it. Find out who she was with, who she saw, where she went, what she ate and how many times she went to the bathroom.'

Davis looks over at me. 'And me, boss?'

'You, Davis, are coming with me,' I say, beckoning her over.

'I had a feeling you might say that,' she says, grabbing her bag.

CHAPTER FIFTEEN

Beth

September 2018

'What do you mean I can't see her? She's my daughter! What the hell is going on, Ms Walker?' Beth addresses the headmistress from across the desk, hands raised in obvious distress. She'd got the call as she'd been driving back from the hospital after a difficult shift. Fear and panic have gripped her alongside confusion and it's not making for a good combination. She wants answers. She wants a cigarette.

'I'm so sorry, Mrs Lawler; it's Beth, isn't it? Can I call you Beth? If we could just calm down a little I can explain things to you until the social services arrive, OK? Can we get you a tea or coffee, something to drink?'

Yes, a double vodka on the rocks.

'I don't want tea or coffee,' Beth snaps, 'thank you. I just want my daughter. Why is she being withheld from me? What's going on?' She thinks she's about to start crying, but she doesn't want to break down in front of the headmistress; she has a horrible sick feeling that she's going to need to stay strong for whatever's coming.

'I understand you must feel incredibly worried and upset, and I'm very sorry for that,' Ms Walker says, although it sounds disingenuous. 'But when it comes to these sorts of things there are very strict guidelines we must follow.'

Beth shakes her head. *These sorts of things?* She has no idea what the woman is talking about. All she can think is how Lily must feel right now, not being able to go home with her mummy. Beth had instantly known something was wrong when she had pulled up at the school. It was like a sixth sense, a wrench in her stomach, a feeling of impeding dread. Then she'd received a phone call from a lady called Rosemary Garrett from the safeguarding team at social services who'd explained that some allegations had been made and that as a result Lily would be unable to leave with her. She told her she was en route to the school to talk to her in person and explain everything. Beth had felt physically sick. Terror had frozen her brain like someone had pressed pause.

'It's a Section 72, Mrs Lawler,' the social worker had said, as if Beth should know what this was exactly. 'Some very serious allegations have been made and we must put measures in place to protect Lily.'

'Section 72? Protect her from what? From who?' she had screamed at the woman down the phone, her panic getting the better of her. 'I don't understand. What allegations have been made? Who by? Who against? What…'

'I will go through everything with you as soon as I'm at the school. Please try not to worry – I will be there soon.'

Try not to worry! Was she being serious? Beth feels a gut-wrenching sense of helplessness as she sits opposite Ms Walker, waiting for this Rosemary woman to arrive. Social services. *Oh God.*

'When you say "these sort of things", what do you mean, Ms Walker?' Beth blinks at the headmistress. She's never had many dealings with her before, doesn't really know her, but she's always seemed a pleasant woman, professional if a little austere. Right now, however, she hates her and vows to take Lily away from this school the moment all this is sorted out. How dare they simply take her daughter from her? On what grounds? Things like this didn't happen in real life, did they?

'Like I said, Beth, if we can just try to stay calm, it will make things a lot easier.'

'Easier for who? You're stopping me from taking my own daughter home and social services are on their way here and no one can tell me why?'

'Once the social worker arrives we can sit down and go through it all and—'

'For goodness' sake.' Beth is crying now, she just can't help it. 'Just tell me what's happened! Why can't I see my daughter? She'll be upset – she'll be expecting me to pick her up, wondering where I am.'

Ms Walker sighs, pulls a tissue from the box on her desk and hands it to Beth.

'I'm sorry, Beth. There's no easy way to say this…' The headmistress pauses, takes a large intake of breath. 'That bruise on Lily's leg, on her left thigh, do you know the one I'm talking about?'

Beth blows her nose, nods.

'Yes of course. I iced it. She came back from an overnight visit from her dad's and there it was.'

'Did she tell you how she got it?'

'She said she'd fallen over in the garden. Then she changed the story a little later to falling off a swing. Evan didn't mention any accident when he dropped her off. He didn't mention it at all. Actually!' Beth suddenly remembers the woman – what was her name, Linda was it? No, Lorraine… shit, she can't remember now, anyway, the nosy gossip from the party. 'One of the other mums told me that she and Evan had taken the girls horse riding and that Lily had fallen off the horse and that's how she'd really got it. I wasn't aware they had even been riding because neither Evan nor Lily told me about it.'

'I see,' Ms Walker says. 'Well, today, Lily asked to speak to her form tutor, Mrs Alcock. She seemed tearful and upset, troubled about something. Mrs Alcock has felt that there's been a change in Lily this last term, that she seems a little more subdued, not her usual vivacious self.'

'OK… and?'

'Well, Lily confided to Mrs Alcock that your partner, the man you live with, Nick, is it?'

Beth's adrenalin is in overdrive and her heart is beating so fast it almost hurts.

'Yes, Nick, what about him? Lily adores him; he adores her. They get on brilliantly and she loves spending time with him, with all of us.'

Ms Walker smiles thinly, nods her French-plaited head. 'I'm afraid Lily, after a little coaxing, confessed to her tutor that your partner, Nick, had given her the bruise.'

'WHAT!' Beth stands bolt upright from the chair. 'That's utterly ridiculous, absolute nonsense. No! No way! Why would she say such a thing? I told you, she came back from Evan's with the bruise. It wasn't there until after he'd brought her home and then this woman… this thingy's mum… God, I can't remember her bloody name… Imogen's mum, she's Imogen's mum, in Lily's class, she told me that Lily had been riding and fallen off a horse. I… I…' Beth's tripping over her words. She can't think straight; she can barely think at all.

Ms Walker looks at her with a grave expression. 'Your daughter claims that your partner has touched her… intimately touched her, Beth, in her private area. More than once.'

Beth thinks she might pass out. She can't believe what she's hearing.

'Oh no! NO! No, no, no! No, no, no…' Beth is shaking violently, the word 'no' spilling from her lips on repeat. Every cell in her body feels heavy with dread. 'This is a lie,' she shrieks. 'Nicky would never touch her – never. I know he wouldn't. He adores her… she adores him, for Christ's sake! There's been some kind of dreadful mistake…' Beth physically begins to back away from the desk, like Ms Walker has pulled a gun on her.

'Please, Beth, sit down.' Ms Walker is calm but her tone has the firmness of a headmistress.

'Lily would've told me, she would've come to me… This is a mistake. He would never hurt her like that – Jesus Christ, he'd never hurt her at all! I need to call my husband, call Evan and get him here right away.'

Ms Walker gives her a strange look. 'Actually, he's already on his way here.'

'What? Why? How does he know? Did you telephone him?'

Ms Walker nods. 'I'm afraid we're obliged to. Mr Lawler pays all Lily's tuition fees and…'

'Oh Jesus Christ!' Beth drags her shaking hand down her face. 'This isn't happening; tell me it isn't happening!'

'I'm sorry, Beth, but the police are on their way too. This is an incredibly serious accusation. It has to be thoroughly investigated – you understand this obviously, for the sake of Lily's safety and well-being.'

'She's lying.' Beth looks at Ms Walker. 'Sometimes she tells lies… for attention, you know? Her dad and I are going through a divorce; perhaps she's made it up simply to get our attention. I thought she'd been taking the separation well. She's never been close to her father. Jesus, Nick has done more with her in three months than Evan has done with her in six years!'

Ms Walker's head lowers a little. 'Beth, I realise how difficult this is to hear but I really do think you need to consider the accusation very seriously. How long have you even known your partner? Are you aware of his background? Do you know—'

'How dare you! Oh my GOD!' Beth feels her panic and horror spill over into rage. 'I've told you, Ms Walker, I know my partner. He's a good, honest, decent man, hard-working, kind… He's not a child molester! I just can't believe Lily would make something like this up; she's only six, she doesn't understand the connotations, the seriousness of the accusations and…'

And then it suddenly hits her, like a wrecking ball in the solar plexus, almost folding her in half. 'Oh my God. Evan… this is Evan, isn't it? He's put her up to it. I know my daughter; I know her better than anyone…'

'I don't doubt that, but—'

'He's told her to say this; he's trying to sabotage my relationship, trying to sabotage my relationship with Lily too. Oh God help me, Ms Walker.' Beth finally sits down, looks into the woman's eyes, imploringly. 'Please, you've got to believe me when I say that this is all lies. It's all been cooked up by Evan – I feel sure of it.'

For a second it looks as if the headmistress believes her but then she says, 'It's like you've said, Beth, why would Lily make up such a terrible lie?'

Beth wants to scream, bang her small fist on the woman's pristine desk.

'Surely you owe it to Lily to give her the benefit of the doubt?'

There's a knock at the door then and a large woman wearing a garish, ill-fitting floral wrap dress enters. She's carrying a folder and Evan is behind her. Beth stands up, desperately tries to gather herself together, but she needs to hold on to the chair for support. The woman introduces herself as Rosemary Garrett from the safeguarding team at children's social services and gives Beth a weak handshake. Beth feels like she's in a dream – a nightmare – as the woman begins to speak. She feels like she imagines those poor souls who are given anaesthetic during surgery, only it doesn't work and they're paralysed on the operating table, helpless, unable to speak up, trapped inside their own body, feeling every cut of the surgeon's knife. She'd heard about it happening on rare occasions at the hospital where she works and it had given her chills.

She can hear the woman talking about an incident in the bath, something about a bedtime story… the bruise inflicted as a means to silence Lily. She can hear the words but she cannot believe they're being said, and her mind is whirring, juddering like faulty machinery.

'We've taken the steps to safeguard Lily by placing her temporarily in her father's care while we and the police make their enquiries. You will be granted temporary visits – alone, of course, and supervised for now. The police have informed us that they will be attending your address to speak to you and your partner, Nicholas Wainwright.'

Horror and fear sweep through Beth like fire. They're taking her daughter away from her. They're going to arrest Nick.

'I understand how upsetting this is for you, Beth,' the woman says, placing a hand on her arm. Beth snatches it away, an involuntary reaction. She doesn't want this woman to touch her.

'It's lies,' she says, tears tracking her cheeks. 'It's all terrible, malicious lies.'

The social worker nods. 'Lily will need to be examined by a doctor, and she will need to make a statement to the police.'

Beth cannot breathe. She can't speak, can't process it all. This can't be happening.

'I want to speak to Lily,' she says. 'I need to speak to my daughter right away. You cannot simply deny me the right to see my daughter; I've been accused of nothing. So why can't I see her, talk to her and get to the bottom of this? I will know instantly if she's telling the truth or not – and I'm convinced she's not – but I will know as soon as I look at her. So can I please see my daughter, or do I need to call my solicitor?'

'It may well be a good idea to speak to a family lawyer,' Rosemary says, her overly gentle and patronising voice making Beth want to smash her teeth down her throat. She has never in her life felt such acute anger. 'But I'm afraid Lily doesn't want to see you right now.'

The words feel like a sledgehammer to her skull. Lily doesn't want to see her?

'But… but I dropped her off this morning,' she cries, her voice cracking with the emotional overload. 'She kissed me goodbye and said, "love you, Mummy". She was absolutely fine… I don't understand this?' She glances between the two women, desperate for answers, for help. 'None of it makes any sense.'

'Lily will be leaving with your husband today…'

Beth wants to say, 'He's not my husband; he never really has been,' but she's not stupid – things are bad enough. 'You know where she'll be and that she's safe and we will arrange a visit, if that's what Lily wants, as soon as possible, OK?'

Beth wants to drop to her knees. Lily doesn't want to see her; her baby girl doesn't want to see her own mummy, and the pain is so real it's like a thousand cuts to her heart.

'So you're OK to take her then, Mr Lawler?' Rosemary turns to Evan, beams at him almost, like he's some kind of saint.

'Of course.' Evan nods sagely, his words heavy with what Beth believes is self-satisfaction. Beth looks over at him and he makes eye contact with her for the first time since he's entered the room but says nothing. He simply smiles at her instead.

CHAPTER SIXTEEN

Dan

October 2019

He died on the Thursday. Vic's full report claims that TOD was between 1 and 2 p.m. A single 9 mm bullet, most likely from a Glock handgun, killed him outright. There were no signs of a struggle or the weapon at the scene. He'd left for work that morning at the usual time of 8.45 a.m., ANPR pick up his plates en route. His secretary, Shanna Brush, a jumped-up, snooty woman who I took an immediate dislike to, informed us that he arrived for work on time, made some calls, drank some coffee and then cleared his diary for the afternoon.

'Why did he do that, Shanna?' Davis enquired when we spoke to her.

She'd shrugged, looked at Davis like she was something she'd just trodden in.

'He didn't say. Just told me to cancel that day's appointments from 1 p.m. onwards and that he wouldn't be back until Monday.'

Or in fact at all, as it had turned out.

The team are checking his incoming and outgoing calls. Someone or something made him change his plans.

'So why do you think Lawler dropped everything and made his way over to his secret apartment that day?' I pose the question to Davis, who's devouring a cheese-and-onion sandwich like she hasn't seen food for a fortnight.

'Got a phone call from someone asking to meet him?'

'Most likely but why there? Beth Lawler says she never even knew he owned an apartment at The Mulberries.'

'Do you believe her?'

'Yes,' I say, 'I do.' But only that she never knew about the apartment, at least not until recently.

'He used it to meet the escort girls.' Davis is thinking along the same lines as me.

'I think Lawler agreed to meet an escort at his Mulberries address. So we need to find out who she is.'

'Boss.' Davis nods and chews simultaneously.

'Run that CCTV back again,' I say and she does.

'There's nothing, boss.' She swallows loudly. 'I've checked it at least five times over. Beth Lawler can clearly be seen answering the front door on several occasions throughout the day of the murder. She signed for her Ocado shopping at 1.15 p.m. and then at 1.56 p.m. she can be seen signing for another parcel. When Mitchell did door to door with the neighbours, she said two of them separately reported seeing Beth on her front lawn around 2.15 p.m. and then again at around 2.45 p.m. They waved at her; she waved back. Camera picks her up again at 3.12 p.m. getting into her car to do the school run. School CCTV sees her arriving at 3.33 p.m. to collect the daughter and she's picked up again on the route home, and both she and Lily are caught on camera returning at around 3.54 p.m. She was definitely at home when her husband was killed.'

I stroke my chin thoughtfully.

'Interview both delivery drivers, and speak to the neighbours again. Find out what she said, how she appeared, if they'd ever delivered to the house before.'

Davis looks at me quizzically. 'OK, boss.'

'Run it again…' I say and Davis rolls her eyes, though does as she's told.

I watch the footage carefully; watch as Beth answers the door. The camera is positioned to the side, but she's visible and the footage, though a little grainy, is good enough for her to be identified. It's all as she said in her statement. The timings match up, almost to the minute. But something is troubling me. It's almost too perfect somehow.

'See what I mean, boss,' Davis says. 'Everything she told us, this corroborates it.'

'Hmm. It certainly looks that way…'

Davis looks at me. 'What you thinking, boss?'

I snap back into the moment. 'I'm thinking, Davis, that I might try that new sushi place up the road for lunch. Fancy it? Anything's got to be better than that cheese and onion sandwich.'

'I would love to, gov, but—' Before she can fob me off, Mitchell enters the room and I can tell immediately she has something important to say. Mitchell is definitely one to watch; I've been impressed with her dogmatic approach to her role, even if she is still a little wet behind the ears.

'Ah, DC Mitchell,' I greet her, 'please tell me you've come bearing good news?'

Her expression answers my question.

'Out with it then,' I say, exhaling.

'The CCTV from The Mulberries, sir, it's not good.'

'How not good? Not clear, you mean?'

'Oh yes, it's clear, sir – crystal in fact. That place is camera'd up to the hilt. One at the gate, one in reception, in the lifts and on every floor.'

'And…? Don't tell me, on the day Lawler was shot the system went down?'

'No, gov. The security there is state of the art; if one of the cameras goes down then it triggers an alert and maintenance are made aware of it.'

'So, Mitchell, you're about to tell me that we have clear footage of Evan Lawler entering The Mulberries? And of the perpetrator who also entered The Mulberries and went on to murder him in his bed, yes?'

'Not exactly, sir.'

'Jesus Christ, Mitchell, spit it out,' Davis says, and I inwardly smile at how much she is beginning to sound like me.

'Evan Lawler is captured on CCTV arriving at The Mulberries at 12.18 p.m. He punches in the security code, which opens the gate, and drives through. A few seconds later we see someone go up to the camera and place a cap or some kind of lens over it. Same thing happens in reception, then in the lift and finally on the floor of Lawler's apartment.'

'So Lawler is trying not to be seen on camera?' Davis asks, clearly confused.

'Oh no, not at all,' Mitchell says. 'I'd say he was making sure to hide the identity of whoever he was expecting.'

'So you saw the identity of whoever put the cap over the lenses?'

'Yes,' Mitchell says, looking at me and then at Davis. 'It was Lawler himself.'

CHAPTER SEVENTEEN

Beth

September 2018

Beth drives home in such blind panic that in hindsight she realises she was lucky not to have crashed her car. Lily's accusations have blindsided her so completely that her hands can't stop shaking at the wheel. She doesn't know what to do next, who to speak to, who to go to for help. She needs to speak to Lily; needs to look in her daughter's eyes to know the truth. Beth can feel her world – a world where she has finally found happiness and contentment, one where the future excites her instead of filling her with dread – collapsing around her with every blurred passing car.

Beth replays the conversation with the social worker over in her mind: '*How well do you really know your partner, Mrs Lawler? Have you ever left your partner alone with Lily, even just for a few moments?*' She shakes away the tears that are streaking her cheeks as she drives. Befittingly, it has begun to rain a little and she puts the wipers on. She tries to recall if she ever has left Lily and Nick alone together; she thinks she might have, but not for any considerable amount of time, not long enough to…

Beth shakes her head in a bid to erase the thought of the man she loves – the only man she has ever truly loved – abusing her baby because it's incomprehensible and inconceivable, isn't it?

'*Surely you owe it to Lily to give her the benefit of the doubt…* ' No. No. Nick always arrives home from work later than she does, then they eat together, she baths Lily, they play for a bit, then it's night-time, a bedtime story… The social worker said something about a bedtime story, didn't she? Has Nick ever read Lily a bedtime story alone? Beth hits her forehead with a tight fist in a bid to recall. She thinks he might have and…

Oh God! This is just absurd! Nicky wouldn't hurt a flower, let alone a little girl. He is a beautiful soul, a wonderful, kind, loving human being. She feels guilty for doubting him, even for a second. But then it strikes her that if she could doubt him, albeit fleetingly, what is everyone else going to think? No smoke without fire?

Beth feels a sense of dread inside her stomach, like a swamp being dredged as she remembers the look on Evan's face as she had fled the school, ashamed and in tears, that sickly, fake smug smile… This was his doing – somehow she feels sure of it. Evan has cooked this up just to hurt her, to hurt Nick, to get back at them both. But how could he do that to his own child? How could anyone be so evil, let alone her insipid estranged husband?

Beth scrabbles for her phone inside her handbag on the passenger seat, her heartbeat knocking against her ribs in time with the rhythm of the wipers. She presses Evan's number, her breath audible as she struggles to retain enough oxygen to keep herself conscious.

'Answer the phone, Evan… answer the bloody phone, you goddamn—'

'Beth.' He picks up after a few rings. His voice is calm, almost jovial even, like he's pleased to hear from her.

'What the hell's going on, Evan?' she shrieks. 'What the fuck have you done?'

There's a pause on the line. 'I've done nothing, Beth. And I'd prefer it if you didn't use bad language. You know how much I detest it *in a woman*.'

Beth is hyperventilating. 'Where's Lily?' she asks, desperately trying to calm herself down, but really she wants to scream down the phone and not stop until her voice runs dry. 'Where have you taken her?'

'Taken her?' His tone is measured, full of hubris. 'I haven't *taken* her anywhere, Beth. She's safe at home, at *our* home, where she should be, where *you* should be…'

He punctuates the word with deliberate over-pronunciation.

'She's always been *safe*, Evan,' Beth retaliates. 'This… these accusations… they're not true, absolutely not true. Nick would never… never… Jesus, Evan, what have you made her say? Why are you doing this? Why? To hurt me? Is she OK? Is Lily OK? Is she scared? Is she wondering what's going on? Let me speak to her. I want to speak to my daughter, Evan!'

There's another pause on the line and she hears him draw breath.

'She's sleeping.'

'It's four-o-fucking-clock, Evan! Let me speak to my daughter!'

She's shouting now, losing control.

'Look, clearly you're in a state. I can understand – I mean, I would be too if I was in your shoes and found out my partner had been abusing our child, but you need to get a grip, Beth. You need to stop being abusive towards me.'

Beth tries to speak but too many words come out at the same time and it all sounds broken and fragmented and nonsensical.

'He… No one has abused… I'm not abusing you! I… I… Just let me speak to her, Evan, you fucking bastard!'

She thinks she can hear him sniggering.

'I'm hanging up now, Beth. Clearly you're incapable of discussing this like an adult. Your lover has abused our daughter and *I'm* the bastard? Do you know what will happen now? They've told me I have to take Lily to the police station. She will be examined by a doctor and interviewed, make a statement. She's going to have to go through a terrible ordeal and all you're worried about is blaming me, just like you did for the demise of our marriage. Selfish to the end, Bethany. But then you always were.'

Beth is so stunned and enraged that she cannot speak. Her jaw is locked tight with anger, frustration and fear.

'I'm going to instruct my legal team immediately. The courts will grant me full custody, given the circumstances. If you're hell-bent on standing by that boyfriend of yours then on your own conscience be it. You will lose your daughter as a result, be lucky if you get supervised visitation rights. She's safer here with me. After all, Ms Garrett was right, wasn't she? I mean, how well do you actually know this Nick character?'

He doesn't give her time to answer even if she could. 'I'm not agreeing to the divorce terms, Beth. I'm not going to allow you to divorce me so that you can marry that… that paedophile; I still care about you and won't allow that to happen. If you just come home, come home and be with your daughter, with… me, then we can deal with this horrible mess together… otherwise, I promise you things are about to get a whole lot worse.'

The reality of what Evan is saying hits her like a brick through the windscreen of her car at 40 mph. Is he blackmailing her? She'd been right; Evan was behind this. Somehow he had got Lily to lie to the authorities and now he had leverage, leverage to use against her to destroy her, and to destroy Nick too.

'Worse? How could this be any worse?' Beth says, but Evan has hung up.

Instinctively, she calls her mum, just like she's always done whenever she's needed help.

'They think Nick has been abusing Lily, Mum!'

'Well, he is amusing, isn't he, Nick? Good sense of humour, very important in a man – in anyone really. I mean, God knows you've got to see the funny side of life…'

Her mum had clearly misheard her.

'Not *amusing*, Mum, *abusing*!'

Lilianne agrees to come over right away.

'We'll sort this out, darling,' she assures her hysterical daughter, though Beth can hear the worry in her mother's voice. 'Don't panic – we will sort this out.'

Beth feels light-headed and -footed, as she pulls up to the ATM outside the bank. She needs to withdraw some cash for household things, shopping and bills. She puts the card into the machine and punches in the pin. Seconds later it is spat back out. 'Insufficient funds,' the message reads.

'Jesus, don't do this to me now,' she wails under her breath as she tries again. Maybe in her stressed state she's punched in the wrong PIN. But the same message appears on the screen. On the third attempt, the machine swallows her card. And that's when it dawns on her; she and Evan share a joint bank account. He must've withdrawn all their funds, including her own wages she'd earned from her job at the hospital! He's taken everything, cleared it all out. Beth feels icy fear run down her spine like the sharp blade of a knife. And she hears Evan's voice as though he is standing right behind her: '*I promise you things are about to get a whole lot worse.*'

CHAPTER EIGHTEEN

Cath

September 2019

Cath dries her hair with a towel and sprays her armpits with antiperspirant. It smells lovely, like expensive perfume. Not like the 99p crap she's been using since she can remember. It's nice to have a proper hot shower too. The water at the bedsit was always at best barely lukewarm and she had never felt truly clean, even after showering. Ivy's place is like a palace in comparison. She has her own room with an en suite and clean sheets that smell of washing powder – she even has her own TV. Ivy has given her clothes too, stuff her niece doesn't wear anymore. It was good stuff as well, some DKNY jeans that fit her like a glove and Ted Baker tops. Her favourite, though, is a black dress from Karen Millen – a designer shop she'd sometimes walked past on the high street and dreamed of one day being able to go inside and buy herself something. It's stretchy and hugs her thin frame, pushes her breasts up, giving her something resembling a cleavage. The moment she'd put that dress on Cath had felt as though her life had changed for the better; finally she was free, she'd escaped, and now she could be normal, or at least try and begin to be.

Three weeks have passed since she bought her train ticket and made her escape to London. Three whole weeks where she has been free of him and the constant fear that she's lived in for years, and although she is still a nervous wreck who jumps at the sound of a rustling crisp packet, she can feel the beginnings of change within her, a trickle of something, something positive, something she'd never dared to feel before – the idea of being happy, and it feels like nectar, like liquid gold trickling through her veins.

Her escape had taken some careful and covert planning on her part. Neve's promise of a friend who could put her up in London had been an incentive she had gripped on to for dear life. And she had come good because her friend, Ivy, had agreed to help her. Carefully, Cath had been squirreling money away, just a tiny amount each week so that he wouldn't notice, with the intention of buying a train ticket to London – a one-way train ticket. Desperate not to get caught, she'd sewn cash into the hem of a dress in her wardrobe, an old one she never wore because he didn't like it, and each week she'd unpick it and hide another five-pound note or a tenner if she could inside and sew it back up again. Saul went through all of her things almost daily – he even checked her tampon boxes. Goodness only knows what he had ever been looking for. That day she had bought her ticket to London had felt like one of the best days of her life.

Cath smiles at herself in the mirror, something she has not allowed herself to do in so long that she isn't sure she ever had. She and Ivy are going out tonight, to Ivy's favourite bar bistro place down the road. It has taken a lot of coaxing from her to get Cath to agree to go – she was nervous of the outside world, fearful of strangers and socially awkward – but she'd worn her down eventually, and the dress had swung it.

Ivy is a lovely woman, wonderful even. She is in her mid-fifties but looks ten years younger and has the energy of a woman in her twenties. She'd been so kind to help her, and Cath had been so grateful that she'd spent the first three days upon her arrival simply crying and saying 'thank you' repeatedly until it had sent Ivy mad.

Ivy is a woman with a past too; she is living proof that you could free yourself from an abusive relationship and go on to achieve great things. She runs her own market stall in Spitalfields where she sells vintage jewellery and clothes. She also has a sun-bed business that her daughter takes care of, which is her 'bread and butter' as she calls it. She's agreed to let Cath work there a few days a week too, when she feels ready and all her bruising has gone. Cath can't wait. A job! An actual real job where she earns her own money – and gets to keep most of it too!

She tries not to think of Saul, but it's impossible not to. She wants to garner some small satisfaction from imagining his face when he had come home that afternoon she had absconded to find their bedsit empty. But she can't. The fear of knowing how angry he would've been erodes any feeling of vindication she could allow herself to experience. Because she knows if he finds her what he will do…

Cath pours herself a glass of Prosecco, enjoys the sensation of the bubbles tickling her nose as she takes a sip. She pulls the black dress up her thighs and struggles with the zip at the back until it's done up. She's put a little make-up on tonight, probably the first time she's worn any in years. Ivy says she looks great with a bit of mascara and lip gloss.

Cath turns the radio on, sings along to the Justin Timberlake song that's playing. She likes this one. She begins to dance a little, forgetting herself for a second. This is what it feels like to be normal, a normal young woman getting ready to go out with a friend, putting on make-up and listening to music, singing and dancing.

Cath feels like laughing out loud suddenly, the sense of emancipation gradually beginning to dawn upon her. She can be happy now, can't she? Rebuild herself and her life; leave behind everything that happened, everything she had endured, all the pain and hurt and grief and loss. She can't forget it – never, especially her Cody – but she can slowly begin to move forward now, on to better things, happier times. Maybe soon, if she saves up enough, she can get her own little place and then Kai could come and visit her. She could be a mother to him again, a proper one, not some burnt-out, abused wreck. This thought alone fills her heart up and she takes another sip of her Prosecco by way of celebration.

She wants to write to her neighbour, Neve, thank her for everything she has done for her too, for making this possible, but she is too scared to in case somehow Saul sees the postmark, finds out she is in London and come looking for her. London is a big place, huge in fact, but her fear of Saul is bigger.

Cath pushes the thought from her mind as she reapplies some lip gloss. Ivy had said that they might go on holiday together; get a cheap deal to Spain or Greece and jet off somewhere. Cath's never been abroad; the furthest she's ever been is here, to London. Ivy couldn't believe it when she'd told her that.

'Well, in that case, my lovely, we'll need to get you a passport ASAP, rectify that right away!' Spain! Imagine that! Her in Spain, on holiday sipping cocktails in the sunshine and…

Cath's phone rings and it startles her. She hasn't owned a phone in a long while. Saul had forbidden it, thought she was texting other men on it. He'd smashed at least three of them up last year – each time she'd got a new one, he would end up breaking it, or selling it for drugs or attacking her over it, so she'd given up in the end. It wasn't worth the aggravation. But Ivy has given her an old iPhone and a new number. No one knows it but Ivy, so Cath picks it up.

'Hey, Ivy, I'm just getting ready and—'

The voice on the other end of the line is silent for a second. 'Hello, babe.'

She recognises it immediately, nearly drops the phone as terror almost cuts her in half like an axe.

'When are you coming home?'

CHAPTER NINETEEN

Beth

September 2018

Blue lights illuminate the outside of the house like a fairground attraction and Beth can see Nick being led out of the front door flanked by police officers. What looks like photographers and reporters are lingering outside, a small bunch of them drawn together in a pack, their voices creating a symphony as they rush forward and all begin to speak at once.

'Nick!' Beth almost falls from her car in haste. 'Nick!'

She makes brief eye contact with him as he's ushered into the police vehicle, his face ashen underneath the glare of the lights.

'It's OK,' he says to her with a thin smile that doesn't reach his wide blue eyes. 'Your mum's inside; I'm sorry.'

'Where are you taking him? Is he being arrested?' Beth can hear the shrillness of her own voice cut through the din. The neighbours are looking; some of them are standing on their front driveways, and she wants to scream at them to get back inside and stop rubbernecking.

'What's going on?' She grabs the arm of one of the police officers. There's so many of them – five, six, maybe more and three cars at least. And what are the press doing here? Who has informed them? Beth feels like she's in the scene of a film; that none of this is real and it's all just an act.

'We're taking your partner to the station, Mrs Lawler. He's been arrested under Section 1 of the Protection of Children Act 1978 for the possession of indecent images of children. Two of my fellow officers are inside – they'll need to speak to you.'

The words resound inside her head like it's a boom box. *Indecent images of children.* The police officer is still speaking but she can't hear him – it's like white noise, a high-pitched ringing in her ears. The atmosphere becomes still around her, like time has frozen and someone has pressed pause, and airless. She glances around her front lawn, turning in circles, the sounds and images of the police cars, neighbours and their houses blurring into one, like a fresh watercolour painting that's been left out in the rain.

Beth can still hear voices as she shuts the door on the rabble outside and is relieved to see her mother hurrying out of the kitchen towards her.

'Oh God, Mum, they've taken Nick… they've arrested Nick!'

Lilianne hugs her daughter, takes her in her arms like she did when she was a child.

'I got here as quickly as I could… Jesus Christ, Beth; they're saying he's been abusing Lily… something about indecent images on a computer. They've seized everything in the house, your laptop, phones, the lot.' Her mum looks ill, pale and sick, worry etched on her face.

'They took Lily, Mum,' she says. 'Evan has her. Social services were waiting for me at the school. They won't let me see her; they're saying she won't see me! There's going to be some kind of conference, police and the school and social services and… It's all lies, Mum; you do know that, don't you? Lily came back from Evan's with a bruise and it turned out she'd been horse riding and… Oh God! Hang on!' Beth remembers something. 'Imogen's mum! Miranda!' She has remembered the name now.

'She can vouch for how she got the bruise! She was the one who told me that Lily had fallen from a horse and…' Beth scrabbles around her handbag for her phone. 'I can call her and she can tell the police…'

Breathless, she retrieves her phone from her handbag, her guts twisting with anxiety. 'It's all a terrible misunderstanding and I know that Evan is behind all of it and… he never even told me about the horse riding and…'

'Beth… Bethany!' Her mother grabs her by the arm, pulls her away from the door with a concerned look on her face. 'They're saying they've found images on his computer,' she says in a low hiss, 'disgusting images of very young girls, of children being abused. How would they have got onto his computer? Why are they there?'

Beth shakes her head. 'No… no, this is all wrong; it's all a mistake, Nick wouldn't… he's not… Evan has done this, Mum; somehow he has convinced Lily to lie… I know he's behind this…'

Lilianne clasps her hands to her chest and closes her eyes for a few seconds.

'Evan? Why would he do something so terrible, to his own daughter? How could he? I couldn't bear it if I thought that little girl had come to any harm; I just couldn't bear it…' She starts to cry then and Beth starts to cry too.

'They're saying that poor Lily will need to be examined!' Her mother shakes her head in anguish. '*Intimately examined*, Beth!' She bites her bottom lip. 'That poor little thing – she must be terrified. Why won't they let you see her?'

Beth swallows hard. Seeing and hearing the fear in her mother's voice only serves to exacerbate her own. Her mother has always been so strong.

'I don't think I can cope with this,' Lilianne says. 'You think Evan is behind this? Why would he do such a thing to his own child? No one in his or her right mind… How sure are you of

Nick? Have you ever left them alone together? Why would Lily ever say such a thing… and the images, Beth…'

Beth blinks at her mother, her head still shaking, like it's coming detached from her neck. Even her mother doubts her; doubts Nick. Beth wants to break something, smash a window with her fist – release some of the tension.

'I don't know, Mum; I don't understand any of it. All I do know is that man hasn't touched my daughter. You've seen him with her – she adores him; he adores her. Somehow Evan has put her up to it, somehow that man…'

Lilianne has her hand over her mouth, her eyes wide with shock.

'But Evan's not like that, is he? He seemed to take the split OK enough. I mean, he hasn't really kicked up much of a fuss about any of it, has he, really? Even when you and Nick moved in together, he didn't say a word.'

Beth's blood feels like it's turned to ice. 'It's not what he's said, Mum, it's what he's done. He's refusing to give me a divorce and has cleaned out the joint bank account…'

'Oh, Beth.' Lilianne holds the edge of the sink and looks out onto the small patio garden, sighing heavily.

'He told me if I come home then all of this will stop.'

'He said that?' Lilianne looks round at her daughter.

'He's blackmailing me… he's behind all of this.'

Lilianne pauses for a moment and the two women stand close together in the kitchen, only the sound of their breathing audible.

'You've got to tell the police. Tell them the truth, get this Miranda to back up your story about the bruise…'

'I will… I will tell them everything.'

'But what about the images, Beth? How have they ended up on Nick's computer?'

'I don't know, Mum. Evan planted them somehow? He must've. You do believe me, don't you?'

Lilianne holds on to the kitchen sink again for support. There's a moment's silence between them.

'You'll never be able to fight him, Beth,' she says with quiet resignation. 'If what you're saying is true – and I do believe it is – then Evan's out to destroy you, to destroy Nick, and it seems he's more than willing to use his own daughter to do it.' She slumps down onto the kitchen table. 'I worried this would happen.'

Beth looks at her mother, blinks back tears.

'As soon as you said you were leaving him. I'd hoped I was wrong, because he seemed to be taking it OK, but men like Evan… they don't go down without a fight.'

'Men like Evan?'

'Oh, he may seem harmless enough, come across as Mr Nice Guy, but I never liked him, not really, always thought he was a bit…'

'A bit what?'

'Creepy,' Lilianne says, a flash of anger crossing her face. 'Still waters, they always run deep; I've been on this planet long enough to know that. I was secretly glad when you left him – worried, but glad.'

Beth is stunned. Her mother had never voiced such opinions until now.

'Don't underestimate him, Beth. You thought he was just going to let you go, move on with your life and be happy with another man?'

Her mother sucks in a breath, straightens herself out. 'Not in this lifetime. Not a man like that. I had my suspicions about him for years.' Lilianne kisses her teeth. 'Wish I'd voiced them a long time ago. This is my fault, all of this; I should've talked to you sooner. But the house… the lifestyle – I wanted you to have it all, Beth, you and Lily… and now look at the mess you're in…'

'You look a bit peaky, Mum,' Beth says, reaching for her hand. 'It's not your fault! None of it! I never thought Evan was capable of being so wicked, so twisted and evil. No one did. I mean Evan has always been… Evan. So… *vanilla*.'

'Well, I had half an inkling of what lay beneath.' Lilianne folds her arms across her chest. 'He never built that successful business being a soft-arse pushover, darling, mark my words.'

'I never thought… I never knew…'

Lilianne sighs deeply. 'You never knew him at all, darling – that's the trouble. You're going to need lawyers, and they cost money – lots of money – and you'll have social services crawling all over you. The bloody press have already been knocking on the door. The whole neighbourhood will know, the mums at the school, and mud sticks, Bethany – we both know that. If that poor man, if Nick is innocent—'

'He *is*, Mum,' Beth interjects. 'I know he is.'

'Yes, and how are you going to prove that? The authorities are going to take a very dim view of you if you stand by him. You'll never get her back, and what if… what if she really is telling—'

'Stop! Mum! He is… he's not a bloody paedophile, for God's sake. He's been set up – we both have.'

The two women are silent for a moment as they digest the horror of the unfolding situation.

'I'm not going back to him, Mum,' Beth says quietly.

Lilianne sighs again, deeply. 'Please, love,' she says, wiping the mucus from her nose. 'Please think of that little girl. If what you're saying really is true then you don't know what you're dealing with. Men like Evan, they don't stop until they win, until you're on your knees and…' Lilianne coughs, clasps her chest.

'Mum?' Beth can hear her mother's laboured breath. 'Mum, are you OK? You've gone a funny colour?'

Lilianne drops to her knees, grabbing one of the kitchen chairs for support as she sinks to the floor. It makes a nasty screeching sound as she drags it forward and collapses onto the tiles.

'Oh God! Mum! Mum! Speak to me, Mum!' Beth hears the sound of people entering the kitchen.

'Mrs Lawler? I'm DC...'

'I don't give a fuck who you are,' she snaps. 'Get an ambulance. She's having a heart attack.'

CHAPTER TWENTY

Dan

October 2019

Digging into Evan Lawler's personal and professional life, it transpires that aside from a liking for escort girls and owning a secret apartment, he was squeaky clean. No bad business deals, no debts and no one with an obvious grudge against the guy – aside from Beth Lawler and Nicholas Wainwright – and I think we can rule him out given that he's dead. Lawler was well liked by business associates, staff and most people he came into contact with, the overriding adjectives used to describe him being 'pleasant' and 'reserved', on the outside at least. I'm not disputing the fact that Evan Lawler may well have been a 'good guy', but from the very beginning my gut has told me that there was more to him because 'good guys' don't tend to turn up dead for no reason.

'Keep digging,' I say to the team. 'Have we spoken to the family yet? Mother? Father?'

'Both deceased apparently, boss,' Harding says.

'Right, well, I suspect Evan Lawler wasn't everything he claimed to be on the outside, or perhaps, more tellingly, he was more than he let on.'

And it turns out that my gut is right – again.

'I met him last year,' the woman says in a strong Eastern European accent. She flicks her long, glossy dark hair back and extinguishes a foreign cigarette. 'At a hotel in London.'

'Which one?' Davis asks, notebook poised.

'Claridge's. It was his favourite. Sometimes we meet there, other times different hotels, or his apartment.'

Davis raises an eyebrow. Like I've always told her, the posher the gaff, the darker the riff raff!

'He was a regular client of yours?'

'Yes,' she says, poised but otherwise unruffled. 'I saw him once or twice a month, every month for almost eighteen months. Up until a few months ago.'

I look at the woman sitting opposite me. I'm notoriously rubbish at guessing a woman's age but I'd hazard she's mid-thirties, or slightly older and she's had work done to her face because it's smooth as a doll's and she has those lips that look like they've been plumped up with a bicycle pump. She's not pretty but she is somehow striking, the kind of woman you can't stop staring at, even if you can't work out if it's for the right or wrong reasons. Her name is Svetlana and she's Lithuanian, or so she says.

'Don't worry; I have all my visas in order,' she explains defensively. 'I am British citizen.' And it looks like this country – or the men of it – has served her well because she's dripping in jewellery and her black clothes are obviously expensive.

'Did you like Mr Lawler, Svetlana?' Davis asks her. 'Did you have a good relationship?'

Svetlana smiles thinly and reaches for her foreign cigarettes but doesn't take one, just plays with the packet instead.

'Like him? Is not really important whether I like my clients or not.'

'Surely it makes a difference?' Davis enquires.

'Do you like your colleague, Detective?' Svetlana shoots back.

'Yes,' Davis says without much hesitation I'm happy to state. She glances sideways at me with a little smile, adding, 'Most of the time, anyway.'

Svetlana shrugs. 'I did not know him well enough to decide. He was a quiet person, not one for the small talk.' She pauses. 'I liked him enough not to want him dead, I suppose.'

'Did Evan ever talk to you about his personal life? About his business, any enemies he may have had, any trouble he was in?'

Svetlana shrugs again. 'He talk about very little in all the time I am knowing him.'

'But you knew he was a wealthy man, yes?'

A slow smile creeps across her cat-like face. 'All of my clients are wealthy man, Detective. The services I am providing are not cheap.'

Svetlana looks proud of this fact and I want to remind her that a brass is a brass, whether you're selling it on street corners for a fiver or in five-star hotels for five hundred, but I want her to keep talking so I keep shtum.

I tilt my head into a half nod and remain silent and wait for her to answer my original question.

'I knew he was married, had a child. I didn't know their names, or anything like this – is better for everyone this way. Is no good to, how do you say, mixing the business with the pleasure.'

'How long have you worked at the agency, Svetlana?'

'Around two years and a half. Is safer. All of the clients are vetted. Payment is in advance, is all done through the office. I prefer this way.'

'Did his wife know that he used your services?' I ask, leaning forward to light her cigarette with her own expensive-looking lighter. I think it might be Cartier, one of those old-fashioned ones that you flip up with a flint. I imagine it's been given to her by one of her wealthy aging clients, like everything else she owns.

She shrugs again. Svetlana likes to shrug.

'If she does he don't tell me, and I don't ask. But I don't think so. 'Van was private person. He liked the fact I am discreet in my job.'

I look at her.

'Is part of the requirement,' she adds.

Davis is looking around Svetlana's swish apartment, admiring her objets d'art and pristine soft furnishings, which are bordering on garishness although clearly top end. She's probably thinking she's in the wrong profession.

'When was the last time you saw Mr Lawler, Svetlana?'

She shrugs again. Three times and it's a habit. 'I think maybe three months ago… I can check my diary… I went to his apartment, The Mulberries. Is where we sometimes met. He like it there – is very quiet, very private. No one can hear you.'

I'm standing now, walking around her apartment a little, surveying it. I notice there's a pile of mail on the granite worktop and pick it up. It's addressed to someone called Sonia Edwards – a council-tax bill and others.

'Hear you?'

Svetlana kicks off her expensive-looking sandals and pulls her manicured feet up onto the cream leather couch. She raises a very dark, arched eyebrow that looks as if it's been tattooed on.

'He have the room soundproofed apparently…'

'What for?'

Svetlana shrugs again. 'Why does anyone do this?' she replies facetiously.

'Can you tell me anything about your encounters with Mr Lawler, Svetlana? Anything of relevance?'

She gives me an amused smile. 'Depends what you are meaning by relevant, Detective.'

I look into Svetlana's eyes. They're dark, almost black and I sense deadness behind them, like someone has switched the lights off a long time ago.

'Did you get on well with him? Did he always pay you? Did he ever buy you gifts?'

She rolls her eyes a little, looks bored by the questions.

'A man is dead, Svetlana,' I remind her gently. 'Evan was shot in the head, his body left to rot. Someone killed him. Do you know who that someone is?'

Her nonchalant expression changes slightly then, which was my intention.

'I have alibi for this day he is dying,' she says, indignant. 'You can check with the agency, with the client, with the hotel we are staying in, CCTV...'

'We already have, Svetlana.' I smile at her, though it's threating to be a grimace.

'You cannot pin this shit on me! I did not like him so much, but I did not want him dead. 'Van was a good client, even if he was a little... He pay well, pay extra.'

'For what?'

Svetlana has snapped back into superior indifference, which appears to be her resting personality.

'He like certain things, you know?'

'No, I don't know,' I say. 'Enlighten me.'

She raises an arched jet-black brow again, gets up from the sofa and goes into the bedroom, returning a few moments later.

'These kinds of things,' she says, throwing the contraptions down one by one onto the couch. I look at them. One of them looks like a harness – some kind of restraint. There's a rope, a black shiny PVC balaclava mask and various whips, paddles, blindfolds and gags.

Davis looks sideways at me. 'So he was into S&M?'

I want to make a gag about wanting to know how Davis knows this but will save it for later.

Svetlana smiles, but it's a crooked, slanted smirk of a smile.

'You are good, Detective,' she says, somewhat sarcastically.

'He was kinky then, liked to be tied up, that sort of thing?'

Svetlana repositions herself on the couch, her silky black blouse dangerously daring to expose her fake breasts.

'Not him…' she says, 'me. He liked to tie me up, whip me, gag me, use the dildo,' she says, like she's reading off a shopping list from *Fetish Monthly*. 'I specialise in giving pleasure and pain, Detective. I am mostly dominant, but 'Van, and the others… well, they pay very well for my services, even though…' She stops.

'Even though what?'

She shrugs yet again. 'Even though there are some things he ask me to do that I refuse, even for money.'

I find this somewhat difficult to believe but don't let on. 'What sort of things, Svetlana?'

For a second I think I see a fleck of fear in her eyes, something that immediately makes her appear more human.

She sighs, looks away as if she doesn't want to answer the question. 'He like to torture… sometimes he ask to do rape scenes, sometimes he ask to hurt me…'

'Hurt you? I thought that was the whole point of S&M?'

Svetlana laughs at me then, like I haven't the first clue.

'You are missionary man, Detective?'

I refrain from answering; I think she's trying to embarrass me, emasculate me even. I glance at the huge black dildo on the couch and inwardly wince.

'The whole point is both people enjoy the experience, Detective Riley.' I'm surprised she's remembered my name and even more surprised she's used it.

'I do not enjoy the idea of being raped, or beaten to a pulp.'

'That's perfectly understandable.'

'What made you stop seeing him, Svetlana?' Davis asks before I can.

She swishes her black hair from her shoulders again, exposing her pale neck. She reminds me of a young Morticia Addams.

'This,' she says, pointing to a large nasty mark on it. It looks like a scar, and whatever caused it must've gone deep because it is still red and slightly raised.

'He attacked you?'

Svetlana shrugs, and I feel like shaking her and imagine her jewellery and false eyelashes falling to the floor as I do.

'Yes,' she says. 'One time he take things too far… and I spend one night in the hospital. I need five stitches. I refuse to see him again after this.'

'You didn't report the assault to the police?'

Svetlana shrugs for the hundredth time. 'No.'

'Why not, Svetlana?' Davis asks. 'He put you in the hospital, gave you a scar… Why didn't you report him? Were you scared? Did he threaten you?'

'No…'

'What then?' I interject. Svetlana looks uncomfortable.

'On the one hand I am glad he is dead; he was vicious bastard to me that night. I could see it in his eyes, that he want to hurt me, cause me pain, even when I am begging for this to stop. 'Van was not everything you see on the surface, everything he show to people. I don't think he like women so much. He want to dominate and degrade. Some men are like this.' She shrugs again. I think it must be some kind of tic. 'Inadequate men mostly, but 'Van…' She looks at me then, makes direct eye contact. 'I think he was going to kill me.'

'Where did the assault take place?' Davis enquires.

'The apartment; the penthouse in The Mulberries. Is very quiet there. No one hear you scream,' she adds sinisterly.

Or gunshots, incidentally. Not one person heard the gunshot that killed Evan Lawler. No one heard anything at all.

'So, if the attack was so severe, why didn't you report him?' I ask her again and I can see that she doesn't want to answer.

Svetlana pauses. 'He pay me,' she says eventually.

Davis looks at me.

'How much?'

'A lot,' she says.

'How much is a lot?'

She lights another cigarette, blows the smoke hard from her inflatable lips.

'In total, around £100K, maybe more if you include the gifts he send to me afterwards. A Cartier lighter – this one' – she holds it up – 'and some jewellery, Cabochon, Swarovski…'

'So he bought your silence, Svetlana.'

'It was a mutual understanding,' she says.

'Was it worth it? Worth being assaulted for £100K?'

She shrugs, gives me a look as if it's a ridiculous question, which I suppose to someone like Svetlana it is.

'Well,' I say, more to Davis than to Svetlana, 'seems like our Mr Nice Guy wasn't quite so nice after all. Thanks, Svetlana,' I say, 'or should I call you Sonia?'

She looks up at me in surprise and gives a wry smile, which changes her face completely.

'Well, you know what they say, Detective,' she says in a perfect and broad cockney accent. 'Never judge a book by its cover.'

CHAPTER TWENTY-ONE

Beth

October 2018

It has been four weeks since Beth buried her mother but still she can't grieve. Her mind and heart simply can't accept that she is gone, so suddenly and so brutally. She feels like she's still here; that she could pick up the phone and call her, hear her lovely voice on the other end, her familiar sing-song tones, her laughter that sounded like cow bells. Beth cannot comprehend that she will never again be able to see her mum's smiling face, the way the corners of her mouth always seemed to turn upwards, giving the impression that she was just about to break into a huge grin, even when she was cross. Her mother had been her rock; a place she sailed to when the waters got choppy and threatened to drown her, an island where she could always find solace, warmth and comfort, a place where she felt unconditionally loved. Where will she sail to now?

Beth has witnessed strangers and friends lose a parent and so has often thought about how she would feel if she was forced to live in a world where her own no longer existed. Her job as a nurse had, perhaps unsurprisingly, presented such dark thoughts to her sometimes late at night… she had imagined the heartbreak, the agonising pain and the grief by proxy, such maudlin visions causing tears to spill from her eyelids and onto her pillow, but still she knew they were just thoughts; they weren't real, they hadn't happened – not to her. But now they were, now they *are* real – very real. And her imagination, when she had dreamed such dark scenarios, had only given her a shallow glimpse into the anguish she now feels.

The shock of her mother dying, right there on her kitchen floor, seems to have frozen her emotions solid, like she stopped being human in that moment. She keeps reliving the scene inside her head, how she had frantically given her CPR, working on her furiously until the paramedics had arrived, physically having to prise her away, her screams punctuating the air like an intruder alarm. But Beth had known, even before they had bustled through her kitchen in their green uniforms with all their equipment, that she had lost her. She had sensed the very moment of her mother's passing, had almost felt her spirit leaving her body. The scene had been surreal, almost like a dream, like a nightmare, like it was happening to someone she didn't know, an actor in a film – a horror film. Only it had been real, all of it.

Beth pushes the door to Lawler & Co.'s offices and marches up the stairs and into the lobby past the curved reception desk.

'Is Evan in?' she asks the receptionist curtly, a young girl with braces who doesn't look old enough to buy a drink in a pub.

Beth isn't sure if the girl knows who she is, but she imagines by the look on her face that she has already guessed this isn't a friendly visit. 'I can check for you.' The girl smiles nervously, exposing a set of silver train tracks. 'Who shall I say wants to see him?'

'Doesn't matter,' Beth says, walking past her and through the double doors towards Evan's office.

'Shanna,' she says, greeting Evan's PA, who looks up from her desk, clearly surprised to see her. Beth has never liked Shanna;

stuck-up cow, she is, ideas above her station and always a disingenuous smile on her pinched little face. She imagines she bullies the girl with braces on reception; she is just the type to do that.

'Hello, Beth,' Shanna says sweetly with a faux smile. 'How nice to see you – it's been ages.'

It takes all the limited composure Beth has left not to tell her to fuck off.

'I'm afraid Evan isn't in the office currently, but I can give him a message when he returns. Is it urgent? Is everything OK?' Shanna knows exactly what's going on, and she's no doubt enjoying every second of it. 'Hey, I was sorry to hear about your mum… I—'

'Go to hell, you jumped-up little bitch,' Beth hisses as she marches past her and into Evan's office.

'What! Hey! You can't just go in there… Beth!' Shanna calls after her. 'You can't do that!'

'Watch me,' Beth says under her breath.

She hears Shanna pick up the phone as she locks the door behind her, pulls the blinds shut and starts searching Evan's office. She doesn't have a clue what she is looking for but there has to be something – something incriminating, and something that will prove Evan had set Nick up. Something she could take to the police as evidence of his malicious intent.

Beth remembers how Nick had returned from the police station the day following his arrest a broken man to find Beth a broken woman, her mother dead, her daughter taken from her. They'd sat across from each other at the kitchen table, arms stretched out, their hands touching. And for a while they couldn't speak. The house was clean and tidy, like nothing had taken place, yet there was debris everywhere, like a bomb had been detonated, the house reduced to rubble around them, the remains of life as they'd fleetingly known it.

Nick had spoken first. 'Oh God, Beth. Oh… God…'

She had looked at him and saw fear for the first time in his grey-blue eyes. 'I'm… I'm so sorry.' And he had started to cry, or perhaps he was already crying, because in that moment, they both knew that nothing, *nothing*, was ever going to be the same again.

In the weeks that followed, Beth has put her grief to one side, shut it away somewhere deep inside of her. Even at her mother's funeral she had been unable to cry. *Unable to shed a tear at her own mother's funeral! She must be a hard-faced bitch, that one!* She knows it's what people think. Evan hadn't allowed Lily to attend, had said it would be 'too traumatic' for her. Too traumatic!

'I'll tell you what's traumatic, Evan,' she had screamed at him down the phone, 'brainwashing your own child into telling wicked lies, making her believe that I don't want to see her, that I don't love her, keeping her from her own mother… Do you know, Evan, the damage you're causing her? Because of you her nana is *dead*. How can you do this, Evan? How? Why? Refusing to divorce me, cleaning out the bank account – that's *my* money too, Evan. You can't do this… you can't get away with it… I will right the wrongs, Evan, if it takes me to my last breath, I will make sure…'

'You're upset, Beth, about your mother. It's understandable,' he'd said patronisingly. 'I will make allowances for that. But Lily has been through enough…' He'd paused on the line. 'Look… why don't you come home? Come and be with us, with our daughter, together… I will take care of you both and…'

'I'll see you in hell first.'

Evan had sighed. 'Not if I see you first, Bethany.'

Beth had thrown the huge bouquet of lilies that Evan had sent for her mother's funeral in the bin. She would grieve for her mother once they were through this. But for now, right now, they had to fight. Fight to clear Nick's name, fight for their future together, for Lily, *for herself*.

'We will come through this,' she had told Nick as they'd held each other. 'Mum always said that you have nothing to fear if you've truth on your side. The truth is non-negotiable.' But she could tell by the sag in his shoulders that he was almost defeated.

'Everyone thinks I'm a child abuser, Beth, a sexual predator, a… a paedophile… My name is in the papers… the police… the images on my PC… I've never seen them before – you do believe me, don't you? He planted them there, someone planted them… broke into the cabin and… You know, you know I would never…'

'Shhh, baby… shhh.' She had soothed him with an inner strength she didn't know she possessed, one she felt, almost certainly, was the spirit of her own mother.

Nick had pulled her so close to him that she wasn't sure where she began and he ended. And they lay there, naked, just holding each other like scared children afraid of the dark.

'He's got money, Beth; he knows people… that lodge he goes to… full of lawyers and doctors and people high up in the community, people with status and money and power… We'll be cast out; I may end up with a conviction, on the sex offenders register for the rest of my life. I'll never get another job. People will hate me – I'll be a pariah.'

'No one believes it,' she said, but she could hear the lack of conviction in her own voice as her words met the air.

'I should go away,' he'd said, breaking their embrace and sitting up. He'd dragged his fingers down his face. He looked as if he'd aged a few years overnight. 'Then you'll get Lily back. You can put it all behind you. Evan wants me gone – that's what he wants, Beth. He's destroyed my life, your life… You've lost your mum… you've lost your daughter. It's all because of me, Beth, because of me.'

She'd sat up too and pulled her knees up to her chest, turning to face him, seizing his hands in her own.

'No,' she said. 'Not because of you, Nick; because of *him*. We're not running. We have nothing to hide. We have to believe in the truth, in the justice system, in each other…' Her voice had cracked with emotion, with the sheer weight of the horror she had faced and of the future horror she sensed was to come. 'We have to gear up for battle – we cannot let Evan do this; we cannot let him win.'

But even as she'd said it she could see the surrender in his eyes. 'Please, Nick.' She was crying again and he thumbed a tear from her cheek – those big hands, like the shovels he used to dig up the land with, yet soft as cashmere against her skin. 'When you're going through hell, you know what they say,' she said.

Nick snorted softly, resignation heavy in the exhalation.

'Keep going.'

CHAPTER TWENTY-TWO

Beth

October 2018

Nick was awaiting trial. He'd been bailed to their home address, given a curfew and a tag – the humiliation and injustice of it all was too indescribable to comprehend. Nick's name had been published in the local newspaper, his identity exposed. She had no idea how the press had even got wind of his arrest, how they had known so quickly and been there that night to witness him being carted off in a police car. But she had a good idea. Evan must've tipped them off. How else would they have known? She also knew that somehow he had planted that filth on Nick's computer, broken into Nick's office and uploaded it. She'd remembered how Nicky had casually mentioned to her one evening how he'd felt someone had been in the office, that a window had been open when he'd returned – one he felt sure had been closed when he'd left – but as nothing had been taken he had shrugged it off, forgotten about it. They both had. Until now.

Had Evan done it alone or had he had help? She needed to gather evidence, evidence that would exonerate Nicky and expose Evan as the malicious liar he was. Then he would be the one carted off like a criminal.

Yesterday she had contacted that dreadful woman, Miranda, Imogen's mum, the one from Lily's school, the one from the party, in a bid to get her to corroborate how Lily had received the bruise that Nick was alleged to have inflicted upon her. She'd got the woman's address and gone round to her house, noticing a brand-new Bentley in the driveway as she'd pulled up. Miranda had looked horrified when she'd opened the door and seen Beth standing there, shock registering on her face.

'Oh! Beth! Hello,' she'd said shiftily. 'What can I do for you?'

Beth knew what they were all saying about her, about Nick. Lily had been taken from her and she was only allowed supervised visitation because Nick had been bailed to their address. She hadn't been allowed to question her daughter about the accusations she'd supposedly made against Nick because the social worker claimed it could be seen as coercion! Coercion! It was all so unjust that she could barely contain her frustration. Lily appeared subdued and sheepish during their supervised visits, and it had taken another piece of Beth's shattered heart to see her daughter so distant and troubled. It was as if Lily had disappeared and been replaced by someone who looked just like her but wasn't her daughter – her happy, innocent, vivacious six-year-old girl who talked of horses and pop music and glitter slime and LOL dolls…

But Beth had been right; she had known instantly that Lily had lied about the accusations – she could see it in her little eyes: worry, fear and confusion. She had felt it when she held her too, her small body stiff and guarded in her arms, as if she was doing something wrong by cuddling her own mother.

Telling her daughter that her beloved nana had gone to heaven was by far the worst thing Beth had ever had to do.

'Nana is with the angels now, isn't she?' Lily had said, her bottom lip beginning to quiver with the realisation. She had begun to cry. And Beth had cried with her.

'Yes, my darling, Nana is an angel now, a beautiful angel looking down on you, on us, protecting us.'

'Is she looking down on Daddy too? Is she looking after Daddy as well?'

Beth had swallowed dryly. 'Yes, baby, she's looking down on him too.' Though she hoped for very different reasons.

'I want to go home,' Lily had said to her, gazing at her with pleading eyes. 'Everyone goes away; Marta and Nana, and you…'

The lump in Beth's throat had felt like weighted granite; she could barely swallow.

'I haven't gone anywhere, darling.' She had stroked Lily's long blonde hair, so much like her own had been as a child, just like her mother had always done to her too, even as an adult. 'I promise you, I will never go anywhere.'

'When are we going home, Mummy? I want you to come home.'

And Beth had sobbed quietly into her hair as she'd held her, eyeing the social worker that was watching her carefully as she hovered nearby.

'You must tell the truth, Lily,' Beth had whispered into her daughter's ear. 'I can come home when you tell the truth. Remember what Mummy has always said to you: "You have nothing to fear from the truth."'

'Daddy said that he would buy me a horse.' Lily's high-pitched baby voice had cut through her heartstrings. 'Daddy said if I tell people that Nick is a bad person then I can have a pony.' She'd looked up at her mummy with sad eyes and it broke Beth's heart all over again to see regret in someone so young, in her own baby. 'I'm sorry, Mummy,' she'd said.

'Sorry to turn up unannounced,' Beth had apologised reluctantly. She couldn't stand this vile woman but she needed something from her – desperately. 'Do you remember Amber's party, a couple of months ago now, the garden party?'

Miranda nods, looks a little flustered. 'Yes, of course – lovely day, hot.'

'You told me about going horse riding, you and Imogen and Lily and… Evan.' She can barely say his name aloud without wanting to burst into flames. 'You said that Lily fell off the horse she was riding, do you remember? Well, I gather you know that some accusations have been made against my partner, Nick, suggesting that he inflicted the bruise that was on Lily's leg, the one you said she got from falling off the horse and, well… it would be very helpful if you could corroborate what you told me to the police as…'

The woman pulls the front door closer behind her, as if she doesn't want whoever's inside to see or hear her.

'I'm sorry, I have no idea what you're talking about,' she says quietly, smiling. 'Oh, by the way, sorry to hear about your mum… Truly,' she adds, casting her a fleeting look of pity.

Beth stars at her blankly. 'Thank you, but yes… you must remember, you told me at the party – you said you and Evan and Imogen and Lily had all gone riding together and—'

'I don't recall that conversation, I'm afraid,' Miranda says, shuffling awkwardly on her doorstep. 'You must be mistaken – probably all that Prosecco!' She does that laugh again, one that sounds like pots and pans falling out of a kitchen cupboard. 'Look, I'm sorry, Beth. I really have to go, got something in the oven…'

'Miranda!' Beth struggles not to lunge forward and seize the woman by the throat. 'This is incredibly important… This is someone's life, someone's reputation… This is about my daughter – she needs me, needs to be with her mum. You're a mother… please…' She can hear the desperation in her own voice, hates having to beg this awful woman, but she knows she must. 'I've already lost my mother… I can't lose Lily as well.'

She thinks she sees a genuine flicker of sympathy in Miranda's smug face, but it's so fleeting she may have imagined it.

'I'm sorry. I really can't help you, Beth,' she says again, softer this time, as if she knows all of this is wrong but can't help putting herself first.

'Can't or won't?' Beth feels that white heat rise up through her like a phoenix. 'That's a nice new car you've got there, Miranda... yours, is it?'

Miranda's demeanour instantly shifts. She stiffens, her faux sympathetic smile disintegrating faster than the hazy heat on the tarmac.

'Yes,' she says, straightening up. 'It is.'

'Nice. Must've cost a fortune. Bonus at work, was it? Oh, no, sorry, you don't actually go to work, do you? Husband buy it for you, did he? *Your* husband I mean, not mine.' She stares straight into Miranda's eyes, and this time she detects a brief look of fear.

'Look, Beth, I am really sorry about your mum, about all of... well, about what you're going through, but please don't come round here again. If you do, I'll call the police.'

'Do it, you fucking bitch,' Beth says, but Miranda has already shut the door in her face. She thinks about ringing the bell again, bashing the woman's door down, demanding she tell the truth, make a scene until someone *does* actually call the police, force Miranda to confess, to tell them about the horse-riding incident. But she knows it is futile.

Beth looks at the brand-new Bentley in the driveway, surreptitiously dragging her key along the side as she slowly walks back to her own car. Evan had got to Miranda first.

CHAPTER TWENTY-THREE

Beth

October 2018

Beth yanks open Evan's desk drawer and begins to pull out the papers it contains. Security will be here any minute so time is of the essence. She stuffs them into her handbag, zips it up and makes to leave.

'Beth? What on earth...'

She looks up. Sees him standing there in the doorway. He's unlocked the door.

'Hello, Evan.'

'What the hell do you think you're doing, Beth? You can't just walk in here and go through my stuff!' He looks so indignant that she wants to laugh at him, at the irony. 'Shanna's called security – they'll escort you off the property. Have you lost your mind?'

Beth stares at him, a high-pitched noise ringing in her ears. The hatred she feels is so strong it has a sound wave all of its own.

'No, Evan, not my mind; my mother, yes, my daughter, yes... but my mind, no. Why? Is that the plan? Destroy my life, everyone I love, so that I'll end up in an asylum?'

Evan laughs. He actually has the brass neck to laugh at her.

'You really do have such an imagination, Bethany Ann. Your talents were wasted as a nurse. You should've been an actress or a writer or a performer or something.'

'Don't call me that,' she hisses at him. 'Only my mother called me by that name, and you know it. Jesus, Evan, I never knew what a truly spiteful, hate-filled, vicious bastard you really are.'

He doesn't flinch; looks at her in amusement.

'Compliments will get you everywhere.' He raises an eyebrow comically. 'And I never knew what a foul-mouthed, cheating, lying whore of a bad mother you are, so it's swings and roundabouts, I guess. What exactly are you looking for anyway?' He walks towards her with an air of arrogance. God, she hates him.

'Evidence,' she says. 'Evidence that will prove you set Nick up, that somehow you – or some crony you paid – broke into his cabin and put that filth on his computer.'

Evan's eyebrow is still raised in a comical fashion. She can see how much he's enjoying himself and wants to grab the crystal rock on his desk – a memento of a cave they had once visited on holiday in Santorini – and bludgeon him to death with it.

'I went to Miranda's house earlier… you know, Miranda, Imogen's mum from the school, the one you went horse riding with? She told me you'd paid her off, bought her a brand-new Bentley so she'd retract the conversation we'd had where she'd told me how Lily had fallen off a horse, how she *really* got that bruise on her thigh…' She's bluffing but he doesn't know that. 'You won't get away with this, Evan… Making your own daughter, a six-year-old girl, tell lies about her own mother… about Nick… dreadful sick, evil, wicked lies, Evan… I won't let you get away with it—'

'No idea what you're even babbling on about, Beth,' he cuts her off. 'Look, I realise you're upset about your mum… I was genuinely, genuinely sorry to hear what happened. Lily's been very upset too…'

'Fuck you, Evan! You as good as killed her… all this' – she throws her hands into the air – 'all this bullshit… her heart couldn't take it.'

'Please don't swear, Beth. You know I hate women who use expletives.'

'Fuck, piss, shit, bollocks, cunt, wanker, arsehole…'

'Bastard,' he says, smirking. 'You forgot bastard.'

'Technically not a swear word.' Beth rolls her eyes, shakes her head. 'You're lying… you and I know it, so does Lily, so does Nick… and so will the police when I get the evidence I need to prove it. Then it'll be *you* they'll cart off in a wagon, humiliated, shamed…'

Evan's really laughing now. 'Good luck with that, Beth. You need to leave now, before security throws you out. Haven't you humiliated yourself enough, living with a man who's abused your own child? Standing by him like a lovesick teenager, blind to the facts, naïve to the truth? It's only because I think you're still in grief that I haven't called 999 already.'

'Do it, Evan, call them – here—' She snatches up the telephone on his desk. 'I will tell them the truth, get them to investigate, expose you for the twisted liar you are.'

Evan sighs, as though she is becoming a dreadful bore.

'We both know it will do absolutely no good whatsoever. Just go, Beth – do yourself a favour and leave. I have a very busy day.' He turns his back towards her dismissively, stares out of the window, just like he did the morning she told him she was leaving him, the morning Marta went missing.

'Did you do something to her?' The words leave Beth's mouth unconsciously, so much so she's not sure she's said them at all.

'To who? Lily? For God's sake, Beth, don't be ridiculous—'

'Not Lily… aside from poisoning her mind and making her tell lies… no, I mean Marta – did you do something to Marta?'

She's not sure why she's asked the question. There had been nothing to suggest that Evan – or anyone – had caused Marta harm, yet she had felt compelled to ask him. Something, a dull nagging sensation inside of her, like the beginning of a headache. She had felt it that morning too, something odd about his behaviour, his demeanour, his body language. He hadn't seemed too shocked, or overly concerned about their young housekeeper's disappearance, had he? Beth's mind flies back to that morning, the doors wide open… calling Marta's name… her phone and passport missing, her car and belongings still there, the scarf… and champagne… Good God, the champagne… that had *definitely* been odd, very out of character, almost like he wanted to celebrate, or commiserate… Had he known she was going to leave him? Had Marta told him, or been forced to? Had…

Evan still hasn't answered the question, still has his back to her and she gasps suddenly; feels the breath leave her body.

'Oh God!' Beth covers her mouth with her hand as if to stifle the scream she can feel behind it. 'Oh my God! You *did*! You did something to Marta!'

At the time, she had put his odd behaviour down to shock; she'd been in shock too, paralysed by panic. Not for moment had she thought, back then, that Evan, mild-mannered, polite and amenable Evan – a man she'd been married to for almost a decade, the father of her child – was capable of hurting anyone, of causing anyone any deliberate harm.

Beth had sometimes wondered how Evan had become so successful, being the beige, basic, almost wet-blanket type he was – or came across as. She'd wondered how he hadn't been annihilated by all those stereotypically ruthless businessmen and women he dealt with on a daily basis, and those bullish, misogynistic, arrogant pricks he socialised with down at that creepy Freemasons' lodge that she'd never liked. But the real truth was that she hadn't really known the true Evan at all, had she?

Beth remembers something he'd said on that day, the day Marta had vanished without trace. They'd been discussing possible reasons for her disappearance, potential explanations. The police had asked her about Marta's private life, friends, boyfriends, lovers… and she had said there were no secrets between them, had been adamant about it because she felt sure she would've known, that Marta would've confided in her, just like she had confided in Marta about her marriage and Nick.

'*Do you really know her, Beth?*' he'd said. '*At the end of the day do any of us really* know *anyone?*' Oh God! Oh dear Jesus…!

Fear cuts through her like a pickaxe. Suddenly she has no idea who Evan is, or who she is dealing with. A malicious maniac? A vengeful murderer? Not Evan – surely he wasn't capable…

Beth hears the security men enter the room behind her and swings round, another gasp exhaling from her open mouth. She recognises one of them, Ravi, a gentle giant with a huge beard that still couldn't mask the kind smile underneath. He looks at her apologetically.

'I'm sorry, Beth…'

She shakes her head, grips her handbag, her fingers digging into the leather like claws.

'It's fine, Rav.' She smiles at him. 'I was just leaving.'

CHAPTER TWENTY-FOUR

Dan

October 2019

'Ah, Dan… come in… good to see you.' Woods looks up as I enter his office. He's used my Christian name and said 'good to see you'. He's even almost smiling. I'm on immediate high alert. This does not sound – or even look – like Woods. I don't think, in all my time working under him on homicide, he's ever once said to me 'it's good to see you'.

'How have you been?'

This is getting weirder by the second.

'Fine, sir,' I reply cautiously. 'And yourself?'

He responds with a curt smile. I suspect that Woods is never 'fine'. He has the permanent demeanour of a man whose trousers are two sizes too small for him.

'You must be getting nervous now?' he says.

'Nervous?' He's right; I am getting nervous. Woods doesn't do niceties, not with me anyway, and yes, it's making me *feel* nervous. 'Why's that, sir?'

'The baby,' he says. 'Must be almost time now.'

I'm flabbergasted he's even given it a thought.

'Oh, right, yes, the baby… Yes, Fiona's due in a few weeks, although she thinks Junior might take his – or her – time in coming.'

'Yes, well, they all worry about that, the women… Mrs Woods was overdue with all three of ours, had to be induced with our Michaela; it wasn't a very pleasant experience if I remember – the contractions come much harder and faster.'

I inwardly cringe. Hearing Woods use the word 'contraction' sounds all wrong; the fact that he's got three children with 'Mrs Woods' forces me to imagine the possibility that he's had sex – more than once – and that's not an image I can entertain for too long a stretch without feeling decidedly icky.

'Well, fingers crossed it won't come to that.' I smile briefly, hoping he'll change the subject.

'Yes, I remember them all well, the births… lots of blood and gore and mess, but at the end of it…'

I'm mentally willing him to stop. 'Mrs Woods really went through it with our last one, Joshua. He was almost 11lbs, don't know how she managed to push him out; she was never the same after that… tore her perineum, had to have stiches and…'

'Sorry, sir, was there a reason you wanted to see me?' I say, desperately trying to erase the image of Mrs Woods' torn perineum from my mind. I think I might need a glass of water.

'Family, Riley,' Woods says, like he's about to break into song. 'It's everything. Becoming a father, it changes you – it *will* change you. Yes, Riley, even you.'

I wasn't going to argue with him.

'Softens the edges a bit. Suddenly, you're not the most important person in your life anymore…' He picks up the photograph of his brood on his desk, gazes at it wistfully, or as wistfully as someone like Woods ever could. 'You'll do anything to protect your family, Riley. It's a man's duty to take care of them, keep them safe, provide for them…'

I want to say, 'Thanks for the pep talk, now what is it you actually want?' but I don't want to appear rude, not least when

Woods is giving me a rare glimpse of his human side, however unpalatable.

'Absolutely,' I agree with him. 'Family is everything, sir.'

Woods replaces the photograph on his desk, gives me a thin smile that tells me he's done with the sentiments.

'Have you thought about paternity leave?' he says, busying himself with papers on his desk. I get the feeling he's avoiding eye contact with me.

'No, sir, I haven't. I'm in the middle of a murder enquiry, in case you'd forgotten.'

He shoots me a derisive look. 'Of course I haven't forgotten, Riley,' he says abrasively, which is a tone I'm much more comfortable with. 'But I think you should consider it. It's important to be there for Fay and the little one, when he arrives.'

'Fiona,' I correct him. 'And it could be a she.'

'Yes, yes, *Fiona*, and the baby. I think it would be good for you,' he says jovially, too jovially for my liking, and it's all coming across as a bit disingenuous. 'It'll be good for you all… take a few weeks off, a couple of months maybe. You'll need time to adjust to fatherhood, trust me – your life will…'

'Never be the same again. Yes, sir, you said. Are you trying to get rid of me?'

My directness alarms him. 'Of course not, Riley,' he says quickly, which only serves to confirm my assumption that he does, in fact, want me off the case.

'How are you getting along with the enquiry anyway?' he says overly casually, which again smacks of disingenuity. 'Any new leads?'

'We're exploring all lines of enquiry, sir,' I say, which we both know pretty much means we haven't got very far. Oddly, Woods seems unperturbed by my lack of progress. Usually he'd be barking at me by now, piling on a little pressure, making noise about how the commissioner 'wants this one sewn up quickly'.

The commissioner wants every case sewn up quickly, so I've never fully understood his need to say it. Only this time he doesn't, so I do it for him.

'I imagine the commissioner will want this all put to bed quickly, seeing as though he was a friend of Lawler's – that you both were, sir.'

'More of an acquaintance actually,' he quickly corrects me.

'You were – are – both members of the same Freemasons' lodge, weren't you? All three of you in fact, am I right?'

'Among many other people, yes.' Woods appears defensive and my interest is piquing.

'So you didn't know him well then, Evan Lawler?'

'Like I've already said, Riley, he was more of an acqu—'

'But you saw him regularly? Did you ever meet his wife, Beth?'

Woods actually looks a little nervous. 'Beth? Yes, once or twice over the years, possibly more. The Lodge is men only, as you know already, but on a few social occasions, yes, our paths crossed. Nice lady,' he adds. 'A nice couple, all told.'

'Did you know their marriage was in trouble? That she was seeing someone else, planning to leave him? That she *did* leave him and moved in with her lover?'

'No. I didn't. We weren't that close,' he says, avoiding the question directly.

'What was he like, Evan Lawler? As a person I mean?'

Woods' discomfort is now palpable and if I were sitting down I'd be on the edge of my seat.

'Decent chap, from what I knew of him. Amenable, quiet, kept himself to himself, seemed quite a humble sort, not overly social. Liked a game of golf. But our paths didn't cross that often.'

He's distancing himself from the victim.

'I was thinking I should visit the lodge, talk to a few of the members there, and see if they can give me any more insight…'

Woods' eyes narrow. 'Insight into what, Riley?'

'Into Lawler's character, sir, find out a little more about him, talk to some of his friends – sorry, associates.'

He's rattled. His eyes won't focus on mine and he's twitching slightly. I've rattled Woods! Now there's a first.

'The Mulberries, where Lawler was found, it's been a target for professional thieves before. I think it would be prudent to follow that up.'

'You think Lawler's death was a burglary gone wrong?'

'It's a possibility,' Woods replies curtly. 'It's something you should consider.'

'We have, sir. Only nothing was taken at the crime scene – no money, jewellery, personal belongings… His Rolex was on the bedside table, next to his wedding ring. A little odd, don't you think?'

'Odd?'

'Well yes, apparently, according to Beth Lawler they had reconciled, given their marriage another go – Lawler hadn't wanted it to end in the first place. Seems strange he would've taken his ring off.'

'Plenty of people take their jewellery off at bedtime.'

'Yes, but their wedding ring? A watch perhaps… and that puts paid to any robbery theory. Even if you were a novice and accidentally shot someone, surely you'd have the nous to grab two very expensive items of jewellery and make a quick escape?'

'Not necessarily so – he might have been spooked. Shot him accidentally and panicked.'

'So you *do* think this was a robbery gone wrong, sir?'

'I didn't say that, Riley, I just said—'

'Did you know that Evan Lawler regularly used the services of escorts?'

'No. I did not,' Woods says quickly.

'Seems Lawler was into all sorts of dark stuff, sadomasochism, bondage, whips and chains and all of that. He liked to inflict pain on women, according to the one we spoke to anyway. The agency eventually banned him.'

Woods' face has dropped slightly, like he's aged a few years before my eyes.

'Yes, he went a bit too far one time – the girl ended up in A&E. He was paying her to keep quiet.'

'Well—' I can see Woods visibly swallow by the pronounced movement of his Adam's apple. 'Each to his own, I suppose.'

'Indeed, sir. Did he ever mention the name Nicholas Wainwright to you?'

'Are you questioning me, Riley?' He stands up, visibly vexed.

'No, sir,' I say, feigning innocence, 'it's just that you knew the victim, and I thought you might be able to…'

'Well, you thought wrong, Riley!' he snapped. 'I've told you – Lawler was an acquaintance, nothing more. We never spoke about his personal life, or preferences for that matter.'

'Did you know that Nicholas Wainwright, Beth's lover, died just a few months ago?'

'Yes. Delaney told me. The man got into an altercation outside a pub and fell over on his way home and hit his head on the kerb. He was drunk. It was an accident. Coroner recorded it as such. Tragic, obviously.'

'Obviously.'

'He was awaiting trial for the possession of indecent images of children.'

'That's right, sir. Only I'm not sure…'

'Not sure about what, Riley? They were found on his computer – he was arrested. He was also accused of abusing the daughter, Lily. Only there wasn't enough evidence to bring him to trial and the girl retracted her statement.'

Woods has shot himself in the foot. He's been following the case avidly and this admission confirms it. The question is: why?

'So did you know that soon after Wainwright's "accidental" death, Beth and Evan had a reconciliation?'

Woods' expression now resembles that of a man with a bowl of soup in a world full of forks. I've never seen him look more uncomfortable in all the time I've known him.

'Yes, I believe so. Are you saying, Riley, that you don't believe Wainwright's death was an accident, because if you are…'

'If I am, what, sir?' The mock innocence is back again. But the truth is, I'm not saying that exactly, because I don't know – yet. Beth Lawler is lying, or at the very least she's not giving me the full picture. When I spoke with her, I got the distinct impression that she was downplaying her feelings for Wainwright. I just didn't buy it – something in her eyes, something deep within her, was silently revealed. Maybe only I saw it, recognised it, because I've felt it too. Agony. Pain. Raw heartbreak. You can't simply cover that up to the trained eye, or to a fellow sufferer.

'For the record, I think Beth Lawler killed her husband.' I say this deliberately, provocatively. I watch him carefully. He's getting even more flustered and to my shame I feel a buzz of excitement.

'She has an alibi, Riley, watertight. She's clearly seen on CCTV at the time of Evan's death by more than one person. Plus, there's no forensics, nothing to support that statement, nothing to suggest she was involved in any way whatsoever.'

He's right, at least so far, and yet my instincts tell me that he's wrong, very wrong, and that Beth Lawler *is* responsible for her husband's murder somehow. I just need to prove it.

'She could've had him executed,' I say, playing devil's advocate. 'Could've paid someone to kill him.'

'Only there's no evidence of this,' he interjects, 'is there? No transfer of funds from her bank account, no large unusual cash withdrawals, no evidence of her associating with any criminals…'

'I didn't realise you were following the case so closely, sir,' I say, and I think I can see him squirm a little behind his desk.

My antenna is off the charts now. Woods is a results man, and he doesn't care how you get those results, just so long as you do.

'Lawler was a very successful businessman; I've no doubt he made a few enemies, disgruntled a few people, particularly in his line of business. He'd been working on a huge housing project, building affordable homes for the...'

I think he was going to say 'poor'. '... for those on a lower income. He was planning to erect two large tower blocks, aiming to house over 50,000 people in total. I know the local residents showed some real resistance to it – there was uproar, real anger among the community.'

I nod. I wisely don't push it further.

'Like I said, sir, we're exploring all avenues.'

Woods nods, but I see him swallow hard again, that Adam's apple bob. They say men with prominent ones are well endowed, though how this correlates I have no idea. I banish the thought from my head along with his wife's perineum.

'I think you should focus on a failed robbery attempt, look into the disgruntled residents – there could easily be a madman among them.'

'Or woman,' I interject, knowing full well the connotation. He knows I'm not going to leave this one alone, that I'll dig and pick and scratch away like a dog with a bone until I get to the truth. That's why he's so rattled. Woods has something to hide. He knows something. Or he knows someone else knows something. But what? He's clearly trying to steer me away from looking into Beth Lawler's life in any great detail, and similarly so is she.

He glances at me as though he's waiting for me to leave.

'I may make an appeal, sir, a public one. Witnesses, anyone who may have seen or heard anything that day, anyone who might know why anyone would want to kill such an "amenable" chap as Lawler. I think it will help, sir, maybe give us a few new leads.' I cannot help myself.

'You'll do no such thing, Riley,' Woods says, looking up at me gravely.

'But sir, I…'

'For fuck's sake, Riley, do as you're told,' Woods barks at me and I stay silent, though I don't take my eyes from him. I want to know why he's so spooked.

'Beth Lawler killed her husband, sir, but I don't know how – yet. But I will find out, and then the superintendent will be pleased, I'm sure.'

Woods has turned his back on me now and is scratching his thinning hair, seemingly in exasperation. I keep pushing.

'You know me, sir. I trust my gut, I work from instinct, and it's never let me down, not so far anyway. I can get to the bottom of this; investigate the wife in more detail. There'll be flaws – there are in every case, and I will find them. Someone always slips up somewhere down the line, even in the cleverest of crimes. And I will find those flaws and slip-ups, I promise you that.'

Woods slumps back down in his seat. He looks defeated. 'Yes, Riley, that's what I'm worried about.'

I'm not entirely sure what he means but don't ask.

'The offer of early paternity leave is a kind one, sir, but I won't be taking you up on it.'

He buries his head in his hands. He knows he can't suspend me – on what grounds? He clearly wants me off the case. It's almost as if he doesn't *want* me to solve it.

'Do yourself a favour, Dan…' He stands up then, comes around his desk and faces me, his earlier brash demeanour all but evaporated. 'I advise you not to push this. You're barking up the wrong tree. Beth Lawler didn't murder Evan. You're wasting time on her while the real culprit is walking free.'

'If you think so, sir,' I appease him. For now.

'Good.' Woods nods abruptly. 'And come to me with anything, and I mean *anything*, you find out first. Is that perfectly clear?'

'Yes, sir.'

'I need you to promise me you'll do that, Riley,' he says. Promise him? He wants me to make a *promise*! This is a day of many firsts.

'I promise,' I say, with my fingers crossed behind my back.

'Good,' he says. 'Thank you.'

I close the door behind me and go back to the incident room where I immediately tell the team to start digging deeper into Beth Lawler's life. 'I want to see bank records, where she's been in the past few months… speak to friends, family, neighbours again. Talk to her colleagues… find out who she's been with, get those shovels out and start digging.'

'How did that go?' Davis perches on the edge of my desk clutching a plastic cup of coffee. 'In there, with Woods?'

I lean closer towards her. 'He told me to lay off the wife, that I was barking up the wrong tree. He invited me – rather told me – to take early paternity leave, which I politely declined…'

Davis's eyes are almost out of their sockets. 'He wants you off the case?'

'Exactamondo,' I say, remembering how much I hate that word, yet can't seem to stop using it.

'Why?'

I raise my eyebrows. 'I don't know, Davis, but I'm sure as shit going to find out.'

CHAPTER TWENTY-FIVE

Beth

October 2018

Beth's adrenalin is causing her to drive too fast as she absentmind-edly shoots through a red light.

'Shit!' The sound of the horns of disgruntled drivers fills her ears but there's no more space left inside her cramped mind to digest them, or care. She needs to get home, to see Nick and talk to him, tell him what she's found out. The meeting with the solicitor had not gone well exactly, but what she's discovered is so shocking and sensational that she's sure it is all the leverage she needs to stop this terrible business in its abhorrent tracks. At the very least it would be something Evan and his nasty little associates won't want people knowing about, *those sick bastards.*

'This may sound harsh, Beth.' Dwaine Simpson, a diminutive yet dogmatic man, had given her the kind of look that someone gives you before they're about to impart some bad news. 'I can't – I shouldn't – sugar-coat anything for you, and I won't because you need to know what you're up against here.'

Beth had raised an eyebrow; she was slowly beginning to understand *exactly* what she was up against, but still she could barely take it all in.

'Your husband is a powerful man, he has money – a lot of money – and he's appointed arguably one of the best legal teams money can buy. As it stands, he appears to be in a much better position than you, financially and arguably, morally – at least on the surface.'

Beth had pulled her chin into her neck in outrage. 'You think coercing a six-year-old child into making false allegations that she's been abused and taking her away from her mother is moral? Do you think that breaking into someone's portacabin and planting child pornography on their PC is moral, Dwaine?'

He'd sighed. 'Of course not, but breaking into your estranged husband's office and stealing papers from his desk was highly inadvisable, Beth. Now you have a non-molestation order against you, which won't work in your favour in court. You need to start thinking with your head and not with your emotions.'

Beth had swallowed back her anger. She'd been incensed when she'd been served with a court order the day after their confrontation in his office – a non-molestation order, against *her*! Evan seemed to be one step ahead; his campaign of hate had blindsided her, and she had been totally unprepared and emotionally ill-equipped for any of it.

'It should be the other way round,' she'd replied miserably. 'This is all wrong, all so very wrong and unjust. I don't know what to do, how to fight him, how to even begin to.'

He'd sighed heavily, like he saw and heard this kind of bullshit every day. He probably did.

'Look, Beth, I'm not going to lie to you, it's going to be a battle, and an expensive one – *a very expensive one.*'

Beth had dropped her head into her hands. She'd felt so exhausted that she wanted to curl up into a ball on the aging carpet beneath her and rock back and forth slowly. 'Nick's life is in ruins.' She'd heard the desperation in her own voice, a voice she hardly recognised anymore. 'He's been condemned… labelled a paedophile. It's been all over the local papers. He's lost all his gardening contracts, he's scared to leave the house and I'm scared for him. The bloody social worker won't let me speak about it to Lily – if I could just talk to her, get her to tell the truth, then all this might go away.'

Dwaine Simpson had looked at her like she'd come down with the last shower.

'That's not going to happen anytime soon, Beth. You need to understand that, be prepared. The CPS feel there's enough evidence for Nick to stand trial, the images… Lily's testimony.'

'Screw the CPS! This is corruption! It's a bloody witch-hunt!' Beth felt the rage descend upon her again, like a black cloak thrown down at her from above.

'I don't doubt you're right, which is why this is going to be extremely tough. Nick will need to appoint someone – someone good, someone who specialises in these cases.'

'But surely the police will have to listen to us? Surely they will investigate, won't they?'

Beth had gone into the police station in person and had spoken to someone, a detective – what was his name again? Delaney, Martin Delaney. She'd told him everything. Told him how Evan had lied, how he'd made his own daughter lie. She'd told him about Miranda, Imogen's mum and the horse-riding accident and how she was convinced Evan had bought Miranda's silence and had given him the woman's phone number and told him to speak to her directly. She'd told him how Evan had made veiled threats to ruin her life, destroy her relationship and that there should be an investigation into the break-in in Nick's portacabin. She had shrieked and cried, become animated as she had protested, over and over again, 'How can this happen? How can this be allowed to happen?' She had implored the detective, looked into his eyes and silently begged him. 'Nick doesn't have a criminal record; he's never been in trouble in his life. He's never hurt anyone, let alone a child, *my* child.' And the detective, a good-looking but somewhat dispassionate and arrogant man not much older than she was, had told her that he would have his say in court.

'There was no break-in reported by your partner, Mrs Lawler,' he'd said. 'No evidence of tampering,' and once again, she'd been asked how well she knew 'this Nick character'.

In her solicitor's office, Beth had felt like she was drowning in a tsunami of helplessness and injustice, unable to catch her breath before the next giant wave came crashing into her, sending her tumbling backwards onto sharp gravel.

'If you want my opinion, Evan's endgame is to destroy you, destroy your relationship with Nick and with your daughter too. In fact, if the judge grants your husband permanent full custody of Lily then *you* may end up having to pay *him* maintenance.'

Beth had stared at Dwaine, wide-eyed with disbelief. 'On a part-time nurse's salary?'

He'd nodded slowly. 'Yes, that's the bottom line, I'm afraid.'

'And the house?'

'I checked; it's in his name.'

'No… no! It's in both our names, he assured me of that! I signed something, I remember, it was after we got married and…'

But Dwaine slowly shook his head.

'I'm sorry, Beth. Your husband didn't tell you the truth. In fact, it seems he's been lying about a *lot* of things…'

Beth's head had dropped into her hands, bent double in the plastic chair she was sitting on. She'd thought she might pass out. He wanted to leave her broken, with nothing, no one, so she would have to come to him begging, cap in hand. *Never. Not in this lifetime or the next.*

'There's more? Such as?'

'Such as his mother being alive for one thing.'

Beth had looked up at him, her eyes wide in shock. 'Evan's mother is alive? But… how… how did you find this out?'

'It was pure coincidence actually, but my former colleague acted on her behalf on the sale of a property some years ago and for some reason I remembered the name and did a bit of digging… anyway we traced her to a hospice in Surrey. Cancer,' he'd said. 'Terminal. She's in palliative care. And no, he doesn't pay her fees, hasn't visited her once apparently. In fact, they had no idea Eileen Lawler even had a son.'

'Why would he say she was dead when she isn't?' Beth hadn't been able to believe it. Evan had told her the story of his mother's death a few times over, how sad he had been, how he had grieved for her.

'That I don't know, I'm afraid – I didn't get that far because something else came up.'

'Something else?'

'I didn't want to tell you this, Beth. I'm not even sure if I should because—'

'Tell me what?' Beth had said, indignant. 'You know something, something about Evan, something that could help me and Nick, help me get Lily back?' She'd blinked at him. 'Dwaine, you have to tell me!'

Dwaine had looked down at some papers on his desk. She could tell he was in two minds.

'What I've found out has the potential to make things even worse for you, which is not something I want to happen… but, if played carefully, well, then it might just be the leverage you need to get Evan to back off,' he'd said, going over to the coffee machine and pressing the button, releasing black liquid into a plastic cup and handing it to her. 'You'll need it strong and black.'

'*Just tell me.*' She'd taken the cup, placed it on the desk.

'I used to work as a private detective, many moons ago now,' he'd said almost nostalgically. 'Those papers you stole from Evan's office were bank statements mainly. I went through them, did some more digging and couldn't help myself. Got a funny feeling about something…'

Beth had been on tenterhooks. 'And…?'

'There were a few transactions that intrigued me, monthly payments, always for the same amount, and also payments to a company with a strange name, Angels and Demons. Anyway, I dug some more, made some phone calls and it turns out that Evan has been using the services of' – he'd coughed into his fist again, awkwardly – 'escorts…'

She'd blinked at him, momentarily speechless. 'Prostitutes,' he'd clarified, as though she didn't know what an escort was. 'And for quite some time too, by all accounts.'

The room had started to spin.

'Evan? Prostitutes!' Not Evan; he'd been practically asexual throughout their marriage and… oh God… Beth had thought back to all the times he had rejected her sexually, how he had seemed utterly indifferent to her and taken up residence in the spare bedroom once Lily had been born and rarely, if ever, shown an interest in any kind of physical interaction with her. And now she knew why. All those years, all those years she had believed that Evan was a quiet, decent, kind man, albeit one with a low libido. And she had blamed herself.

'There's more I'm afraid.' Beth had reached for the coffee and wished there was a brandy in it. 'Much more.' Her hand had shaken as she held the plastic cup to her lips.

'It seems your husband – among others – regularly attended private S&M sex parties organised by this escort agency.'

'Orgies, you mean?' Beth hadn't been able to believe what she was hearing.

Dwaine had nodded. 'I traced a few payments to a woman named Svetlana, although her real name is Sonia. It seems that Evan was paying her off, paying her to stay silent over something.'

Beth had been too stunned to swallow her coffee and it had sat burning the back of her throat.

'It transpires that he and Svetlana had been involved in a sex game gone wrong and that she'd been injured – quite badly injured by all accounts.'

She had felt physically sick at hearing that.

'Svetlana was one of a few girls at the agency who specialised in degradation… female degradation,' Dwaine had clarified, almost wincing as the words left his lips. 'Evan paid to abuse her. They all did.'

'They?'

Dwaine had sat down, leaned in close to her.

'Do you know who your husband associates with down at the lodge, Beth?'

She had shaken her head. 'Fellow Freemasons, I presume. He plays golf with them… I didn't take much interest… all seemed quite boring – all those middle-aged men talking about their handicap and business.'

Dwaine had raised another eyebrow. 'Doctors, lawyers, police commissioners, MPs and politicians, businessmen, local councillors, judges… all members of the same lodge.'

It had felt like Beth's sphincter muscle had fallen through her backside. 'Good God… they were all in on it together? All keeping this dirty, perverted little secret.'

'So it would seem.' Dwaine had leaned back into his swivel chair and let Beth digest the information he'd just given her for a moment – or try to. 'You can imagine, I'm sure, if something like this came out into the public domain it would be a scandal of national proportions. The press would think all their Christmases had come at once.'

Beth's mind had been spinning in time with the room.

'So it *is* a conspiracy. They've all got each other's backs… protecting each other…?'

Dwaine had shrugged. 'It would seem so, yes. But before you get overexcited, if that's the right word, you must understand that the agency, these girls, they were – or still are – being paid off, and handsomely too. They're not about to sell out their cash cow to help you win a custody battle and clear Nick's name… not unless you've got the resources to match them. And besides,' he'd sighed, 'these men are incredibly powerful people; they're pulling the country's strings. They'd no doubt get a press injunction if anyone threatened to expose them, granted by one of the judges involved, and you'd be hung out to dry – you and Nick both.'

'I think he killed Marta.' Beth's hand had been covering her mouth, so she hadn't been sure if she'd said the words aloud or not.

'Sorry, who?'

Beth had shaken herself out of her paralytic fog.

'Marta, our housekeeper; my friend. She disappeared a year ago. I came home one morning and she'd just vanished, left Lily alone upstairs, the back doors wide open. No note, no phone call, no nothing. I think Evan did something to her.'

'And the police… you called them?'

'Yes of course. They came, forensics, all of that. But her passport and phone were missing. They… they never really followed it up. Said she'd probably just had enough and left… no foul play suspected, no body… no Marta.'

Dwaine had looked genuinely shocked.

'That doesn't sound right.' He'd pulled his chin into his chest. 'A woman goes missing like that and there's no real investigation? What makes you think it has something to do with Evan?'

Beth had paused. She'd stopped trying to battle with the dread that was filling her entire body, threatening to spill over onto Dwaine's plastic desk and just let it flow through her instead. Some battles you just couldn't win.

'At the time, nothing, but now, everything,' she'd said.

Dwaine had blown air through his lips.

'Jesus, Beth, you don't understand what you're dealing with here. I'm genuinely concerned for you. If this is some kind of conspiracy then you won't be able to fight it. If you really want my advice then you'll do what I suggested and steer clear of Nick until this blows over and you've got Lily back. These are men who would stop at nothing to ensure this doesn't come out, and I mean *nothing.*'

Beth had looked up at him.

'I'm so sorry, Beth,' Dwaine had said, with gravitas. 'You never really knew your husband at all, did you?'

'No,' she'd answered, fighting back tears of horror and frustration. 'But then again, do we ever really know anyone?'

CHAPTER TWENTY-SIX

Cath

September 2019

The ticket feels sharp and cold like a razor blade in Cath's shaking fingers as she boards the 3.15 p.m. to Bristol and searches for aisle seat number 25b. He'd found her, but then again, deep down she's always known that he would, *that he always will.*

'I got the address out of that pissed-up Irish bitch across the hall in the end,' he'd said. 'Quite a tough old bird, given her size and the amount of whiskey inside of her.'

Neve. Oh Jesus.

'You didn't hurt her, did you, Saul?' she'd asked knowing full well it was rhetorical. Saul hurt everybody.

'She'll get over it, silly old alky – probably don't even remember.' He'd laughed, pleased with himself. 'Give her half a bottle of scotch and she'd tell you she liked kiddie fiddling, that one.'

Cath had felt the nausea rising inside her stomach again. For a few weeks it hadn't been there, that feeling, that omnipotent sickness inside of her. And it had felt like a lightness she hadn't felt for as long as she could remember, or perhaps even experienced at all. His call had plunged her straight back into that dark abyss once more, only this time she could feel, could see the end coming. And in a way, she knew no one, no one perhaps on this entire planet, could ever understand that she actually welcomed it.

Cath knew that if she didn't come back, come home to him, that he would find her eventually and kill her anyway. She'd been running away from him forever inside her mind, had managed it physically a few times too, but now… now she was done with running. Now she simply wanted to take a slow, gentle pace towards her fate. She knew that if she had tried to resist, if she had objected or gone against his will, then Neve would be hurt, maybe even killed, if he hadn't killed the poor woman already. And then he'd come after Ivy too.

Saul thought nothing of the law; he wasn't frightened by the idea of being incarcerated. After he killed her she imagined he'd be happy to give himself up. 'I'd have a permanent address and three meals a day, wouldn't I?' He'd said this enough times for it to be convincing. 'With you gone, there'd be nothing else to live for anyway, Cath.' He was a master at making this kind of statement; one that made no sense whatsoever, but one that she fully believed with what was left of her shattered heart and diminished soul. Saul's own life was cheap to him, which in turn made hers and everyone else's. He had no fear of consequences or death and that's what made him so dangerous.

'No one is beyond help, Catherine – everyone can be fixed if they want to fix themselves.' That's what her social worker always used to say – well, one of them anyway; she can't remember which, there had been so many. But Cath knows that this is just something they say, these educated people who have trained and studied and gone to university and never in their comfortable lives experienced a moment of the things she has. And they were wrong – some people *were* beyond help. Saul was. And perhaps she was too. She had no option but to accept it. There was a name for such a thing – what did they call it? She'd read it somewhere, in a book, back when she could focus on something for long enough… it was a French saying…

Cath shakes her head gently. She can't quite remember and it mildly irritates her. She can't quite remember anything anymore. Fear was a governess most people did not understand, not really. It muddles your mind. No one understands anything until they have truly lived it. Like people who think they would fight and kick and scream if attacked but faced with the true reality of such horror find themselves paralysed and mute with fear instead.

Cath knows that today she is making the journey to her own death. Maybe he won't kill her straight away; maybe it will be a matter of weeks or months or – God forbid – years. He probably won't even *mean* to kill her, but his anger will be worse than anything else she has already endured, because this time she had escaped, she had almost beaten him, and for that she knows she will pay the highest price. Or perhaps it's no price at all and her death will be her freedom, true emancipation.

She looks at her phone. It's 3.04 p.m. The train will be departing soon and she feels a stillness settle upon her like an ethereal butterfly. She will have a glass of wine when the woman with the trolley comes round, maybe even a couple; she'll look forward to that. Ivy won't be back from work for a good three hours or more; she won't get the note she's left for her, which simply reads: 'Thanks for everything. Goodbye, x' until then. She was done with explaining, with even trying to. This was the best way, *the only way*. There would be no one else to hurt after she was gone. Kai would expect it; so would her mother and sister. They might not understand it, but they would expect it. She would be the sacrificial lamb, and she would be with Cody, where she should be, where she should've always been and… God, what was the name of that French saying about accepting something that was already decided for you…?

Cath's thoughts are interrupted as the door to the carriage opens with a hiss and a woman gets on and looks right at her.

CHAPTER TWENTY-SEVEN

Beth

September 2019

Beth's feet feel like bricks cemented to the platform as she waits for the 3.15 p.m. to Bristol to grind to an ear-splitting halt. Her mind could not rest; it hadn't been able to ever since the day she had left Evan and Marta went missing, the day that had changed everything. *What a difference a day makes.* She'll get drunk on the train, yes, that's what she'll do, *get drunk* and swallow one of those pills – who *wouldn't* after all she had endured? On top of everything, a judge had recently awarded Evan continued temporary full custody of Lily in her absence; she'd been too ill, too traumatised by everything to attend court. Dwaine Simpson had asked for an adjournment given the circumstances, but Evan's team of dynamic barristers had argued that she was in no fit state to care for her daughter for the 'foreseeable future'. Foreseeable future! Wasn't *that* the irony! They had portrayed her as a basket case in court, a woman in need of psychiatric treatment; unpredictable and incapable of caring for herself, let alone a child. She'd been left high and dry, hung, drawn and quartered by her vengeful estranged husband, a deviant man whose capabilities for evil had been so well concealed that it had enabled him to blindside her and subsequently strip her of everything. Evan had ensured that she had been brought to her knees; and it had been as easy as taking candy from a baby.

The one and only justice that had come out of any of it was that Lily had finally retracted her statement about Nick and the abuse. She'd told that social worker, Rosemary, that she'd only said it because she'd been 'sad about Mummy leaving Daddy, and had wanted her to come home'. Beth didn't believe it; Evan was still manipulating their daughter, coercing her into telling lies, pulling her little strings and working her like a marionette. Besides, it was of little solace now, the damage already done. Beth doesn't blame her daughter. Evan has used their little girl as a pawn in his wicked game; a game he appears to have won.

Beth automatically presses the large illuminated button on the train door and steps inside the carriage, her tired eyes searching for seat 25c. That's when she sees her.

CHAPTER TWENTY-EIGHT

Beth

September 2019

At first sight, she assumes that she knows the woman sitting opposite her but just can't place her and instinctively acknowledges her with a smile.

Her memory races to identify her. Did they go to school together, nursing college? Was she a sister of a friend or a former boyfriend? Were they *related*? Anyway, she's sure she knows her. A strange and bizarre thought involuntarily pops up in her mind; she's not sure where it has come from. *Could she be her long-lost twin, a sister she never knew about, one her mum had kept hidden from her all these years*? No, that's preposterous and absurd and impossible and…

'Hello,' she finds herself saying.

The woman smiles back at her timidly. 'Hi.'

'Do I know you… or…' Beth is confused, and she can see confusion on the stranger's face too. *Is she drunk?* She wants to sit down, *needs* to sit down, but all she can do is stare and gawp. Sunlight has hit the side of the carriage, causing shadows to move and dance behind them, illuminating their respective profiles, making the moment feel almost cinematic somehow. Adrenalin courses through her like rapids as she studies the woman's features;

her facial expression suggests she was on the verge of breaking into a smile, just like her mother's; just *like her own*.

She sits down in the seat opposite. She is aware she is staring but is unable to take her eyes from the woman's face; it's like looking in the mirror. She is absolutely convinced that they must somehow be related – they *have* to be.

Another bizarre thought enters Beth's mind – perhaps she was dead and was hovering somewhere between life and death, waiting to cross over. You had to face yourself in death, didn't you? That's what they said, and this is what she imagined it felt like. But she wasn't dead. She was on the 3.15 p.m. to Bristol and this was real. *She* was real…

'This is… a bit mad, isn't it?' The woman opposite giggles in what appears to be nervous confusion, her eyes darting awkwardly from side to side. She doesn't need to explain why though because it is, quite literally, staring them both in the face.

'Hello,' she replies. 'My name's Beth.'

CHAPTER TWENTY-NINE

Beth & Cath

September 2019

'Have we… have we met before?'

'No, I don't think so,' the woman replies. 'I'm… I'm pretty sure I would've remembered.'

They both start to laugh then, awkwardly at first, gradually building into absurd hysteria.

'It's not just me, is it?' Beth says. 'But… but we really do look alike, don't we? You can see it too, can't you?'

The woman nods; she appears to have gone into some sort of momentary shock.

'Yes,' she says. 'I can… I can see it… I…' She closes her eyes briefly, opens them again as if she's checking her vision is intact.

'Are we… do you think we might be related?'

Even her expressions appear familiar somehow – small nuances, gesticulations Beth recognises in herself.

'I'm Cath… Catherine.' The woman's accent is different, broad Bristolian by the sounds of it, but even her voice – soft and high-pitched – bears a similar tone to her own. Although they are dressed differently, Beth can see that she is of a similar build; their hair and eye colour are almost identical.

'Well, this really is bizarre, Cath,' Beth says, 'but then again…' She was about to add 'everything in my life is right now' but remembered that the woman was a stranger, yet at the same time she feels an immediate affinity towards her, something inexplicable, like a kind of cosmic pull.

'You're not related to the Walkers are you, by any chance?' Beth takes a stab in the dark. She has to know. 'Are you from London, originally I mean?'

'No.' Cath shakes her head. 'My surname is Patterson – that's my family name – and I grew up in Bristol, all my life, more's the pity.'

'So you definitely don't know the Walkers…?'

Cath shrugs. 'My mum's maiden name was Westbrook, and her mother's name was O'Hennesy – Irish,' she adds. 'But I never heard no one speak of any Walkers.'

Beth feels slightly embarrassed. 'Thought I would ask, given that… well, I guess you must be my doppelganger then.'

The woman blinks at her. 'They say it's an omen, don't they?' she says. 'If you meet your doppelganger, your double… it's supposed to be an omen, or so I read somewhere.'

'Oh…' Beth says. The faintest tracings of an idea begin forming inside her subconscious but they've not yet broken the surface. 'Do they? Well, I hope it's a good one.'

'Me too,' Cath answers quickly.

Beth senses the woman is carrying a deep unhappiness inside of her. She can almost smell it, like a cadaver dog sniffs out death.

'So, you were visiting London, Cath?'

'Something like that,' she replies with a polite smile, looks down into her lap. She appears nervous, scared almost, as if she's doing something she shouldn't by talking to her.

'Family?'

'No. I don't really have any of that anymore.'

Beth gives a gentle melancholy snort. 'No, me neither.'

'And you?' Cath asks. 'You have family in Bristol?'

Beth suddenly thinks of the bottle of pills inside her handbag, about taking one.

'I did have… well, I would have done… put it that way.'

Cath nods as if she understands perfectly. Perhaps she does.

'Listen, do you fancy a drink?' Beth says, pulling a bottle of Chardonnay from a plastic bag. 'I went to M&S at the station, got plastic glasses and everything! I know how to live, me.'

Cath giggles like a schoolgirl, glances around the carriage as if she's checking it's OK to say yes. 'Why not?' she says.

'Well, we've got the next two hours to get through and I don't know about you but I could do with a drink!' Beth can hear the strain in her forced joviality. She wonders if Cath can hear it too. There is a moment's pause as she decants the wine into the plastic flutes.

'You said you *would've* had family in Bristol?' Cath's head is cocked to one side and Beth translates the gesture as her seeking elaboration.

'Yes,' she says, trying to keep her emotions in check. 'I'm visiting my partner's mother, my dead partner's mother actually.' She pauses, adding, 'He died a couple of months ago. I never got to meet her, his mother, when he was alive, so I figured, as he died because of me, that I would do the decent thing and go and see her.' Beth sloshes a little of her wine onto the carriage floor. The woman adjacent to her gives her a sideways glance and she silently dares her to make a remark so that she can tell her to mind her own business, expunge some of the anger that's constantly rising and swelling inside of her.

Cath looks at her with sadness that she's convinced only they share in that very moment. 'I'm so sorry,' she says. 'How did it happen?'

Beth welcomes the woman's interest. She feels like an open wound.

'That's just it.' She snorts derisively. 'No one really knows exactly. The police told me that he'd got into an altercation in a pub and had fallen and hit his head on the pavement. He never regained consciousness – died of an aneurysm a few hours later, alone in hospital. I was going through a messy divorce you see… my estranged husband, he was out to destroy us, made allegations about Nick – false allegations – that he'd been—'

Beth swallows back the wine – and the lump at the back of her throat. 'That he'd been interfering with our daughter, planted images on his computer – all lies,' she adds, supping more warm wine from the plastic glass. 'Dirty, filthy lies…' She shakes her head, unable to stop now that she has started. 'We were hounded, you know, by the press, had graffiti scrawled on our garage door. Nick lost his contracts because of it – he worked as a gardening contractor, schools and public places mostly. It destroyed him, *those lies,* they killed him. I lost my mum a few months before… and my daughter has been taken from me and… Oh God, I'm sorry,' she apologises. 'What must you think of me? I'm not in a good place right now… I'm sorry.' She apologises again.

Cath suddenly leans forward and takes Beth's hand. 'It's OK,' she says, squeezing it. 'I understand…'

It's like seeing her own reflection staring back at her as Beth's eyes meet with the stranger's – one she feels like she instinctively already knows.

'Yes,' she says, 'I think you do.'

They lightly tap each other's glasses, the plastic making a dull thud in place of a musical 'ding'.

'You've lost someone you love too?' Beth can feel the warmth of the alcohol hit her empty stomach and welcomes it.

The woman doesn't answer; she doesn't need to.

'Want to tell me about it?' she says.

Cath looks up at her but doesn't let go of her hand.

'You first,' she says.

CHAPTER THIRTY

Beth

September 2019

The train journey had passed quickly in a blur of alcohol and conversation. Beth had learned that Catherine Patterson had spent her entire life in Bristol, had also once thought about training to be a nurse and, at thirty-three years old, was just three months her junior.

Beth had never heard anything like Cath's story before, not first-hand anyway, and she had listened, silent and horrified, as she had recounted the years of abuse she had suffered at the hands of a monster called Saul Bennett, how he had robbed her of everything – her family and the life of their unborn baby, a little boy she had named Cody and had been forced to give birth to, stillborn. It had been a catalogue of sheer horror; abuse on a level that Beth could barely stand to listen to much less comprehend. She felt in awe of the fact that Cath, despite her nervous disposition, had somehow survived through it, but Beth could see the toll it had taken on her.

'I thought,' she'd said, 'that this time I had truly managed to escape…'

Her hands had trembled constantly as she spoke, her movements jerky and her eyes darting nervously from side to side.

She had appeared to be in a constant state of hypersensitivity mixed with paranoia, flinching when the door made a hiss and a passenger walked through the carriage. 'But he found me.' Beth had seen the fear in her eyes as she spoke quietly – it was almost tangible. 'Somehow I knew deep down that he would… that he always will, and that I will never be free of him, never all the time I have breath left in my body.'

Every word she'd spoken had compounded Beth's anger and disgust. As truly awful as it was listening to a brief synopsis of Cath's tragic life, strangely it had also given her a modicum of comfort. She wasn't alone; she wasn't the only one at the bottom of a black hole, trapped in a dark abyss of hopelessness and heartbreak. There were others out there suffering as much, if not worse than, she was.

'And so I have to go back… do you understand?' Cath's voice had been barely audible, like she was becoming a ghost right before her eyes.

Beth had reached for Cath's hand this time and squeezed it tightly.

'Yes,' she'd said. 'I do.' But she had felt frightened for her, frightened for them both. Both of them were equally trapped, let down by a system designed to protect them. Cath lived on the breadline in a constant state of fear, a miserable existence, but she was – just about – living proof that money made scant difference when it came to living with psychopaths *and* murderers. No money in the world could buy back her mother, or Nicky, her daughter or Cath's sons.

Saul Bennett and Evan Lawler, though different in their methods, were cut from the same cloth; their only difference was that one was overt and the over covert – but the damage they had done was respectively on par.

'What are you going to do, Cath?' Beth had asked her as the train had crawled into Bristol. She had wanted to tell her to go to the police again – after all, that's what most people would've advised, but Beth heard the futility in her voice before she'd even said it. What would the police do? Lock him up for a few years at best? And after that? A restraining order that he would inevitably breach? A new identity and a life spent looking over her shoulder, living in constant fear that one day, *one day*, he just might find her? Wasn't that a life sentence in itself? The system wasn't foolproof; even if the police *did* protect Cath, they couldn't be with her 24/7 – they couldn't protect her from monsters like that, hell bent on destroying you, on killing you…

Beth had felt the hopelessness of Cath's situation as acutely as her own as they'd stood on the platform, facing each other. She'd wanted to say something profound, something that would help this poor woman who was so like her in so many ways but instead she'd said: 'It was so good to meet you, Cath.'

'You too, Beth,' she'd replied, hugging her. And Beth had felt a strange sensation as they had embraced, like somehow this woman had been sent to her – that they had been sent to each other – for a reason, destined to meet on the 3.15 p.m. to Bristol. She had felt an inexplicable emotional shift as they said their goodbyes. The hopelessness she'd felt when she'd embarked on the journey had diminished slightly. Cath and her diabolical story had instilled a sense of strength, of camaraderie within her. *And it had given her an idea.*

'Take my number, Cath,' Beth had said. 'Please promise me you'll stay in touch, and use it if you ever need it.'

Cath had nodded and punched Beth's digits into her phone. 'And vice versa, Beth,' she'd said.

They had hugged again for a few moments longer, neither one of them wanting to break away.

'What you said earlier, about meeting your doppelganger… I think it was a good omen…' She had kissed Cath on her cheek, turned to walk away.

'Beth?' Cath had called out to her.

'Yes?'

'What's that saying, it's French… and it means something that has already been decided before you know about it… It's been on the tip of my tongue all day.'

Beth had smiled.

'A fait accompli,' she'd said, as she walked away. '*A fait accompli.*'

CHAPTER THIRTY-ONE

Dan

October 2019

'Right, people, what have you got for me?' I address the incident room jovially, though it belies the nagging feeling I have in my guts. The conversation I had with Woods is seriously bothering me. Something's amiss, and if it is what I think it is then I could be opening a Pandora's box of epic proportions. As a result, I'd asked Harding to collate a list of all the members of Lawler's Freemasons' lodge and my heart sank as I'd read through it: judges, barristers, lawyers, local MPs, councillors, Woods himself and, most notably, Commissioner Spencer Dunlop-Jones. It read like a who's who of VIPs, of men with status and power – with a lot to lose.

'Marta Larssen,' Mitchell kicks off proceedings. 'I contacted MP for her file but it appears to be missing, gov,' she says. 'They can't locate it.'

This does nothing to put water on the fire of suspicion that is beginning to form inside my mind – and gut.

'I see,' I say. 'Keep on at them; apply a little pressure, yeah? Make a nuisance of yourself.'

'Shouldn't be difficult,' Baylis ribs her and Mitchell pokes out her tongue playfully.

'Yes, gov,' she says. 'But I do have something interesting for you – a couple of things actually.'

'Go on, Mitchell.' I watch Delaney at the back of the room, study his expression. I've also learned that he was the one who had spoken to Beth Lawler when she'd come into the station to make allegations about Evan setting up Nick Wainwright some months ago, but he has yet to mention this. I'm hoping for his sake he does.

'Well,' she says, looking extremely pleased with herself, 'Evan Lawler's parents were dead, that's what he told everyone anyway, that his father had died when he was eighteen and his mother had passed away when he was' – she checks her notes – 'nine years old.'

'OK?'

'His mother's still alive, gov. Eileen Lawler – she's in her early eighties, lives in a care home in Surrey, has done for decades by all accounts. She's not in a good way though – she's paralysed from the waist down and is in the final stages of cancer, hasn't got long left. Think we need to go down there ASAP, boss.'

'Yes, we do. Why was Lawler hiding the truth about his mother?' I say this mainly to myself. 'Good work, Mitchell… You said you had something else?'

She beams, seemingly chuffed to be in the limelight. 'I do, boss. I've gone through Beth Lawler's bank statements, and a little over two weeks before her husband's murder, she bought a train ticket to Bristol.'

'That's where Wainwright's mother lives,' Davis interjects. 'She might've been going to see her.'

'I checked,' Mitchell says, 'she was. Only three weeks later, a day after Evan Lawler was murdered, she bought another ticket to Bristol.'

'To see Wainwright's mother again?' My interest is piqued.

Mitchell shakes her head. 'Nope. I spoke with Joyce Wainwright and she confirmed that Beth had only been to see her the once, a few weeks before. Seems a bit odd, doesn't it, boss?'

A bolt of adrenalin hits me like lightning. 'Who was she going to see?'

'Wainwright. He's buried there, in Bristol,' Davis interjects again. 'Anyway, Evan's body wasn't discovered for five days; she wouldn't have even known her husband was dead at this point.'

Unless she killed him. I think this but don't say it.

'Get all the CCTV from the train stations – go through it with a fine-tooth comb.'

'Request is in already, gov.' Mitchell sits back in her chair as if she's waiting for a round of applause. I'm inclined to indulge her, but it's not the done thing and I don't want her to get cocky.

'Any luck with the weapon?'

'Nothing, boss.' Harding gives me a regrettable look, glancing at Mitchell, who is still basking in a glow of glory. 'It was army issue, a 19 most probably – 9 mm ammo… easily available in the underworld… Nothing registered to Beth or Evan Lawler. He never owned a weapon – wasn't killed by his own gun by the looks of it.'

'The gun is somewhere in Bristol,' I say. 'Maybe that's why Beth Lawler made the journey the day after – to get rid of the weapon. Talk to Bristol City Constabulary, the guys up there… give them the heads-up that we're looking for a 9 mm Glock… see what it throws up… Anyone else?' I glance over at Delaney and our eyes lock briefly. 'Martin?'

'Yes, boss, um… Beth Lawler came to the station last year to file a complaint.'

'Complaint about what?' He's mentioned it – not a moment too soon I should add. I'm actually relieved. I don't want to dislike Delaney, but my instincts tell me I can't fully trust him.

'About her husband… she claimed he had set the boyfriend up, coerced the girl, the daughter, into making false allegations against him, said it was all malicious lies. She thought that Lawler had somehow planted indecent images on Wainwright's computer.'

'And it was looked into, right?'

'I took the statement, boss.' Delaney looks calm and unruffled. 'No break-in reported at his portacabin and nothing came back from forensics when it was searched. She was hysterical, highly strung, if I remember. She was trying to protect the boyfriend. Didn't want to believe the truth about him.'

'We don't know if it was the truth, Martin,' I remind him. 'Wainwright died before it went to trial, and the girl retracted her statement. Besides, there's something off about Wainwright's death, which is why I've put in an application to the Home Office for an exhumation of his body. I'm not entirely convinced it was an accident.' This is not actually true, but I've said it for a reason.

Davis looks at me wide-eyed. But it's Delaney's expression I'm interested in. The coroner who examined Wainwright's body – a name I'm not familiar with – is on that list and I think back to the conversation Davis and I had with Svetlana/Sonia when we returned to ask her some follow-up questions. '*We organise sex parties for men… a lot of men with a lot of power… people like you, Detective, people who get to say what happens to other people's lives… and deaths…*' She'd refused to give any names, claimed she didn't know them, so I'd spoken to the madam of Angels and Demons and requested her client list.

She'd laughed at me down the phone. 'Out of the question!' she said. 'We pride ourselves on protecting the identity of all our clients. It'll put me out of business!'

'And I pride myself on solving murders,' I'd replied. 'The murder of one of your clients, Ms…'

'Adams… Marion Adams.'

'And you'll be out of business anyway if I link you to Evan Lawler's murder. Incidentally, he was lured to his death, to his apartment, on the pretext of meeting one of your girls…'

It was a lie of sorts, but a necessary one. I heard the measured cadence of her voice.

'My girls had nothing to do with Evan Lawler's murder… you have no proof.'

'I wouldn't be too sure of that, Ms Adams. I don't want to expose anyone; I just need names… I'd rather not have to obtain a warrant…'

The anonymous email was sent to me within an hour.

Delaney doesn't flinch but his poker face isn't quite as honed as he thinks it is and I think I see his pupils dilate.

'I want that CCTV footage.' I turn to Mitchell. 'And I want you, Delaney, to go to the Freemasons' lodge and talk to the other members, find out what they knew about Evan Lawler, their connections to him. You'll need to be sensitive, given who these people are.'

Delaney looks pleased, which is just how I want him to look and is all part of the plan.

'Gov.' He nods.

The team begin to disperse back to business and I grab my car keys from the desk.

'Let me guess,' Davis says, picking up her handbag, 'Eileen Lawler?'

'Exactamondo,' I reply.

CHAPTER THIRTY-TWO

Beth

September 2019

'She's really not a very well lady,' the nurse behind the desk says as she pins a visitor's badge to Beth's shirt. 'She's in a wheelchair, obviously, and is practically blind now, poor thing. Cataracts,' she explains with a look of sympathy. 'The cancer came not long after... terrible really, the life that poor lady has had... anyway, we take good care of her,' she says, brightening up. 'We keep her comfortable and make sure she has her favourite treats, a little tot of whiskey and a Chelsea bun every now and again, although she struggles to keep most things down anymore...' Her tone returns to maudlin. 'She's one of our favourites, not that we should really have any,' the woman says, biting her bottom lip. 'But she's been here forever it seems; we're like her family... her only family – well, until you showed up. A long-lost niece... just as she's dying as well...' The woman smiles at her but Beth knows what she's getting at.

'I had no idea of her existence until a few weeks ago,' Beth says. 'And I'm certainly not interested in any potential inheritance, if that's what you're getting at. I'm perfectly wealthy in my own right. I just want to see her, that's all. How long has she been here?'

The nurse gives her a thin, slightly apologetic smile.

'No offence meant, Mrs Wainwright, but you can understand… anyway, she's been here since 2002. She was ever so young when she arrived, youngest we've ever had, but all her family were gone and she had no one to take care of her, being paralysed…'

'Paralysed?'

'Accident, in her thirties, poor love. Fell down some stairs and broke her spinal column. Her mother took care of her until she died, arranged for her to be sent here when her time came.'

'Can I see her?' Beth looks down the corridor of the hospice, at its sparse and clinical interior. The place smells of mild disinfectant and impending death.

'Yes, yes, of course – come this way.'

'Morning, Eileen. Guess who I have here, next to me… it's your niece, Beth. You remember, I told you she had called and asked to visit you – you remember, don't you?' The nurse speaks to the frail-looking woman in the bed as if she's a toddler.

'She has trouble speaking. Can't for too long – wears her out,' the nurse quietly tells Beth.

'I won't keep her,' she says, nodding at her, signalling for her to leave them in private. The nurse hovers a little before closing the door behind her.

'Hello, Eileen.' Beth's nursing instincts kick in as she approaches her on the bed, her inflection gentle. 'I'm Beth.'

The tiny woman in the bed looks almost dead already.

'Come and sit down, dear.' Eileen's voice is surprisingly clear and robust, belying her fragile appearance. 'They told me you're my niece, but I don't have one of those,' she says. 'So who are you really?'

Beth smiles at the woman's directness. 'I'm sorry I lied,' she says. 'I thought you might not agree for me to come if you knew who I was.'

'Can you plump up my pillow, dear,' Eileen asks. 'I can't do it myself anymore. Can't do anything anymore… haven't really been able to do anything for years and years…'

Beth feels a wave of sadness wash over her as she fluffs up Eileen's pillow.

'You're his wife, aren't you? Beth… Am I right? I wish I could see you. I suspect you're young and beautiful, like I was once upon a time.'

Beth's stunned. Had she been expecting her? 'How did you know?' she asks.

Eileen sighs gently. 'I knew that one day someone would come. Did he send you?'

'No… no, absolutely not. Evan doesn't even know I'm here…'

Eileen gives a little snort. 'I suspect you never knew about me, did you, dear? How did you find out? What's he done now?'

Beth stares at her in shock, a thousand questions running through her mind, too many to single out just one.

'He told me you were dead,' she says. 'Evan told me that you died when he was nine years old, and that your husband, Evan's dad, died some years later when he was eighteen.'

'Is that what he told you, was it?' Eileen smiles but sadness radiates from it, almost filling the room. 'Why are you here, dear?' she says, holding her papery thin hand out for Beth to take, which she does immediately. 'Ahh, lovely soft hands… You're a mother, aren't you, Beth? I can tell.'

'Yes,' Beth feels the emotion rise up through her diaphragm, hears the crack in her voice. 'A little girl, Lily. She's six.'

'Ahh, such a lovely age.' Eileen smiles again. 'Enjoy those years… years when they're young and dependent on you and still believe in Santa… because you never know what they might grow into, what they'll become…' Her smile fades.

'Why didn't Evan tell me about you, Eileen? Why did he tell me you were dead?'

'Has he hurt you, Beth?' she asks suddenly. 'I know you're here for a reason… Tell me…'

Beth isn't sure where to begin and suddenly feels terrible that she has come here. 'I left him… I left Evan and fell in love with someone else…' She tries to explain everything that has happened since, with Lily and Nick and her mother; the prostitutes and sex parties and her suspicions about a conspiracy and Marta too, but when she says it all aloud it sounds so bizarre and absurd that she wishes she hadn't. She doesn't want to add to this poor woman's suffering.

Eileen listens, doesn't speak as Beth talks. There's a long silence after Beth has finished, so long that she wonders for a moment if Eileen is still breathing.

'I left when he was nine years old,' Eileen eventually says. 'I walked out on his father; he was a violent man, abusive and aggressive. Thought nothing of giving me a good hiding, daily in the end, but he was emotionally abusive too, which was somehow worse, I think. Years of control, telling me I was mad, an unfit mother, a whore, a useless good-for-nothing mad whore. I plucked up the courage to leave eventually, but I couldn't take Evan – he'd never have let me take him, would've killed me first. Back then… well, you didn't leave your husband, not without terrible consequences. My mother helped me escape, kept me hidden so he couldn't come after me. I shall never forget the look on that boy's face when he saw me go out the back door. It has haunted me all of my life, and will until I take my last breath. It was the hardest thing I've ever had to do…'

Tears trickle down the sides of Eileen's sun-spotted skin. Beth wants to wipe them away for her but is too scared to touch her.

'He never forgave me, Evan. Grew up under that evil man's regime until he mercifully died some years later. But the damage was already done. When I found out his father had passed, I made contact with him. Naïvely, I thought we could try and rebuild our relationship; that I could try and be his mother again. But he was filled with such poison… such hatred and rage…'

She winces, as though it physically hurts to remember.

'He pretended he wanted to come and visit me. I had never been happier – the thought of seeing my son again... Just nine years had passed and he looked like a different person – he was a young man, handsome, his whole life ahead of him...'

She's crying now and Beth grabs a tissue from her handbag and places it in Eileen's hand. She wants to tell her to stop, that she's sorry for upsetting her, making her relive such painful memories, but she can't bring herself to – she *has* to know.

'He was cold as ice as I hugged him for the first time in all those years, stiff as a board, he was, like a breeze block. I shall never forget it.' She dabs at her milky eyes with the tissue. 'I could see it in his face, behind those eyes, a darkness, like my Evan was no longer there. I tried to explain... I tried to get him to understand why I'd left. We'd doted on each other, always had done. He was a mummy's boy from the moment he opened his eyes... You understand why I left him, don't you, Beth? Tell me you understand?'

Beth's crying too now as she hears the agony in Eileen's voice. 'Yes, Eileen. I do – I really do.'

'He did this to me.' She says it so quietly that Beth isn't sure if she's heard her or not.

'Did what, Eileen?'

'*Fucking bitch, fucking evil, cold-hearted bitch* – that's what he called me... among other things...'

'What did Evan do to you, Eileen?' Beth pushes her gently, mindful of her fragile condition.

'He pushed me down the stairs... top to bottom... bang, bang, bang...' Beth's blood turns to ice. 'I think he intended to kill me. I wish he had,' she says. 'But I suffered a fate worse than death. Severed spinal column, a life confined to a wheelchair, paralysed from the waist down, unable to walk, unable to feel anything at all. That was a more suitable punishment for me wasn't it, in the end?'

Beth almost recoils in horror. 'Oh my God. Eileen… I'm so… Oh my God… why didn't you tell the police? Why didn't you have him sent to prison? His own mother…' Beth suddenly sees the true horror of this tiny, dying old woman's suffering at the hands of her husband and her own son and suddenly it makes sense… Evan's campaign of terror, his need to destroy her… She had left him, just like Eileen had, and now she too was paying the price.

'Guilt,' Eileen says through mucus tears. 'If I had never left him then he wouldn't have become what he is today. He wasn't born a monster, Beth – monsters are made.'

CHAPTER THIRTY-THREE

Dan

October 2019

The drive to Sunnydale Hospice is taking longer than I'd hoped thanks to the rush-hour traffic.

'Don't you think, Davis, how much easier life would be to navigate if we all had a musical soundtrack as a backdrop?'

Davis is doing something on her phone and doesn't look up but I can tell she's listening. She's a woman; they multitask.

'What do you mean, gov?'

'You know, like in films when the music warns the viewer that danger is approaching…' I hum the theme to the film *Jaws*. '*Der da… der da… der der der der, dar der da der…*'

Davis glances at me like I've lost the plot.

'It would!' I protest. 'Imagine how many lives would be saved, how many bad decisions would be diverted if life gave you musical prompts. I mean, the girl in *Jaws* would never have even got into the water if she'd heard that menacing oboe, would she? Nope. She would have gone, "You know what, I think I'll give the skinny-dipping a miss tonight, thanks all the same."'

Davis is laughing. 'It was a tuba actually, not an oboe.'

'Well, all right, Mozart, but you get my point.'

Davis shakes her head in amusement. 'The way your mind thinks, boss… it's something else.'

'I'll take that as a compliment,' I say, though I'm not clear either way.

We both laugh, but actually, in a way, it's what I liken my sixth sense to, some sort of inner soundtrack guiding me. It's the closest analogy I can get to it, anyway.

Besides, the banter is a bid to sidetrack me from the thoughts sprinting round my mind; dark, dangerous thoughts that if proven correct could bring down a lot of people.

'Penny for them, boss,' Davis says without looking up from her phone, like she senses my troubled mind.

'I'm not sure I want to share them at this stage, Davis. If I tell you, I may have to kill you.'

She drops her head on her neck. 'You still think Beth Lawler killed him?'

'Yes, Davis, I do. But that's not all I'm thinking.'

I reach for my phone. Press Fiona's name. She sounds sleepy as she picks up.

'Dan? You OK?'

'Shouldn't it be me asking you that?' I say.

'You know I'd ring you as soon as… we've *had* this conversation already.' I'd made Fi promise to call me the second she feels a twinge or her waters break or she gets any indication that Junior is on the way. I could be miles away and even though I'm as squeamish as hell, I think I really do want to be there at the birth, to see my son or daughter take their first breath into this crazy world. I want them to know I was there with them, for them, and I want to be there for them for all their firsts – smiles, words, steps, haircuts, bike rides… just like my own dad was for me.

'What you doing?' I ask her.

'Lying on the sofa watching *Sky News* and eating taramasalata straight from the pot with my finger. I needed a pee about an hour ago but I need a hoist to get me up off this sofa. I'm so bored, Dan...'

I feel a wave of affection for her childlike grumbling and wished more than anything in that moment that I was deeply in love with her, like I was with Rachel. 'Well, I've got a task for you... I need your help with something.'

'Oh?' I can almost hear her sit up. 'Something to do with the case you're working on?'

'Exactamondo,' I say, and Davis looks at me. I must stop saying it. I'm turning into my father more and more each day. 'Nicholas Wainwright. Does the name ring a bell?'

'Yes. He was arrested for having indecent images of kids on his computer. Died in an accident, hit his head after a fight in a pub. The gardener?'

I smile. Fiona has a photographic brain. It's the reason she's a brilliant journalist, I'm sure.

'That's the one.'

'What about him?'

'Your lot were already there and waiting the day of Wainwright's arrest. Find out who gave you the tip-off.'

'Come on, Dan, you know the rules – you don't reveal your sources.'

'There's a tub of cookie dough Ben & Jerry's in it for you,' I say. 'And I'll pick up some chicken gyozas from that Japanese place you like on the way home.'

'It's a deal,' she says without hesitation.

'How's Junior?'

'Lively. He or she hasn't stopped wriggling about all morning.'

'I miss you,' I suddenly say, though I've no idea where it came from.

Davis glances at me surreptitiously, but I caught her.

Fiona pauses. 'I miss you too, Dan,' she says softly. 'We both do.'

After I hang up, Davis looks at me.

'You think Wainwright was set up?'

'Yes, I do. I think Evan Lawler planted those images on his computer and got the girl to lie about being abused. I also think Evan Lawler was directly or indirectly linked to Wainwright's death.'

'Had him bumped off? But the witnesses at the pub said he left on his own.'

'No phone. No CCTV. No witnesses to the actual accident… an anonymous passer-by called an ambulance. And the coroner who did the autopsy was on that list. George somebody or another, a Freemason.'

Davis looks alarmed, and rightly so. 'You think it's a cover-up, gov? That they're all in on it?'

'Let's say, for example, Lawler stitches Wainwright up, wants to get him out of the way, revenge for going off with his wife. He recruits the help of his high-up Freemason friends, or at least asks them to cover up for him.'

'But these are doctors and lawyers and judges and… oh God, the commissioner… and Woods!'

I'm nodding slowly. 'That's right – men in authority, men with power, men with the capability to bury things, make them disappear.'

'Yeah, but murder, gov? Would they risk it, I mean… Woods! He's as straight as the day's long.'

'Maybe he isn't part of it, but I'm sure he knows something… He was worried, Davis, nervous and worried… I don't know, maybe Lawler was blackmailing them, threatened to go public about the sex parties unless they helped him…'

'Eww, do you reckon Woods—'

'Don't even go there, Davis,' I cut her off. 'I've not long had my lunch.'

She laughs, but I can see by the look on her face that my theory has shocked her.

'You sent Delaney down there, to the lodge…'

'Deliberately. He's in on it too somehow. He's Woods' inside man, reporting back to him – I'm sure of it. Delaney took Beth's statement when she came into the station that time shouting about Wainwright being set up. Seems a bit odd, don't you think, that he was the one asked to deal with it specifically?'

Davis is shaking her head.

'So you think someone at the lodge had Lawler killed?'

'No. I think they all thought it would die down, Wainwright would go to prison and that would be that. But the plan went awry and Wainwright ended up dead.'

'Do you think Beth Lawler knows this? Do you think she knows about the prostitutes and the parties?'

'I think Beth Lawler knows everything. I think she knew about the apartment, about his mother, about the set-up, the "accident".'

'Is that why you've put in a request to the Home Office to have Wainwright exhumed?'

'It was a bluff, Davis. I want to see if Delaney goes back to Woods with it, although it's not such a bad idea. It could answer a lot of questions. Good job the man had specified that he always wanted to be buried, become part of the earth. I guess it was the gardener in him. Now he might be able to help us from beyond the grave.'

'You'll need Woods' approval,' she says.

'How can he refuse me?'

'How can anyone refuse you, gov?' She bats her eyes at me playfully and I laugh, though it belies my inner fears. If I'm right about this then some serious shit is going to hit the fan.

'So you think Beth Lawler killed Evan in revenge for Wainwright?'

'Yes. Among other things. I think she faked a reconciliation with her husband to get the daughter back and planned to kill him.'

'But how did she do it, boss? We've been through this before… not a shred of evidence, not even anecdotal… she was where she said she was.'

'That's the six-million-dollar question, Davis,' I say. 'I don't know – yet. But I will find out. *We* will find out.'

We make our way into Sunnydale Hospice in silence, both of us digesting the seriousness of my theory and how, if I'm proved correct, we plan to approach it.

'DS Lucy Davis and this is DI Dan Riley,' Davis says, displaying her badge to the woman on reception. 'We're here to see Mrs Eileen Lawler… we put a call in earlier…'

'Yes… yes of course,' the woman says, looking a little flustered. It still makes me give a little smile, the way people often react to the presence of the police, like we somehow know their secrets. 'I'm so sorry, Detective,' the woman behind the desk says, 'I'm afraid you've had a wasted journey… I don't quite know how to say this but Mrs Lawler, Eileen, died in the early hours of this morning. She was very ill, had been for a long time…'

'Shit,' I say under my breath, but she hears it. '*Shit.*'

The woman looks at me apologetically, as if it's her fault.

'OK,' I say, 'thanks for letting us know.'

'Perhaps you can tell her niece, let her know her aunt has passed on. It was peaceful in the end. Poor Eileen,' she says, her voice trailing off. 'At least she got to see her before she went. Came in a few weeks ago. Only visitor that woman ever had – well, only one I can ever remember anyway, and I've been here since time immemorial.' She laughs, a little too loudly. I can tell she's upset, that she was fond of the woman. 'She didn't leave a number, the niece, nor a forwarding address. We'd like to send on Eileen's things.'

'We'll see what we can do,' Davis says. 'What was her name, the niece?'

The woman scrabbles around on the desk for something.

'Ah yes, here it is,' she says, 'Beth. Beth Wainwright.'

CHAPTER THIRTY-FOUR

Cath

September 2019

Cath felt a terrible sense of foreboding as she'd put the key into the lock of her tiny bedsit, her heartbeat thudding like bass inside her head. She was expecting Saul to be there, waiting for her, hovering behind the door, perhaps even holding a weapon, waiting to kill her the moment she entered. But the place had been eerily – and mercifully – empty. Audibly exhaling, she'd scanned the small room. It looked even more filthy and dishevelled than when she'd left it; dirty cups and plates and cutlery littered the floor, clothes and laundry were haphazardly strewn across the furniture and rubbish discarded on the carpet. The air smelled musty and sour, cloying in her chest, and Cath had pulled the makeshift curtain back and opened the small window in a bid to let in some air and light. Her first thought was to go and see Neve across the hall, see if she was OK and to apologise to her, but there had been no answer when she'd knocked on her neighbour's door.

'You can keep knocking, dear, but you'll get no answer,' the old man, Mr Jenkins, who lived upstairs on the next floor had said as he'd shuffled towards her on the stairs in his slippers. The lift must've been broken again. Poor beggar had to be in his nineties and could barely walk he was so hunched over. Cath got the impression that he too was simply waiting to die, a thought that only compounded her misery.

'She's gone, love. Last week. That maniac you live with threatened to set fire to her flat, burn it down in the night with her in it...' He'd tutted his contempt. 'Should've stayed away, love...'

'Do you know where she went to?'

'I couldn't rightly say,' Mr Jenkins' voice was scratchy and crackled like an old record. 'Just upped sticks and off. He got his comeuppance though...'

'Who did?'

'That drug-riddled maniac... fell down the stairs he did, off his head, the silly bastard, shattered his leg, done a few ribs too no doubt. Top to bottom he went...' Mr Jenkins had chuckled. 'Ambulance came and carted him off... Not that I called it, mind – would've left the mongrel right there on the floor...' He'd shuffled past her slowly. 'Should be put down, people like that. No good to man nor beast, his type – waste of oxygen. When I think I fought for this country... people like him... Shame he didn't break his neck.'

'Which hospital?' Cath had asked him. 'Do you know which one he went to?'

Mr Jenkins had shrugged as he continued on his laboured journey.

'Couldn't tell you, love. The Royal, I suppose.'

He'd stopped then, halfway up the flight of stairs, and had looked at her with his watery green eyes that seemed to tell a thousand stories. 'Where's that wee baby of yours, eh, love? Last I see you, you was fit to burst... someone take him away, did they? Ah well, can't say I blame 'em... no life for a little one... drug addict for a father and a—' He'd stared at her sadly. 'You should've stayed away, love, while you had the chance. You should've never come back... why did you?'

Cath had swallowed back the need to tell the truth; that it was through fear she had returned. It would be futile.

'A fait accompli,' she'd replied as she'd watch him finally reach the top of the stairs. 'A fait accompli.'

CHAPTER THIRTY-FIVE

Cath

September 2019

Perhaps the woman on the train, Beth – her doppelganger – had been right and that the gods were watching over her. Saul's accident had at least bought her a little time if nothing else.

She'd been to visit him at the hospital, let him know she'd done what he'd asked and returned home.

'This is all your fault, Cath, you know that.' They'd been his first words to her. 'It's because of you I'm lying here like this, with me leg shattered. Look at me!'

Cath had wanted to smile as she surveyed him, his leg in traction, strapped up to machines. 'I'll be in this fucking place for weeks! Can't even have a piss on me own... Did you get the stuff?' She'd nodded, handed him the small wrap in silence. 'And the syringe?'

She'd fished around inside her handbag, handed it to him.

'Good girl.' He'd seemed pleased with her. 'That methadone stuff... load of shit it is. I told them to poke it. You'll have to keep bringing it in,' he'd said, instructing her to pull the curtains while he prepared to shoot up.

She'd done as he'd asked.

'I've missed you, Cath,' he'd said, and somehow she had mustered up a fake smile, but it was getting harder and harder to manage. She'd watched him inject himself, his leg hoisted above him, his hair greasy and unwashed, his jogging pants stained and covered in cigarette burns, and suddenly in that moment she'd seen how truly pathetic he really was; a pathetic, dirty, drug-addicted, violent and sick man who had murdered their beautiful son, her beautiful boy, a boy who had his whole life ahead of him, one who was pure and innocent and good. Saul Bennett wasn't worthy or deserving of this earth, a waste of oxygen. Mr Jenkins had been right – they all had.

'But I haven't forgotten what you done, Cath,' he'd said, almost as if he could sense her thoughts. 'I won't be in this hospital forever. When you've helped me get back on my feet, I'll make sure we'll square everything between us.' He'd looked at her with those narrow menacing dark eyes – rat's eyes, that's what they looked like. In fact, the more she'd looked at him, the more rodent-like he'd appeared and Cath wondered if people really did end up with the face they deserved in life, just like her nan used to say.

'Yes, Saul,' she'd said, 'we'll square everything.'

Cath is lying in bed now. She's washed the sheets and cleaned the place up a bit, not that it had made much difference – it resembles a prison cell more than ever now that she's had a tiny taste of freedom, but she couldn't sleep; her mind kept playing out the scenarios of what might happen when Saul returned. She figured he'd need her around while he was recovering, so perhaps she was safe – as safe as she could be anyway – for a little while longer at least. But then what?

Tossing and turning, unable to rest, Cath's thoughts turn once again to the woman on the train, to Beth. She hasn't been able to stop thinking about their strange encounter; one she couldn't help but feel was destined somehow. She smiles as she recalls the moment both of them had clocked one another, how they had done a double take as they'd simultaneously recognised their uncanny likeness. She wonders what Beth is doing now; wonders how she is coping… Beth's life was different to her own and yet in another way it couldn't have been more similar; both trapped by wicked, evil men out to destroy them. She isn't the only one fighting a battle; she supposes everyone is in their own way.

Restless, Cath decides she needs alcohol to anesthetise herself to sleep but it is late now and the off-licence will be shut. Besides, she has less than ten pounds in her purse and needs that to make sure she has the means to travel to the hospital. Then she remembers that Saul often stashed quarter bottles of cheap vodka around the flat, hiding them in places she wouldn't find them. Not that she ever went looking – she doesn't drink vodka; in fact she rarely drinks at all because Saul doesn't like it – the more for him she supposes.

She begins searching the squalid bedsit. There is nothing in the cupboards – literally, except for a couple of cheap tins and some packet noodles – and the drawers prove equally as fruitless. Sighing, Cath fishes down the back of the filthy sofa, pulling up the cushions – nothing except grime and fluff and around thirty pence in small change. She checks underneath the bed, empty bottles and pop cans littering the carpet and she crouches, disappointed, as she retrieves them and throws them into a makeshift bin – a black sack in the corner. Frustrated, she lifts the old mattress up, slides her hand underneath.

She feels something cold and smooth at the tips of her fingers and reaches for it, sliding her arm until she can get some purchase on it, pulling it out from underneath. Cath sits at the side of the bed staring in shock as she holds it in her hand. It isn't a bottle of vodka; it isn't a bottle at all – *it is a gun.*

Cath's phone rings, the noise startling her, causing her to gasp aloud, the weapon falling onto the bed. She feels breathless, a bit like she did in the morning after having a strong coffee. Her heartbeat pounding in her ears, she checks the time – 11.05

p.m. The caller's ID has been withheld but it's no doubt Saul demanding she bring more drugs, more food, more cigarettes…

Shaken, she picks up. 'Beth?' she says, recognising the voice on the other end almost immediately.

'Hi, Cath. How are you?'

Cath stares at the gun on the bed, unable to take her eyes from the metal glinting back at her, almost mesmerised by it. Why does Saul have a gun? Is it for protection, or is, as she fears, he planning to use it on her?

'I don't know how to answer that question,' Cath says, her voice shallow with adrenalin.

There's a pause on the line.

'Listen, Cath, there's something I need to talk to you about, something I think might solve our problems, a way we can help each other – a way in which we might be able to *kill two birds with one stone.* Can we meet?'

Instinctively, and with her eyes still fixed upon the weapon, Cath thinks she understands.

'When?' she says.

CHAPTER THIRTY-SIX

Beth

October 2019

'You're not really going to use that thing.'

She's standing at the end of the bed pointing the Glock 19 directly at his forehead.

Even now with a loaded gun staring him between the eyes he's still arrogant and dismissive.

'And what makes you so sure?'

He smirks at her. 'One word,' he says. 'Lily. You don't want Lily to grow up without a mother *and* a father, do you, Beth?'

'Well, technically that's more than one word, Evan,' she replies, looking around the apartment, the gun still pointing at him. 'Nice place this. Very you. Bit cold and clinical for my taste though. Is this where you'd bring them?'

'Bring who?'

'The prostitutes… women you paid to torture and degrade…'

He raises an eyebrow. 'Is this what this is about?' He sighs, exasperated. 'I thought we were back on track. You said you wanted to "put everything behind us and be a family again", start over… we even talked about renewing our wedding vows.'

She throws her head back and laughs. 'Guess what, Evan? I LIED. I faked a reconciliation with you so that you'd call off the lawyers and the social workers. Our marriage has been a sham from start to finish. *Renew our wedding vows!* And you actually *believed* me!' She laughs again. 'You really are deluded, aren't you?'

A look of anger flashes across his face. 'So I lied, you lied. We're quits. A lot of men use prostitutes, Beth – don't be so naïve…'

'Yes, they do, you're right. But do they also commit murder? Do they kill people like you do, like you have?'

'Stop it; you're being ridiculous. This is ridiculous. Put the gun down. We can talk. Think of Lily… you're just upset.'

'Upset?' She puffs her cheeks out. 'I suppose I have to hand it to you, you really kept your true self well concealed, didn't you? I mean, I always thought you were rather bland, Evan, boring even, not much in the way of personality – or libido. You could hardly get it up for me, could you? And now I know why.'

Beth suddenly thinks of Lily, how withdrawn she is now compared to the lively bundle of trouble she was before all this had started. She had been pleased when Beth had come home but her daughter isn't the same.

'You'll go to prison, for murder, spend the rest of your miserable life in a six-by-eight cell if you pull that trigger.' He reaches for a cigarette from a packet on the bedside table, lights it. Beth is stunned. He'd always told her he hated smoking and smokers. He'd always forbidden her to touch them. *Who was he?*

'Enjoy that cigarette, Evan – it will be your last.'

He snorts derisively at her. 'Always were the drama queen, weren't you Beth?'

He doesn't believe her. He doesn't believe she'll do it.

'Let's play a game,' she says breezily. 'Truth or dare.'

Evan shakes his head, crosses his feet as though bored by the whole thing. 'Is that thing even loaded?'

She smiles. 'Want to find out?' He snorts again but doesn't answer. 'Truth or dare? I'm going to ask you a question and you're going to answer with the truth, OK?'

'That's not how the game works,' he says.

'It is now.' She waves the gun at him, thinks she sees the first flash of real fear cross his features and it gives her a sliver of satisfaction.

'Guess who I went to see a few weeks ago?'

'A psychiatrist?' he retorts, sniggering.

'Come on, guess…'

'For God's sake, Beth, I haven't got time for this nonsense. I was supposed to be working today.'

'Yes, I know, but as soon as you received a text from one of your "escorts" you dropped everything, didn't you? Very unwise move. Guess, Evan…'

He sighs heavily again. 'I don't bloody know… another fancy man?'

'I'll give you a clue…' She takes out her phone, starts to play some music. Dexys Midnight Runners – 'Come On Eileen'.

She watches as Evan's expression changes, can almost see the contempt coming over him.

'That's right, Evan. Eileen… *your mother*. Remember her? The one you told me had died. The one you pushed down the stairs and paralysed from the waist down… the one you tried to murder…'

Evan is silent for a second or two. 'My, my, you have been busy, haven't you?' he says.

'Not nearly as busy as you have. Truth or dare?'

'Lily will have a murderess for a mother on top of everything else you are. Imagine what that will do to her – you kill me and you'll destroy your daughter's life.'

'You've already done that,' she says, although she won't allow herself to fully accept this. She hopes that in time she can undo the damage he's caused and that at six years old she's still young enough not to remember, but only if he's not in the picture. She knows she'd never stand a chance otherwise.

'You poisoned her, Evan – your own daughter. You made her lie and you made her believe and say the most terrible things… You sacrificed her to hurt me, for revenge. She's been nothing but a weapon to you, like this gun here.' She waggles the Glock and he eyes it more cautiously now. 'Your mother is dying, Evan – did you know that? She has terminal cancer.'

'That bitch died a long time ago,' he says caustically.

'When she walked out on your abusive father, you mean? Is that why you hate women so much? Why you want to hurt them, destroy them?'

'She abandoned me – and my father. Went off with some sailor… a proper cliché. Filthy old whore…'

Beth shakes her head. 'She escaped from an abusive relationship. She had no choice. Your father beat her, abused her… She told me not a day had gone past since where she hadn't felt sadness and regret at having to leave you. She went through hell, Evan, and then you… you punished her in the worst way. You tried to kill your own mother but ended up doing far worse… She lived and will die in purgatory.'

He blows a smoke ring into the air. 'You've never fired a gun in your life, Beth. Where did you even get it anyway?'

'Truth or dare, Evan.'

'You're being pathetic. You're mad, just like the rest of them.'

'You framed Nick and had him killed. It wasn't enough to ruin his life; you had to take it from him. Take him from me.'

'Boo hoo, Bethany… but you're wrong – about the last part anyway. It was never my intention to kill him; that was simply a happy accident. A bonus, if you like.'

Beth feels a sickening rage bubbling up inside of her. 'So you did have him killed?'

Evan extinguishes his cigarette. 'No… I just wanted him out of the picture. It was an accident.'

'An accident? You planted indecent images of children on his computer, Evan. You labelled him a paedophile.'

He smirks – he actually smirks. 'Like I said, I just wanted him out of the way so that you'd come back to me. I didn't know he was going to fall over and hit his head and die.'

'I don't believe you,' she says. 'You know what you did. Nick knew it too – we both knew. You killed him, Evan.'

He kisses his teeth. 'Nick killed *himself*, Beth. I had nothing to do with it – and you can't prove otherwise.'

Her hand is shaking a little now. She's been holding the gun up for at least ten minutes and her arm is beginning to burn.

'You're right,' she agrees with him. 'I can't prove otherwise. Those friends of yours in high-up places made sure of that… but they won't mourn you – no one will. They'll be glad you're dead. No one to blackmail them, no one to leak their sordid stories to the press…'

'Except for you, Beth. They'll have you bumped off or put away and silenced for life. You've no idea what you're dealing with… none.'

He's smirking again.

Blow the sick fucker's head off, Beth. Do it! Do it for Lily, do it for Nick, do it for Mum and Marta and Cath… DO IT FOR YOURSELF!

'Truth or dare?'

He shakes his head. 'This is all getting rather boring, Beth.'

He bristles a little, reaches for his phone on the bedside table.

'Don't even think about it.' She shakes her head slowly, tries to steady her trembling hand by gripping her wrist with the other, a cold trickle of sweat travelling down her cleavage.

'Look,' he snaps but doesn't pick it up. 'You're not going to shoot me and we both know it. This is just your little way of getting back a bit of power over me, isn't it? You've really lost the plot this time though. Attempted murder? You're looking at seven years minimum. You'll never get to see your daughter after this. For every action there's a reaction, Beth.' He pauses, waits for her to respond but she silently holds his gaze.

'Put the gun down, Beth – stop this bullshit now and maybe we can talk rationally, OK.'

She's trying to silence the screams inside her head that are telling her to pull the trigger. She knows that killing him – killing anyone – is wrong and that she will have to live with it on her conscience for the rest of her life. But there's no other option, there's no other way out of this.

'You'd never get away with it for starters.' His tone reverts to cocky. 'No one gets away with murder these day. You know that – you've watched enough of those police programmes….'

'Don't they, Evan? Why not? You did.'

He laughs. 'Touché, Beth, but let's be realistic for once, if you can be. You shoot me and you'll be the first person the police look at. You're the only one with a motive – the only one who stands to gain anything. You'll be prime suspect number one.'

She raises an eyebrow. 'The world stands to gain from your death, Evan – it'll be a better place without you in it. But at least you admit I do have motive, that I have reason to kill you – good reason, reasons plural, in fact. Gosh, that almost sounded like an actual admission of guilt for a moment.'

'Yes, yes, very clever, Beth.' He looks irritated now. He's always hated the fact that she was clever, despite her lack of education, compared with his anyway.

'I know you're bitter about Lily, about the fact your daughter wants nothing to do with you, and you blame me for it. I know you blame me for your mother's death too, although I couldn't possibly have known she had a dodgy heart… Anyway, that's what they'll say, the police – and everyone will back it up – it's not exactly a secret that you hate me, is it? You really haven't thought any of this through properly, have you? You always were impulsive and irrational.'

'I'll take my chances,' she says, in a measured tone. 'But you're wrong; I've thought *everything* through – every last tiny detail is planned and honed and pored over down to the last second. The police may very well *think* it was me who killed you, they might even *know* it was, but they'll never be able to *prove* it.'

He hears the conviction in her tone and she's happy to see his self-assured expression drop down a notch.

'What about DNA? And the weapon? It's got your fingerprints all over it. There'll be CCTV, tyre marks, ballistics reports… they'll get something on you; you're not clever enough, Beth. *Silly bitch,*' he mutters under his breath.

'It won't matter, Evan.' She smiles, light-headed with adrenalin. 'My DNA, tyre marks, ballistics… none of it will be enough on its own. Will I be investigated? Yes, I expect so. Will I be arrested?' She shrugs. 'Possibly. Will I be disbelieved? No doubt, but know this, Evan, you despicable piece of shit, go to hell knowing that I will never, *ever* be convicted of your murder.'

He's stopped smiling now.

'Truth or dare, Evan? What happened to Marta?'

Evan shrugs. 'No idea what you're talking about, Beth – you're crazy.'

'You did something to her, didn't you? Where is she?'

That smirk is there again.

'I know you were involved somehow… Did you kill her? Did you find out that she knew about me and Nick and kill her?'

He holds his hands up. 'Actually, I knew about your sordid affair long before you think I did. I knew almost immediately. I like to keep tabs on my investments, Beth. I knew about it even before you confided in that two-faced little bitch.'

'Where is she? Tell me, God help you or I'll blow your fucking brains out!'

A slow, wicked smile crawls across his face. 'She never left the house, Beth. She was never missing at all.'

She stares at him, confused.

'She was quite the dark horse, was Marta. You trained her well, Beth, made her your loyal little servant, didn't you? An alibi for your treachery.'

'She was my friend, Evan.'

'She was digging around trying to find dirt on me, *me*, who paid her wages and gave her a roof over her head, ungrateful bitch. She found out about this place, the apartment, threatened to tell you. I had to protect myself, my reputation, my marriage…'

'So you killed her? You killed an innocent young woman because she was going to tell me she'd found out you used prostitutes and were into all sorts of depraved stuff? Oh, God, Evan… no… Tell me this isn't true?' Beth feels physically sick. Part of her had hoped she was wrong about Marta, that there was another explanation – that her friend and housekeeper was still alive and had come to no harm. Now her hopes are fading fast. 'You said she never left the house.'

'That's right, Beth. She didn't. She's still there…'

Beth's hands are shaking, her mind racing in time with her heartbeat. What had he done with her… OH GOD!

'The swimming pool!' Coldness descends upon her whole body, turning her blood to ice. 'The builders…' She remembered they had come in and concreted it over the next day. 'You put her under the swimming pool.'

Evan's expression remains poker straight. 'Like I said, she never left the house.'

Beth can feel the room spinning. *He's a psychopath – a full-blown, cold-hearted, murdering psychopath.*

'What did you do to her, Evan?'

He exhales loudly.

'I strangled her with her own scarf. It wasn't intentional, OK?'

Beth blinks at him, wide-eyed. Her hands begin to shake uncontrollably. 'Wasn't intentional?'

'She threatened to tell you about… about my *preferences*. No idea how she found out about them, nosy bitch. Anyway, I just saw red. I'd given that girl a job and a roof over her head and that's how she repaid me, threatening to blackmail me? I knew she knew all about your extra-curricular activities and was keeping it from me. So incredibly disloyal…'

His nonchalance is scaring her.

'What did you do with her?'

'I put her body in the hole that had been dug out for the swimming pool, covered her with some of that sand my boys had left.'

Beth thinks she's going to be sick.

'Look at things this way,' he says calmly, like they're discussing the weather. 'If you shoot me, then you'll have to keep quiet about Marta, won't you? How will you explain to the police that you have a body beneath the swimming pool? They'll pin it on you, alongside my murder – a double murder charge, Beth. Think about it – they'll throw away the key. And the judge who convicts you? Well, he'll no doubt want to make sure you stay silent, lest he or his comrades are exposed. And even if you don't kill me, if you go to the police and tell them, they won't believe you. I will tell them that Marta and I were having an affair; that you found out and murdered her. Your DNA will be all over her. I made sure of it – made sure that it will all point to you.'

Beth swallows back naked fear, partly because she knows he's right. How would she explain to police that she knows Evan murdered their housekeeper? He's set her up, just like he did Nick… Marta's face flashes inside her mind and her fear turns into rage again. *Kill him, Beth – pull the goddamn trigger. Avenge them all.*

'Bit of a conundrum, isn't it? If you kill me you'll have to live with the knowledge that you have a Norwegian nanny at the bottom of your garden; tell the police and you'll be convicted of both our murders anyway… ah, choices, choices…'

Beth shakes her head. 'The police, they won't be able to *prove* it. I've planned the perfect murder, Evan – yours – from start to finish. A plan so sublime that it could've only been a gift from the gods themselves.'

'Sublime!' He laughs. 'What are you talking about? Gift? What gift? You're off your head, do you know that?'

'The perfect gift,' she continues, doesn't rise. 'One that will allow me to eliminate you and get away with it.'

His laugh has a little wobble in it. 'And you call me delusional. Whatever you think you believe in your fucked-up fantasy world, that's up to you, but killing me won't change a thing; you still won't have the man you love, will you? Your pathetic, spineless gardener… or your mother, or even Lily… She'll never fully trust you – that's if she'll have anything to do with you ever again.'

'You're wrong. I'll always have the people I love, right here.' She thumps her chest and he rolls his eyes.

'That's extremely touching. Now put the gun down and stop this nonsense right now. I know you – you couldn't even kill a bug let alone shoot someone dead.' He sighs. 'We both know you haven't got it in you to pull that trigger so piss off and let me get on with my day, OK? We can talk about this tonight, over dinner. I'll forget this ever happened and we can get back to being a normal family again.'

She looks at him, completely incredulous, sees him for the true maniac he really is and always has been. *She has to do it now.*

'That's never going to happen.'

Her arm feels like it's on fire; she can't hold the gun up for much longer.

'OK, Beth. Have it your way. I'll call my friends in the force; tell them you're mentally unstable and tried to kill me. You'll never see Lily again. She's much better off without you anyway; she knows it and so do I.'

She looks at his twisted features, his face contorted by such hatred that she can almost smell it, like gas in the room.

'Why, Evan? Why all of this? Marta, Lily, Nick…'

She's doing it again; wanting him to give her some sort of rational answer to it all, something she can begin to try to understand, to grasp hold of and make sense of.

He stares at her for a moment as though he's thinking how to answer her in the worst possible way.

'You still don't get it, do you? You left me, Beth; you discarded me like a defective toy, traded me, *me* in for a *gardener* – a two-bit nobody with nothing to offer you except a big dick – after everything we had built, everything we had achieved together. I loved you, Beth.' He says it like he's the true victim here. 'I loved you more than I've ever loved anyone in my entire life.'

She blinks at him. '*Loved* me? You destroyed everything, *everyone*, because you loved me?'

'No, Beth, *you* destroyed everything.'

'No one ever leaves the late, great Evan Lawler, do they? Not without paying a severely high price. Not without great pain and loss and suffering. Isn't that right? You use the word "love" but you didn't love me, Evan. I was simply a possession to you, like your Range Rover or your golf clubs. It enraged you that I had the audacity to walk away, to say "no more". This was never about *love*. It was about power and possession and ego and control. But never, *ever* love.'

Her hands are visibly shaking now and it takes all her strength to keep the gun up and pointing at him.

'You really do hate me, don't you, Beth?' he says, almost surprised.

For a moment she doesn't reply, then: 'What was it you said, Evan? For every action there's a reaction?'

He shifts himself upright on the bed and this sudden move unnerves her and she cocks the gun, causing alarm to register on his face.

'Jesus Christ, Beth, you moronic bitch, for God's sake, just put the fucking gun—'

The sound of the weapon discharging is deafening, causing her to gasp and take a step back. The smell of gunpowder hits her nostrils around the same time a fresh surge of adrenalin floods her body, causing her to violently shake. She begins to hyperventilate, gasping noisily for air as she opens her eyes.

He's half slumped on the bed with his feet still crossed. His white towelling dressing gown is open, exposing a little of his naked torso, his slightly protruding stomach hanging over the elasticated edge of his underwear. Half of his head is missing, exposing strange white macaroni shapes that she realises must be his brain. Blood and bone and tissue have decorated the headboard behind him and his left eye is missing but the right one is still intact and is open, registering a look of complete shock and surprise. She feels like she's having an out-of-body experience, like she's standing on the outside of herself looking in and that the macabre scene in front of her is not truly real at all but a scene from a film or a play. A strange sense of calm descends upon her, like a delicate silk scarf gently settling upon her shoulders. It's not euphoria exactly; it's closer to relief.

'You always did have to have the last word, didn't you, Evan?'

CHAPTER THIRTY-SEVEN

Cath

October 2019

Cath stares down at him on the hospital slab.

'It's him,' she says to the police liaison officer standing a little way behind her. 'It's Saul.'

The woman nods gently by way of acknowledgement. Ironically, she thinks how peaceful he looks. Saul had never looked peaceful while he was breathing; even when he slept he'd always somehow had a sneer across his face, but now that he was dead his face bore a strange sense of serenity.

'He'd not long come out of hospital. I was supposed to be looking after him. When did it happen?'

'Sometime yesterday afternoon,' the liaison office says. 'He was found this morning, at your address.'

'Who by?' She looks at the officer, her eyes filling with tears.

'A neighbour… Mr Jenkins. He claims the door was left open and he looked inside and found him.'

'Maybe it was the pain,' she said. 'Maybe he overdosed because of the pain.'

The liaison officer nods again. 'Yes, Cath, maybe,' she says kindly.

'I should've been with him.' She starts to cry then. 'If only I hadn't gone and got myself into trouble… I was just trying to get us some food, some medicine for him, vodka… help with the discomfort you know?'

'It's OK, Cath,' she says. 'I'll give you a minute to say goodbye in private. I'll be outside waiting with the detective. She'll need to speak with you, when you're ready.'

Cath nods, wipes her eyes. 'Thank you,' she says, watching as she shuts the door behind her.

'Alone at last, Saul,' Cath whispers as she stands over his corpse, staring at his greying features. The final stage of Beth's plan had gone exactly as she had said it would – and it had worked. Saul was dead, gone forever, and finally she was free. It hadn't felt like murder as she had stuck the needle in him; it had felt more like a mercy mission, for him and for herself. He'd not even flinched. He'd been out of it on vodka and painkillers, probably wouldn't have known a thing. Afterwards she had lain down next to him on the filthy mattress, listening to his breathing as it became more shallow and laboured until it had stopped completely. In that moment, she had felt calmness descend on her; still and soft like feathers against her skin.

She'd ended up drifting off… then awoken with a start and had immediately panicked, checking the time. It was just after 1 a.m. Gathering herself, Cath had taken her handbag and, careful not to make any noise, she had quietly left the bedsit, taking one final look behind her before gently closing the door.

'Catherine… Catherine Patterson?' The female detective approaches her as she leaves the hospital mortuary. 'Can I speak with you for a moment?'

Cath nods. She knows to all intents and purpose she looks like the grieving partner with her tear-stained face and hunched shoulders. The tears are real enough; she's not had to fake them. But they aren't for him.

'I'm Detective Sacha Barnes of Bristol CID.'

CID? Cath feels a flutter of fear settle on her stomach. Why CID? Saul's death was clearly an OD. Just another dead junkie off the streets, died doing what he loved and did best. She shouldn't panic. Beth has everything covered; she'd assured her over and over again, told her not to worry about anything, that the police would know nothing and to stick to what she's told her to say, word for word, parrot fashion.

'I'm so sorry for your loss,' the detective says. 'It must've been a shock.'

'Not really,' Cath says softly, her eyes to the floor. 'Saul was an addict. Gripped by the gear long ago… I tried to help him so many times, get him off the stuff, but it had such a hold on him, you know?'

The detective nods as if she's seen it all a thousand times. 'I know it hasn't been easy for you, Cath – I can call you Cath, can't I?'

Cath nods.

'I've seen his record…'

Beth had pre-empted this – she knew that they would bring up his record of violence. But it doesn't matter. Nothing matters anymore now that he is dead. She has nothing left to fear. She finally has her freedom. And she has the perfect alibi too.

'Stay around for a while. Let them put you in sheltered accommodation for a bit. Answer all their questions as best and truthfully as you can.' That's what Beth has told her. 'I will give you a sign; I will let you know when the time is right to leave, Cath. And then you disappear. You take the money and you go.'

'I know you must be distraught, and exhausted. You got into a bit of trouble last night?'

'I feel so ashamed,' Cath says, surprised by her own acting skills and the confidence with which she delivers them. 'I'd been drinking, you know, for a bit of Dutch courage. I was only trying to get him some things he needed – we had no money, see, and he needed more painkillers, begged me to get him vodka... and food. I didn't know what else to do. I've never been in trouble with the police in my life; never stolen anything before... I put it all back and the police let me sleep it off in the cells. I would've been with him, could've stopped him. If only I hadn't been so stupid then he might still be alive...'

'It's OK.' The detective nods. 'I understand, Cath. It's not your fault.'

She nods, wipes her nose with the sleeve of her cardigan.

'I'm not interested in the shoplifting, Cath. I'd probably have done the same myself. Desperate people do desperate things. Sometimes we have to do what we have to do just to survive.' She looks at Cath, pauses for a moment. 'I want to talk to you about something else. Something we found when we searched the bedsit.'

'Oh?' Cath thinks of Beth again, about the stranger she believes was sent to her from the gods to save her. She would be at home by now, back in London, picking up her daughter from a friend's house. They did it; it's over, she tells herself. It's really over.

The detective hands her a tissue and says, 'Do you know anything about a gun?'

CHAPTER THIRTY-EIGHT

Dan

October 2019

Davis and I are on our way to see Beth Lawler when the call comes in.

'They've found a gun, boss,' Mitchell says. 'We've just had a call from Bristol. A Glock 19 turned up in a junkie's bedsit after he'd fatally OD'd. Saul Bennett – does the name mean anything to you? Nasty little bastard by all accounts. His sheet's as long as your arm – DV, shoplifting, drugs…'

'No. Never heard the name. Is it our weapon?'

'It's with ballistics, gov. I've asked for a priority turnaround; we'll know in a couple of hours.'

So I was right about the Bristol connection.

'You think this Saul Bennett is involved in Evan Lawler's death?'

'If he was he did it with one broken leg, boss. He'd not been long out of hospital, was on crutches…'

Damn.

'There's more, boss. CCTV from the train station – from Euston station, the day Beth Lawler travelled up to Bristol, the day after Evan Lawler's murder, it came in from transport.'

'And?'

'And I think you need to get here as soon as possible.'

'Do a U-turn, Davis,' I say. 'And put the lights on.'

'It picks Beth Lawler up as being at Euston station the day before Lawler's murder, platform 7,' Harding says, pointing to the screen. 'Look, there she is.'

I watch carefully as she comes into view.

'So she was going to Bristol. As far as I know, that's not a crime on its own,' I say. 'She could've been going back to put flowers on Wainwright's grave… fancied a train ride out, anything… It proves nothing in itself.'

'Yeah but just wait, boss… wait till you see this.' He flicks to another screen. 'Note the time on screen one. It's 9.37 a.m. and we see Beth Lawler waiting on platform 7, yeah?'

I'm practically licking the screen, can almost see my breath on it.

'And here, almost at the same time, it picks her up again alighting from the train from Bristol with only seconds in it. It picks her up twice in two different locations in the station at virtually the same time?'

'How would that be possible?' Davis says.

'It wouldn't,' Harding responds. 'There are 327 steps from platform 7 to get to platform 3 where we see her alighting. Not even Usain Bolt could've made it in 7.5 seconds.'

My mind starts shooting off in all directions like a faulty firework. 'The time on the cameras was wrong maybe? Rewind it. Can you go in closer, run them simultaneously?'

'Checked with the station already, boss. They claim the time on the CCTV is running correctly.'

Harding whirs the tapes back and freeze-frames them alongside each other.

I stare at the two images. They're a little on the grainy side, and the angle isn't perfect, doesn't show her face clearly on either sighting, but you can see it's the same person – same hair, same clothes, carrying the same handbag, holding an identical coffee cup. The three of us stare at the images in silence, our collective thoughts whirring in tune to the tape.

'Gov?' Baylis pokes her head around the door, enters. 'Saul Bennett, boss. A 38-year-old heroin user from Bristol, died of an OD three days ago – a week after Evan Lawler. He was discovered by an elderly neighbour. Lived with his partner, Cath… Catherine Patterson. Right piece of work by all accounts, lots of DV on his file but no convictions. She checks out too; was brought in to South Mead nick for attempting to shoplift. She was in custody when he died.'

'Thanks, Baylis,' I say as she closes the door.

'Hiding it for someone else maybe?' Davis suggests. 'The gun?'

'Possibly.' I tap my lip with a pen. 'Speak to this Cath woman, the partner; we'll bring her in if we have to. She might be able to shed light on the weapon, where it came from, why Bennett had it.'

Baylis nods. 'Oh, and Woods wants to see you, gov – says it's urgent.'

Yeah, I think as I stare at the two images in front of me and I get that strange feeling again, the one where I feel like there's a trapped fly bashing against glass inside my head, trying to tell me something I already know deep down somewhere in my subconscious. *I bet he does.*

I'm exhausted by the time I make the slow drive back to my apartment via the twenty-four-hour garage. It doesn't sell Ben & Jerry's, nor gyoza, but it does have a small tub of Häagen-Dazs chocolate chip. I'm saved. It's 3 a.m. by the time I put my key in the door. The TV is still on, the light throwing shapes out into the small living room, flickering and dancing against the walls, illuminating the ancient soft furnishings that Rachel and I chose together and I've never got round to replacing.

Fiona's asleep on the sofa, a cushion propped up underneath the large bump that contains the heir to my fortune. I sit down gently on the edge next to her; place the ice cream on the coffee table. It's started to melt. 'Just think, Junior,' I whisper as I lightly touch her protruding belly, 'one day, all this could be yours.'

Fiona stirs, opens her eyes. 'Jesus, Dan... what... what time is it?'

'Late,' I say. 'Or early, depending which way you're coming at it.'

She stretches, struggles to get up into a sitting position so I give her a helping hand and a gentle pull. 'You should go to bed, Fi,' I say.

'What, and miss out on ice cream and gyozas?' She looks at the sad little tub on the table and smiles.

'It came with its own spoon,' I say hopefully, handing it to her.

'We need to talk, Dan,' she says.

'About the ice cream?' But I know what she really means.

She mock frowns at me. 'No, stupid, about...'

She rubs her swollen belly. It's so big now that her pyjama top doesn't quite cover it and her skin looks tight as a drum. Suddenly I think how beautiful she looks, like a precious egg. I'm scared to touch her, but I'm even more scared of talking to her. *What a guy!*

'About this... about... us.'

'What about us?' I mentally kick myself.

She looks at me, looks into my eyes. 'When Junior arrives...' she starts to say.

'You can stay here,' I butt in. 'All of us, for a while anyway. Then we'll see what's what.'

She blinks, looks down at her belly and sighs. 'I love you, Dan.' She says it so quietly I'm not sure I've heard it.

'Pregnancy hormones,' I say, stroking the side of her cheek. 'I've read all about it; they turn your brain to blancmange.'

She smiles but doesn't look up at me. 'I guess so…' Her voice trails off for a second.

'Cots, prams, those bouncy-type chair things… we'll get whatever we need. We've got a couple of weeks left, haven't we?'

She nods.

'Well then, we'll go this weekend, to that big baby shop…'

'Baby World?' Her eyes light up and I feel a sudden wave of affection wash over me.

'You can choose anything you like. We'll fit it all in here somehow,' I say, looking around the cramped front room. 'We'll manage.'

'Will you be there?' she says, and I'm worried she's about to cry. I'm completely useless when women cry; I fall to pieces and say all the wrong things. 'At the birth?'

'Yes,' I tell her. 'I will.'

'Promise?'

'I promise,' I say, hoping it's one I can keep.

She seems to cheer up a bit then. 'Anyway, I did what you asked,' she says, peeling back the lid on the ice cream and taking a spoonful. 'It wasn't easy but I dug around, called in a few favours…'

'About the tip-off?' I say. In all that's been going round my head today, I'd almost clean forgotten about the task I'd set her earlier.

She glances at me, gives me that look she sometimes does that says 'you're an idiot, Dan Riley, but I forgive you'.

'Yes, Dan, the tip-off.' She has chocolate round her lips and suddenly I feel compelled to kiss them. But something stops me. Something always stops me.

'And?'

'Delaney. Someone called Martin Delaney. Ring any bells?' She takes another mouthful of ice cream.

'Yes,' I reply. 'I'm afraid it does.'

CHAPTER THIRTY-NINE

Beth

October 2019

Beth looks out of the window at the swimming pool in the back garden and feels the nausea rise and swell like ocean waves inside her tightening guts. Was Marta really buried there, underneath the water in a concrete grave, or was Evan bluffing in a final act of cruelty? Whichever way, it is messing with her head and she feels angry that even beyond the grave he can still manage to play mind games with her, like somehow he's had the last laugh.

It's strange, she thinks, how it troubles her more to think that poor Marta is possibly there, alone, her grave unmarked, her death ungrieved than it does knowing she blew her own husband's head off. Evan had got what was coming to him; in the absence of justice – and the knowledge she would never obtain it through the usual channels – she had taken her own. Did it make her a cold-blooded killer, meting out her own punishment for the horrible crimes he'd committed, for all the deviancy, the deceit and lies and the pain he'd caused? She can't believe she'd actually pulled the trigger, made herself a murderer in the process. It makes her no better than him, does it? Her conscience gnaws at her as the image of Evan's face flashes up in her mind like a still frame from a horror film, his skull shattered and broken, his left eye missing. *An eye for an eye.* It's what the Bible says, isn't it?

Beth closes the kitchen blind. The police will come back soon; she senses it. That detective, Dan Riley, the one with eyes that reminded her of Nick's, he'd known she was hiding the truth, she sensed that *he*'d sensed it and that he wasn't the type to stop until he got what he wanted. Well, he can dig away all he wants, she assures herself; he can suspect her, make her prime suspect number one if he hasn't already done so, but he won't be able to prove anything – that is the best part – nothing at all. She's covered every base, every eventuality. For every question she has pre-empted an answer, an explanation, *an alibi.* She has succeeded where others had failed; she has committed the perfect murder. Only in her mind she has decided it wasn't really murder at all. It was justice.

Beth goes to the fridge and pours herself a glass of champagne, sits down at the table and lights a cigarette. She wants to contact Cath, can't stop thinking about her, but she can't, not yet, not for a while anyway, not until the heat is off and things have died down.

'Wait for my signal,' she'd told her.

Once the coast was clear, Cath could do what she'd planned to and take off somewhere. Beth had given her a little money – £5,000 from the safe and a diamond ring Evan had given her to mark their five-year anniversary that was worth double that. She'd promised to give her more once it was safe too. She'd help set her up, help her to start again. It was the least she could do really, because without Cath… without their chance encounter, Beth knew what she would be faced with. And now she didn't have to worry about that – or him – ever again.

'What happens if the police start asking questions? I'll fall apart – I'm not strong enough. I'm not intelligent like you,' Cath had said, fear evident in her voice.

'I will protect you, Cath, I promise.' And she meant it. 'And even if they do, they'll have nothing – we did it, Cath, *we did it!*'

She takes a swig of champagne, wishes she were enjoying it more than she is. She should be celebrating, shouldn't she? Evan and Saul were gone, no more. Even if the police somehow did link their deaths, they won't have enough solid evidence to prove it in a court of law, she reassures herself. She will just have to hold her nerve and can only hope Cath will do the same if it comes to it. She has every faith.

Beth had scrubbed the scent of the police cell from her body upon returning home to London. She'd changed clothes at Bristol station, worn a cap she'd bought from a kiosk and bought some reading glasses. It wasn't a disguise as such, just an attempt at altering her appearance. As far as the police were concerned, Cath Patterson had been in a police cell when Saul Bennett had taken his fatal overdose. Another useless junkie who'd accidentally killed himself was off the streets and out of their hair. They wouldn't be looking for anyone.

The gun was the potential sticking point. She'd given it back to Cath after cleaning it until it had shone, told her to put it back where she'd found it. She hoped they wouldn't find it, wouldn't think to look for a gun at a junkie's obvious suicide. But even if they did find it, it was unlikely they would link it to Evan's death, wasn't it? It was a standard issue Glock, commonplace among criminals. They'd never be able to prove that the bullet fired from it was the one that killed Evan. She'd disposed of the shells in the Thames; they wouldn't find them, wouldn't waste all those resources looking for them. Besides, she was absolutely convinced that Evan's associates – the ones she is sure had been in cahoots with him over Nick's set-up and subsequent 'accident' – would want this glossed over as quickly as possible. It was a case of 'bring one down, bring them all down'.

Maybe they'll somehow pin Evan's death on Saul Bennett – even better. They won't want to dig too deeply; they can't be sure how much she knows, wouldn't want to risk it, would they, just in case she blows the whistle? Besides, she has Dwaine Simpson as an insurance policy. If anything happens to her, he'll make sure it all comes out, the escorts and the sex parties. They can't silence *everyone*.

Beth picks up her phone. She'd told Cath she'd give her the nod if she felt it was the right time for her to disappear. A message from her would signal it was time for her to escape, and that she would know it when it came. She pulls Cath's contact details up. She's in her phone as 'Dee' – for doppelganger – and types the words 'A fait accompli' before pressing send.

Feeling better, Beth pours herself another glass of fizz. Lily is in bed upstairs, exhausted after her sleepover with Amber. That little girl has been through so much; losing her nana and then her father. But Beth has done it for them, for Lily, to save her from her father, a man who cared nothing of destroying his own daughter.

'So Daddy is with Nana in heaven too?' she'd asked after Beth had told her her daddy wasn't coming home.

Beth had held her tightly. 'Yes, darling, he's in heaven with Nana, and they're having a tea party with all the angels looking down on us.' It is another lie that needed to be told and Beth can only hope that soon they will be able to get back to normal, that all of this will become a distant memory to her daughter and that, as she grows, these memories will gradually fade, like photographs in the sun. They will move, Beth decided. Sell this house and move away, start over again, just the two of them, and she will fill Lily's head with happy thoughts of her father, lie about the man he was, tell her how much he had loved her, loved them both.

She thinks of Marta again – poor, innocent, kind Marta, whose life had been snuffed out because she knew too much and had wanted to protect Beth, her friend. The idea of leaving her behind is almost a wrench too far, but how else can she do it without incriminating herself in the process? Evan might've been right – that if she tells the police the truth, she could potentially put herself in the firing line to become their number-one suspect. If Marta really was dead then nothing would bring her back and she had already avenged her housekeeper's murder. Marta had been one of life's givers, her name befitting of her. *Marta the martyr*. What choice did she have?

Beth glances up at the collection of framed 'family' photographs on the kitchen wall, beautiful moments in a fleeting time, captured forever. Lily as a baby in her arms, the two of them on her first day at school. There's one of her daughter and her mother together, her mum crouched down next to her tiny granddaughter, squeezing her closely to her side, her eyes sparkling with happiness, both of them smiling like it hurt. There's only one of the three of them together; her, Evan and their daughter. Beth's wearing a red dress and Evan's standing a little way off next to her, their daughter in front of them, her hands on her small shoulders. She realises, for the first time looking at the photograph, that none of them are smiling. Their faces are almost poker straight and emotionless. She stares at it, focuses on Evan in particular, his unremarkable features, someone you could pass by in the street and never give a second glance. He was the stranger she married; a man she never really knew. *Do we ever really know anyone?*

The sound of the doorbell startles her and she snaps back to reality, gives a small sigh of resignation. She'd been expecting them, sooner in fact.

'Just coming,' she says softly.

CHAPTER FORTY

Dan

October 2019

Sleep was impossible – I was a fool to even try, so I get up, kiss a sleeping Fi's forehead and belly and throw on yesterday's clothes before making my way back to the station.

I'd been right about Delaney being Woods' snitch, although this doesn't make me feel any better. Like I'd suspected, he had put Delaney on my watch simply to report back to him, give him the heads-up. I've never trusted Martin Delaney and rightly so it transpires, but Woods? Now that's a whole different kettle of fish.

I text Davis on the way in, ask her to get out of her pit and get down to the nick pronto. She's the only one I can trust. I rub the grit from my eyes as I drive through London in the early hours of the morning, the crisp and low winter sun threatening to rise once more, and I'm overcome by a strange sensation, one I can't explain, a sort of melancholy feeling of imminent change. This case has taken its toll on me. I know Beth Lawler killed Evan Lawler and I'm pretty sure why. Who wouldn't want to kill a man like that? A deceitful, pathological liar, one who had used his own daughter to destroy another man's life, maybe even to kill him or have him killed.

Evan Lawler was a psychopath, a classic example really – cunning and devious with the ability to fool a lot of people.

I realise now that they're everywhere, men – and women – unassuming and unremarkable, yet the well-crafted mask of normality and respectability they present conceals the hidden depths of their depravity and bad intentions, their lack of conscience and empathy. Even the trained eye cannot spot them, the murderers and serial killers, the hate-filled, vengeance-fuelled monsters, but they're there, among us all, smiling as they serve you coffee or help you pack your shopping. They're there as they talk you through a mortgage application or buy you dinner, or wash your windows or style your hair…

I throw my jacket onto the back of my chair and boot up my computer, my head throbbing with all the information it's trying to process – and what I should do about it. I look up at the whiteboard, the names and faces, the facts and the assumptions, at the spaghetti junction of a muddled case scrawled upon it in my appalling handwriting. The answers to this puzzle are somewhere on that whiteboard, staring me in the face, only I can't see them. It's like looking at a particularly difficult word search and the more I scrutinise, the more the missing word seems to evade me. Sometimes if you look too hard, it's worse than not looking hard enough.

Ballistics will be back in a few hours; I'll chivvy them along at first light. I'm pretty convinced the weapon found in Saul Bennett's bedsit is the weapon that was used to kill Evan Lawler, but I've no idea how it came to be there. I run a check on Saul Bennett on the system, watch as his rodent-like face pops up immediately, the epitome of a washed-up druggie with black holes for eyes and pockmarked skin. I can almost smell him, unwashed and edgy, searching for his next fix.

I read his record in more detail. It's a catalogue of violence, theft and antisocial behaviour. Saul liked to beat his girlfriend up, a lot as it turned out, judging by the records. 'Domestic disturbance, partner slashed with a penknife, domestic disturbance, partner taken to hospital with injuries to face and ribs…' On and on it reads, abuse going back years. I'll bet the poor woman was relieved he'd OD'd and…

Suddenly a thought catches me. The girlfriend. Catherine Patterson. I run a new search on her, put her name through the system. Nothing comes up. I retype the name Cath Patterson, then Cathy, then Cat and all the variations of her name I can think of. Nothing. Zero. She's not there.

I curse, sigh, tap my fingers on the desk. For the first time in my career I feel a level of despondency I've never encountered before. The frustration of knowing what I know deep down and not being able to prove it is sending me sideways. If this case goes unsolved it will be the first of my career – and the last if I don't find what I'm looking for. I get up, pace the room, grab a watery coffee from the machine; try to ignore the trapped fly inside my head that's practically committing hara-kiri.

I run the CCTV footage from the train station again, watch as Beth Lawler comes into view. Transport have assured us the time on the footage is legit – no glitches, no mistakes. Even the techs couldn't explain it – so how would it be possible for her to have been in two different places at once? *Think, Dan, think!* There's an explanation for everything. Sometimes it's not obvious, sometimes you just have to look and think outside of the box, but it's there… it's always there.

I run and rerun the tape, five or six times, watch as she moves along the platform, meanders towards the edge, towards the oncoming train that's slowing to a halt. I study her, the jacket she's wearing, her jeans and black boots. I zoom in on the handbag, the profile of her face, partially covered by her long hair and down at the coffee cup she's holding, Costa, with a cardboard holder round the middle. Then I do the same with the second piece of footage where she's picked up again on a different camera, on a different platform no more than a few seconds later, a physical impossibility, no less given the heeled boots she's wearing. I study the second piece of footage again; note the exact similarities of the hair, the clothes, the handbag and the coffee cup. I run it and rerun it again, back and forth, jumping between the two and… hang on…

I feel a jolt of adrenalin shoot through my body like electricity, stand so quickly I send my chair reeling backwards, my jacket falling to the floor. I rewind the second image a little, zoom in on the coffee cup; it's identical, Costa, little paper band round the middle, only…

Good God! She's holding it in her left hand! I spill my coffee as I place it down onto the desk, flipping back to the first image. Jesus Christ, I'm right. In the first image, Beth is holding the cup in her right hand… switch to the second image and it's in her left!

Immediately I locate the CCTV footage from Beth Lawler's house, the one from the day of Evan's murder and slot it into the machine. I'm hyperventilating as I watch the delivery man ring the bell and she comes to the door, the angle of the camera above the door only really giving a bird's-eye view of her head and the bridge of her nose. The delivery guy hands her the groceries and she puts them behind her in the hallway, steps out of the doorway a little to sign for them and… they speak, exchange a few words, she's holding the pen in her left hand, she signs for them with her left hand – *she's left-handed.*

CHAPTER FORTY-ONE

Dan

October 2019

I'm practically doing a celebratory jig as Davis walks in and startles me.

'Someone's in a good mood for this unholy hour,' she remarks, catching the look on my face. 'This had better be bloody good,' she says. 'I was in the middle of a dream about Tom Hardy when your text woke me up – just at the good part.'

I smile. 'This is better,' I tell her.

'Impossible,' she replies, making her way to the coffee machine. 'So you found something then?' She takes a sip, pulls her lips over her teeth and leans over my desk behind me. She smells good, even fresh from her pit.

'I knew it, Davis,' I say. 'I knew there was something amiss.' I shake my head. 'My, my… what a clever girl our Mrs Lawler is… I almost missed it…'

'Missed what, gov?' Davis is practically foaming at the mouth with anticipation. 'Tell me.'

'Better still, I'll show you.' I run the tapes, the two pieces of footage from the train station. 'Watch closely,' I say, 'and spot the difference.'

Davis pulls up a chair next to me, moves in close to the screen and rubs her tired eyes.

'What am I looking for, boss?' she asks. 'We've already been here. Transport has to have it wrong – the timings don't add up. She couldn't have made it to platform 7 in time – it's not possible.'

I shake my head, wonder how many more times I will need to run the footage before she spots it, secretly, competitively hoping it won't be less time than it took me to. I'm already three goes in.

'You're enjoying this,' Davis says as I run them again for the fourth time. 'I can't see anything, boss. It's Beth Lawler practically in two places at once.'

'You said yourself, how would that be humanly possible?' She's right though; I am enjoying this.

'Well, it wouldn't, so it must be an error. The time on the footage has to be wrong, gov – there's no other explanation.'

'Oh but there is, Davis, there is. If you look closely enough.'

Davis exhales. 'Give me a clue then.'

I smile. 'One lump or two?'

She looks at me bemused, turns back to the screen. I run it once more.

'The coffee?' she says, confused. 'The…'

I laugh out loud as I watch her face change and her mouth form an 'O' shape.

'Jesus, she's holding the coffee in a different hand…'

'Exactamondo,' I say. And this time I don't care.

'But so what? She switched hands. It's nothing – proves nothing really, boss.'

I smile again. 'Perhaps not, Davis. But look at this.' I run the CCTV of Beth Lawler on the day of the murder, watching once more as she signs for the groceries with her left hand.

'So she's left-handed. Beth Lawler is left-handed?' Davis looks a little underwhelmed. She's killing my buzz.

'If it actually *is* Beth Lawler,' I say.

Davis looks at me as if I've lost the plot.

'Are you sure you're not the one having the baby, gov; I think you've got pregnancy brain by proxy.'

'Run a check for me,' I say. 'Do a search on a Catherine Patterson.'

'The junkie's partner? I already did gov – zilch.'

'So did I, but use a K this time, not a C.'

She starts the search and we watch as the system flicks through faces and names like thumbing a deck of cards until…

'Oh! Here we go,' Davis says as the image begins to download. I can hear her breath, heavy like my own as it comes into view and after a few moments, we look at each other. And neither of us says a word.

CHAPTER FORTY-TWO

Dan

October 2019

Davis was onto ballistics as soon as it was light and I watched her on the phone as she gave me the nod.

'It's inconclusive, gov, but they're pretty sure it was the same weapon that fired the bullet that killed Lawler. It's not enough on its own but coupled with this…'

A few of the team have arrived now, bodies milling about, tired faces in need of caffeine to kick-start the day ahead. I watch them. Good, honest, decent coppers, coppers with determination, prepared to put in the graft, the hours, the sacrifice, to see the job through to the end. Delaney breezes past, leaving a trail of aftershave behind him, and a nasty smell behind that.

'Morning, gov.' He nods at me and I nod back.

'Keep shtum, Davis,' I say, 'for now. Just keep what we know to ourselves, OK?'

'Course, boss,' she says, adding, 'What are we going to do?'

I know what she's really asking. We arrest Beth Lawler and she'll expose the lot of them. It all makes sense now – why Woods wanted me off the scent and tried steering me in a different direction. It's why he got that snake Delaney to keep tabs on me so he could stay one step ahead.

'I want you to stay here,' I say in hushed tones. 'I'm going to pay Beth Lawler a visit.'

'To arrest her, boss? Are you going to bring her in?'

I nod. 'We get her dabs and then we've got her. I'd bet my baby they'll match the prints the police took from Catherine Patterson the night the junkie died…'

'So how do you think they're connected, Catherine and Beth? You think they're family, secret sisters… *twins*? Because there's nothing in the paper trail that links them together, boss – nothing we've found anyway.'

'I don't know,' I say. 'That's the bit Beth Lawler's going to tell me.'

'Are you sure you know what you're doing, gov?' Davis looks at me, nervously. We both know what she's getting at but before I can answer her, Woods pokes his head around the door.

'Riley,' he says with what I detect is forced amenability. 'Can I have a word…?'

'I'll be with you in a minute, sir,' I say, holding my hand up.

'No, Riley,' he says, his voice dropping an octave. 'Now.'

CHAPTER FORTY-THREE

Dan

October 2019

'You don't know what you're doing, Riley,' Woods says immediately once the door to his office is closed. 'You have no idea.'

I feign ignorance as to his real meaning. 'Actually, sir, I do. I'm about to arrest Beth Lawler for the murder of Evan Lawler. I've found new evidence. If I get a confession then it's all sewn up, and even if I don't then there's enough to satisfy the CPS, enough for a conviction…'

Woods is pacing the room, chewing his stubby fingers. 'What evidence?'

'Catherine Patterson, sir. Catherine Patterson and Beth Lawler used each other as alibis and…' Suddenly it strikes me. The junkie… the wife-beater, Saul Bennett – his death wasn't an accident. Cath Patterson murdered him, made it look like an OD while Beth Lawler gave her an alibi. It was a pact between them.

'Dan.' Woods looks at me gravely. 'You're not going to arrest Beth Lawler. Sit down.'

I do as he says. I want to hear him out. 'You know, Riley, deep down, how much I've always respected you.' I'm inclined to give a derisory snort but he sounds genuine. 'You're the best detective I've ever worked with.'

I raise my brows. He's using flattery? Surely he knows me better than that.

'I'm being truthful here,' he says. 'You've got to let this one go. Trust me, for your sake, you must let it go.'

I maintain my feigned ignorance. 'Beth Lawler murdered her husband, and I'm pretty sure Catherine Patterson murdered her partner too. Nick Wainwright may or may not have been murdered, but for argument's sake let's say he was, and a young Norwegian woman has disappeared off the face of the earth, I suspect meeting a similar fate. At best we have two murders; at worst, four. How can you ask me to "let it go", sir. I don't understand.'

'Yes you do,' Woods hisses. 'Yes, you bloody well do, Riley. You know everything.'

I meet his eyes; see the fear in them.

'Were you in on it, sir?'

'Oh Jesus Christ.' Woods smacks his forehead, drags his palm down his face. He looks like he's aged overnight. He sits opposite me, exhales loudly in time with his sagging shoulders.

'Do you know why I became a copper, Dan?'

'To catch bad guys, sir?'

He snorts, laughs a little. 'In laymen's terms as you put it, yes, that's exactly why. I wanted to make a difference to the world we live in; make it a better, safer, more peaceful place for future generations. I wanted to rid the streets of crime, lock up those bad apples that spoil it for the rest of us and make other people's lives a misery.'

'So what happened, sir?' I feel anger bubbling up inside of me, although it's more like a feeling of betrayal really, of bitter disappointment. I've always had a love/hate relationship with Woods, but I had always thought he was one of the good guys deep down. And although I can barely admit it to myself, let alone him, I've always sort of looked up to him.

'Are you part of it, sir? The conspiracy to cover up Evan Lawler's crimes... the sex parties at the lodge. Did you know about them? Did you... were you...'

'Good grief, Dan, what do you think I am?' Woods looks genuinely offended. 'Of course I wasn't... didn't even know about them until this— How can you even ask me that?' He shakes his head.

'They won't let this thing come out, Dan. They'll have your badge first; they'll have Davis's too.'

'She doesn't know anything,' I snap, furious. 'Leave Davis out of this.'

'They'll sacrifice Lawler; they'll sacrifice you... and Lucy too. A dead junkie? You really think anyone cares about a dead, wife-beating junkie...'

'What about Wainwright?' I remind him. 'An innocent man accused, set up, *murdered*. His only crime was falling in love with a woman whose husband was a covert psycho; he had nothing to do with any of this. Is he another sacrifice?'

Woods buries his head in his hands. 'I don't like it any more than you do, Dan.'

'So let's blow the lid,' I say. 'We'll come out the heroes and justice will be served to those who deserve it. Wainwright's mother, for example,' I add.

'We don't know he was murdered,' Woods says. 'The coroner said...'

'The coroner was on that list!' I can hear myself beginning to shriek.

'They'll find a way to silence you, Dan. You can't win against these people. There's too many of them and they're too powerful. We're talking government ministers, judges held in great esteem, powerful businessmen with enough money to feed a starving continent, for fuck's sake... Look – Evan Lawler was a psychopath, a twisted bastard, and the world's better off without his sort in it. Beth Lawler knew she would never get justice and that Wainwright's witch-hunt and subsequent death would never be answered. Saul Bennett was a piece of scum, the lowest of the low. Did you know he killed his own unborn son? Kicked that poor woman's stomach until the boy inside her died and she was forced to give birth to him – a dead baby.'

'How do you know this, sir?'

Woods laughs a little, but there's no humour in it. 'You think I'm a bumbling, grumpy old fool past his sell-by date; waiting for retirement so I can spend the rest of my days on the golf course, living off my fat pension – and you'd be partly right.'

'About which bit, sir?'

'Facetious as ever, Riley,' he snaps. 'But I've dedicated my life to this job, this profession. I got here because I'm like you, Riley. I'm a good copper: honest, decent – *straight*.'

'And you don't want to leave under a cloud of suspicion? You want to bow out in a blaze of glory?'

'Beth Lawler took the law into her own hands and meted out her own justice. She did them all a favour. They were concerned he'd taken things too far with Wainwright. No one was complicit in his murder, if indeed it even was a murder.'

'So they just agreed to have him stitched up instead, labelled a nonce?' I shake my head.

'Birds of a feather stick together, Dan. It's a big boys' network; you must know that. You scratch my back, I'll scratch yours… You think those things haven't been going on for years?'

'Yes, sir. I just didn't think you were complicit in them, that's all.'

He glares at me, eyes aflame. 'Aware? Yes. Complicit? No. I knew this stuff went on all the time and I stayed well away, had no part in it.'

'So Beth Lawler and Catherine Patterson get away with murder because Lawler was a psychopath and a murderer himself and Bennett was a scumbag wife-beating junkie? Even if I agree that both men were deserving of the ends they met, it doesn't work like that and you know it, sir. If that were the case then there would be no place for us. Society would simply become lawless, morally bankrupt, everyone avenging their own injustices, real or perceived. This is what the system is; we can't deviate from it just because a group of men don't want their wives to know they like to be spanked. That's not how it works.'

Woods looks like he's about to burst into tears, or flames. 'I'm not saying I disagree with you, Dan. I'm saying, *I'm telling you*, please, I'm begging, for your sake, for the sake of your unborn baby and that lady of yours, Fay…'

'Fiona,' I correct him.

'Her. Do it for them. They'll annihilate you, Riley. They're capable of it and they *will* do it if you insist on arresting Beth Lawler. They can't risk it, can't risk her outing them and exposing the force as a load of…'

'A load of what? Bent bastards, stitch-up merchants who think they're above the law? No one is above the law, sir. You're the one who's always told me that.'

'Jesus Christ, Dan, you really don't get it, do you? These people, they *are* the law, and you and I… we're just foot soldiers.'

We're both silent for a moment as he gathers his composure.

'Mark the case as unsolved. We'll tell the press we're looking into leads that Lawler was mixed up in some bad business deal. Leave Wainwright's death alone. The man is dead and buried; let him rest in peace. Beth Lawler has suffered enough and Lord only knows the other one…'

'So a junkie's life is less important than, say, a banker's or a doctor's?'

'A child-murdering, wife-battering, leech-off-society junkie, Riley.'

'So we *are* judge and jury, then? No, sir. I can't do it. This is not what I signed up for. I'm a civil servant; I represent the people of this country. They put their trust and faith in me, believe in me. I'm a vehicle for justice. A jury will decide what's right and wrong and what punishment is befitting of the crime; they'll look at the facts, take everything into consideration… I won't go along with it. I'm going to arrest Beth Lawler and Catherine Patterson too. I'll take my chances.'

Woods takes a deep breath and a quarter bottle of scotch from his desk drawer, takes a swig as he turns his back on me in his swivel chair.

'On your own head be it, Dan,' he says, his tone heavy with resignation. 'Just don't say I didn't warn you.'

CHAPTER FORTY-FOUR

Dan

October 2019

I leave Woods' office in haste, forgetting my coat. My adrenalin is off the chart as my worst nightmares are realised. Woods' words are resonating inside my mind as I cross the car park to get to my car. '*For the sake of your unborn baby… for that lady of yours… Do it for them… They'll annihilate you, Riley…*' What could they do to me? Throw me in prison? Put something on me? Was my life in danger? Was Fi's?'

I hear Davis running up behind me. 'Gov! Gov! Where are you going? I'm coming with you!'

'No!' I swing round. 'You'll stay here, Davis. You'll stay here and you'll keep your mouth shut. They ask you questions, you feign ignorance; you know nothing about that list and who's on it. You know nothing about hookers and S&M parties. You have no idea that anyone was in cahoots with Evan Lawler to fit up Nick Wainwright… You know nothing, you say nothing.'

'But, gov, I…'

'DO YOU HEAR ME, DAVIS?'

I shout so loudly she takes a step back. I've never raised my voice to Davis; I've never had to before. But this is for her own good, her own protection. 'You get back in there and act like it's just another day in paradise. Start running some leads on Lawler's business associates… Do it, Davis.'

'What will you do, gov?' she says. She's tearing up; I can see it in her eyes. And I think about how much I care about my protégée, how young she is, how good she is – too good for her own good.

'The right thing,' I say as I get inside my car and slam the door.

CHAPTER FORTY-FIVE

Dan

October 2019

Woods is blowing up my phone as I race to get to Cheyne Gardens where Beth Lawler is waiting for me. She answers the door almost instantly, like she somehow knew I was on my way.

'Have you come here with news, Detective, about Evan?' She presents calmly enough but I sense the nervousness just beneath her shallow affability.

I glance around the kitchen, see the condolence cards on the mantelpiece, but the room is spotless, smells freshly cleaned, nothing out of place, not as I would expect. In my experience, the last thing people worry about when their spouse has been murdered is keeping on top of the housework. Unless of course they're the one who has murdered them, perhaps.

We sit down at the kitchen table facing each other.

'We need to search the house again, Beth,' I say, lying. 'Just another formality, I'm afraid. I'll need your signature if that's OK?'

'Of course,' she says obligingly.

I pull out a form from my pocket. I think it's part of an insurance document I'd been in the middle of renewing, but it'll have to do. I hand her a pen. 'Anywhere is fine. You've read it before – nothing different.' Her eyes flicker as she looks at me, takes the pen and signs it.

I feel no elation as I nod my thanks. I suppose a part of me had hoped she'd sign with her left hand and that I had got it wrong. Sometimes being right isn't always satisfying.

'Do you want a drink, Detective?' she asks. 'Something alcoholic perhaps… I know I could use…'

'Yes,' I say swiftly. 'Yes, that would be great.'

She fixes us a large bourbon, a Jack Daniel's – mine and Rach's tipple of choice, incidentally. *Although technically it's not actually a bourbon.* I hear her voice inside my head clearly, like she's in the room. *It has to be made in Kentucky for it to technically be classed as a bourbon, a bit like champagne… it was a gentleman's agreement.* I always loved the fact that she was a fount of knowledge about nothing in particular.

'You're closer to finding out who killed Evan?' she asks unconvincingly, taking a sip from the tumbler. She doesn't strike me as a JD kind of girl. Then again, neither did Rachel, I suppose.

'Yes,' I say, holding her gaze. 'An arrest is imminent.'

'I see,' she says measuredly, placing her glass onto the kitchen table.

'Where's your daughter, Beth?'

'At school. Amber's mum is picking her up tonight. I needed to be alone for a bit, what with everything…'

She knows. We both do. And my chest feels heavy with resignation.

'Have you ever lost anyone close to you, Detective? Someone you love so deeply you can't imagine life without them?'

I nod. 'Yes, Beth, I have.'

'I thought so,' she says, her voice loaded with pathos. 'My mum… Nick… and even Lily… she's still lost somehow… different now. Maybe she'll never be the same again. Maybe none of us will be.'

My heart muscle contracts inside my ribcage. And I think of the shitty drunk driver who knocked Rachel down, killing her and the baby we should've had together. It's sad and strange and unavoidable how other people, even complete strangers, can shape and change your life forever.

'Maybe,' I say, pausing. 'I know you would never have got justice, Beth.' I lean forward towards her, my throat tight with emotion. 'And I know why. I understand why... why you did it – why both of you did.'

'Both?' she says swiftly. 'I don't know what you mean, Detective.'

I manage the smallest smile. I admire her for trying to protect Catherine Patterson. Beth Lawler is fundamentally a good person, a good person who terrible things have happened to. But it doesn't make what she did right, does it?

I can feel my phone buzzing inside my pocket again; ignore it. I'll deal with whatever's coming later.

'I don't blame you, Beth. Either of you. Your husband was a sick man. What he did... it was wrong, unforgivable – evil even. I know you suffered; I know what you lost...'

'Do you? Do you really?' She looks at me with her blue eyes and for a moment I think I might be able to see tiny flecks of violet in them.

'He would never have stopped... would never have been brought to task, never made to pay... he would've destroyed everything, everyone.' She takes another gulp of her drink. 'Lily was – is – all I had left in this world, the only thing left, and he would've taken her too, destroyed her life. I couldn't let him do that, not to my child, not to my daughter... Do you have children, Detective?'

'I'm about to become a father,' I say. 'A couple of weeks left...'

She smiles gently, knowingly.

'Then soon you'll understand,' she says. 'When you see that child for the very first time, the need to protect them, it overrides everything, a base, primeval instinct that would see you dead before they came to any harm. Evan, he tried to make out that Nick had hurt her but instinctively I would've known if that were true, and it wasn't – none of it. And it killed him, Detective, completely destroyed him on every level. Even if he'd lived—' She paused, took a deep breath. 'He would've carried those mental scars with him forever. It broke him, what Evan did. And it broke Lily too. He used his own daughter…'

'I know what Evan did, Beth, what he *was* doing. And I know that Catherine Patterson lost her child in the most brutal way too…'

She stares blankly, but it's there in her eyes, the gentlest flicker of recognition at the mention of her name, her body betraying her.

'I don't know anyone called Catherine Patterson.'

I smile at her again, drop my head a little. 'It was good, Beth. Really good. You know, no disrespect to your profession but you were wasted as a nurse.' I sip my bourbon, the oaky smoothness of the liquor easing a little tension at the back of my throat. 'You very nearly pulled it off. You're a clever woman.'

'I'm just a mother,' she says. 'A heartbroken one.' But I sense she's dropped the façade a little. I can hear it in her cadence.

She stands from the table, goes to fetch the bottle of JD. I don't object.

'Tell me how you and Catherine Patterson met?'

She says nothing for a moment and the air hangs heavy and oppressive above us, like impending rain.

She pours herself another measure into the fat tumbler on the table, the neck of the bottle chiming with the glass, almost like it's signalling the end of something.

'I should never have married him, you know,' she says quietly. 'I knew it was a mistake, knew I was doing the wrong thing, for all the wrong reasons and yet I still… I thought, naïvely, back then, that it didn't matter if I didn't really love him. I wasn't even sure what love was, not then. I just thought that it would be enough, you know?' She looks at me briefly almost for affirmation. 'A nice husband, a nice house, a beautiful child… It worked for past generations, didn't it? Marriages of convenience, people sticking together for the sake of appearances, for the kids.'

'Yes, and no doubt they were deeply unhappy too,' I say. 'Those were different times, Beth. How did you meet Catherine Patterson?'

'I really didn't know who Evan was,' she continues, ignoring my question. 'Probably because I never took the time to find out, to dig deeper. I never asked the right questions – don't think I asked him any, in fact. I just took him completely on face value because the truth is, I just wasn't that interested, Detective – not really. If only I had been,' she berates herself. 'I married a stranger, a man I never knew. And this – this is what it led to.' She pauses briefly. 'Do you think I'm stupid?'

'On the contrary, Beth,' I reply. 'I think you're quite remarkable.'

She seems pleased with this comment though not arrogantly so, more like welcome recognition. She lights a cigarette, takes a deep pull on it.

'Do you know, I never even knew Evan smoked,' she says eventually. 'Made no bones about what a disgusting habit he thought it was, and yet when I—'

'When you what, Beth?'

She filters herself, stops short. And turns towards me. 'Are you going to arrest me?'

She sounds almost childlike as she says it, causing me to exhale some of my regret.

'Yes, I am. How did you and Catherine Patterson meet? Are you related somehow? Is she your sister – twin sister?'

Beth's head wobbles and she pinches her nose as though the words are about to come from her nostrils. 'I've told you I don't know anyone by that name.'

She's not budging, not yet.

'The CCTV at the train station. Aside from the fact it would be impossible to be on two platforms at once, you were holding the coffee cup in your right hand. And just now, you signed this document' – I hold it up briefly – 'with your right hand.'

'Of course,' she says., 'I'm right-handed.'

I nod. 'But Catherine Patterson was holding her coffee cup in her *left* hand, just like she held the pen in her left hand when she signed for the groceries at your front door on the day of Evan's murder when she was pretending to be you.'

I look at her and the light seems to have dimmed in her eyes.

'She is left-handed, Beth…' I say this apologetically because I am sorry – in a way I really am. 'You didn't think to ask her, did you? And she didn't think to tell you.'

She snorts through her nose softly and drops her head slightly but doesn't speak.

'I have to say though, the alibi you gave her in return was inspired. What better than being in police custody at the time of a murder… and spelling Catherine's name with a K was sublime. We didn't find you at first… didn't link it. But I'm sure once we take your fingerprints, and Catherine's, it will become clear, because they will be your dabs on the system, won't they, Beth? She helped you, and you helped her. Two women doing the ultimate service for each other, emancipating themselves from men who had destroyed them. It'll be taken into consideration at the trials. Everything will come out, Beth – I'll make sure of it.'

She sits down again now and I lean in towards her across the table, seize her hands in my own. They feel small and clammy, the tips of her fingers cold from the glass. My phone is buzzing again; Woods must be desperate.

'They'll know about the conspiracy, about Nick being set up. We'll have the body exhumed and looked at again and if it transpires that there's any sign of foul play then I will bring the culprits to justice; these men who covered up for your husband, the very ones that should've helped you – we'll expose them, all of them and their dirty secrets. We'll bring them down together.'

'Will we?' She shakes her head, disbelieving. 'I don't think so, Detective.'

'Catherine was let down by the system just as much as you were, Beth. Domestic violence… the baby… the jury might even let her off after they hear the catalogue of abuse she endured.'

'I don't want her involved, Detective.' She sits up straight now, adopts a more businesslike demeanour. 'I'll tell you everything if you leave her out of this.'

I can't make this promise to her, and I think she knows it. 'I'll do whatever I can, Beth. I can promise you that much.'

She sighs, shuts her eyes tightly and vigorously rubs her hair with both hands. I say nothing, wait for her to speak.

'We met purely by chance,' she says eventually. 'Although I'd prefer to call it fate. I was on my way to Bristol, to visit Joyce, Nick's mum, not long after he… well, anyway, the resemblance between us—' She shakes her head, laughs a little, as though she still can't quite believe it herself. 'It was incredible really. I mean, have you ever met your doppelganger, Detective?'

'Luckily for both of us, no I haven't.'

'Well, let me tell you, it was the strangest feeling… seeing her there, sitting on that train, it was as if I was looking into a mirror, like meeting myself. It was so bizarre that at first I thought we had to be related, that I might even have a sister I never know about… so, so bizarre… Instinctively I knew there had to be a reason for such an encounter, a message… something. I mean, it's not every day of your life you meet a complete stranger on a train could easily pass as your double, is it? These things, they don't just happen by chance, do they?'

I shake my head. 'I don't know, Beth. Perhaps not.'

'Well, I believed she had been sent to me, that we had somehow been sent to each other, predestined to meet, some kind of higher power at play. I thought,' she says, looking away as though slightly embarrassed, 'I thought that maybe... after my mum died, oh, I don't know, it sounds ridiculous, but I thought that somehow she had something to do with it, had sent her to me as a lifeline...' She lowers her eyes. 'You think I'm mad, don't you?'

I shake my head. 'No. No, I don't.'

'Anyway,' she says, snapping back to the present, 'it was all my idea. I came up with everything – the plan, the details. I was the governing force behind it all. Cath simply did what I said because she's used to doing that. I coerced her into it, used her. It was all me. Please, Detective, don't go after her. I'll give you what you want. Leave Cath out of all of this. She has suffered so much already.'

Her desperate pleas resonate but I won't make promises I know I can't keep.

'Do you know where she is?'

'Gone,' she says quickly. 'And I have no idea where. I gave her the means to disappear, to start over again. She deserves that, Detective. I hope I never see her again.'

'Talk me through the day of the murder, Beth... tell me what happened.'

I'm coaxing her gently into a confession, trying to make it feel like she isn't really confessing at all.

She goes silent for a moment, looks into her glass before eventually picking it up and finishing it. 'She's buried underneath the swimming pool,' she says, audibly swallowing the contents back. 'There, outside, beneath the concrete.'

'Who is?' I turn to look outside.

'Marta. Our housekeeper, the one who went missing, the day this whole thing started.'

Instinctively I go to the window, look out into the garden, at the swimming pool at the end.

'He confessed, didn't he?' I say. 'Before you killed him, he told you she was there. And he knew, didn't he, Beth, that by telling you, you would have to live with that knowledge, the knowledge he'd killed her and buried her there, that if you told anyone it would incriminate you – that you might even be accused of her murder…' I'm pacing the kitchen now in disbelief. 'Good God…'

She says nothing for a moment and her silence speaks volumes.

'What will happen to Lily?' She looks at me from across the room, her eyes windows to the worst pain I think I've ever witnessed in my life, and I have to look away. 'She has no one left. Will she go into care?'

She breaks down then and I go to her, comfort her. She feels tiny in my arms; broken like a china doll, and I know that even with all the glue in the world to stick her back together, she will never again be the same.

CHAPTER FORTY-SIX

Dan

October 2019

'Beth Lawler,' I say as I hold her tightly, 'I'm arresting you for the murder of Evan Lawler. You do not have to say anything, but anything you do say…'

I cuff her because I have to rather than want to and she doesn't object. Beth Lawler is a prisoner once more.

She's largely silent on the journey back to the station and I know that what she told me off the record in the kitchen is probably as much as I'm going to get from her, for now at least.

'I want my daughter to go and live with Joyce Wainwright while I'm gone.' Her voice is a monotone, void of any real emotion. I can almost see her setting like concrete next to me. 'I discussed it with her, when I went to visit. She said she would take care of her if ever anything happened to me.' She turns sideways to look at me and I glance back, taking my eyes off the road for a second. 'With my mum gone, there's no one else – she has no other family. Will you arrange that, Detective? Will you make sure that happens and that she's not slung into some awful care home someplace where the word "care" is nothing but a misnomer. I couldn't bear that. It's bad enough that she'll have to know what I've done, that her mother is a—'

'I'll do everything I can,' I say, trying not to picture the scene where Lily learns that her mother has killed her father and is going away. I grapple with my rising anger. Why is it that children always suffer the most for the mistakes of their fathers and mothers? At six years old, Lily Evans has seen it all: messy divorce, death, murder and deceit. She will grow up knowing that her father was a murderer who used her as a weapon to destroy another man's life, to seek revenge on her mother until it drove her to kill him, making her a murderer in the process. I can't even imagine the amount of therapy that little girl will no doubt need as a result of such a mess – a lifetime's probably. It makes me yearn for simplicity, for an easy, uneventful life. It makes me yearn for the impossible.

There's a strange kind of stillness back at the nick as I book Beth Lawler in, the sort of feeling you get when you wake up and look out of your window to see everything covered in a fresh blanket of snow – only without the excitement. There's nothing exciting about arresting a young, damaged woman for the murder of her murdering husband and subsequently making their daughter an orphan – or as good as.

And that's not all that's on my mind. I know that in arresting her I've opened a can of worms, a whole factory in fact. And I have no idea how this will impact on me, on Davis, on Woods, on my career… There's every conceivable chance that Beth Lawler will blow the whistle on 'The List', but if she doesn't then I might just have to. My integrity won't allow me not to. But when I get to my desk, I find that it's gone, disappeared. Someone's taken it. I scrabble around for Marion Adams' phone number, the madam at Angels and Demons, though I suspect it's more of the latter.

'The number you have dialled has not been recognised…'

Shit! I go to boot up my computer and suddenly Davis crashes into the room. She's pink in the face, like she's just been for a jog.

'She's in the cells,' I say. 'And some bastard has stolen the list. Delaney no doubt, Woods' little bitch,' I say bitterly. 'I suppose he's been in here, asking for me and…'

'Gov, I've been trying to get you on the phone… you haven't been picking up…' She's breathless, struggling to get the words out. 'It's Fiona… she's in labour. You've got to get down there now, boss… The baby… it's coming!'

CHAPTER FORTY-SEVEN

Dan

October 2019

'God help me, Riley, you bastard…'

These are Fiona's first words to me as I burst into the hospital room, a sweaty, mess of a nervous wreck.

'Is green my colour?' I say, motioning to the scrubs in a pathetic attempt at humour.

'You said you'd be here. You promised me, you fucking bastard!'

'Push, Fiona!' the midwife says. 'Just a few more.'

'But I didn't think it was time… a couple more weeks you said…'

The midwife laughs at me like there's a village somewhere missing an idiot. 'It's not an exact science, I'm afraid,' she says. 'They come when they come!'

Fi's screaming, her face crumpled like paper in pain and she thrashes about. I rush to the bedside, hold her hand.

'I *am* here, Fi,' I say, seriously this time. 'I'm going nowhere.'

'Oh God, Dan, it hurts… I'd forgotten how much it… huuuuuurtsss!' She grits her teeth and makes noises that don't sound human.

Anna-Lou Weatherley

'They design it that way.' The midwife smiles at her pitifully. 'You're almost there, Fiona…'

'I can't do it… I can't…'

'You can,' I say, desperately trying to remember what it had said to say in the pregnancy books I'd seen lying around the flat. 'You can do anything. You're Fiona Li; journalist extraordinaire, the nosiest cow this side of the river… and you make a mean chow mein and… try not to tear your perineum.'

'Shut up!' she screams, her body jerking forward. 'Just shut up, you idiot…'

'That's it, Fiona!' the midwife is almost screaming herself. 'We can see the head… That's it, love, another big push… Come here, Dad,' she says. 'Watch your son or daughter be born.'

I swallow dryly, not an ounce of saliva in my mouth, my lips sticking to my teeth like I've been chewing a Bostik. This was the bit I was dreading, but I do as I'm told. I'm outnumbered. *And I'd made a silent promise to my unborn child.*

Fiona lets out a piercing noise that could shatter glass at a hundred paces and suddenly, in a split second, they're here. A tiny person, covered in blood and white stuff that looks like cottage cheese, purple with anger, screaming as they gasp for air, taking their first breath in this godforsaken life. Then it seems all hell breaks loose as they begin wiping and cleaning and fussing as I stand in shock.

'It's a girl!' the midwife says, turning to me. 'Congratulations – you have a daughter!' They take my daughter and begin to clean her up, wrap her in a receiving blanket and place her in Fiona's arms. I think I'm crying as I crouch down on the bed next to her; something else I said I wouldn't do.

'You nearly didn't bloody make it, Dan Riley,' she says, unable to take her eyes from our girl. *Our girl.* We have a girl!

'But I did,' I say. 'I made a promise.'

'Hold her,' she says, handing her to me. 'She's yours.'

She places her in my shaking arms and I feel it instantly, the moment my eyes meet her face. Beth Lawler had been right – until now I couldn't possibly have known what she had truly meant. But I feel it move through me like an entity, that rush – that unexplainable, potent rush that people talk about, the purest love you will ever feel. *A daughter.*

I study her tiny face – her eyes screwed shut, like she doesn't want to open them and realise where she is; her teeny nose, perfect rosebud lips, and her soft tuft of dark, dark hair, like her mother's. She snuffles in my arms, the scent of her purity and newness permeating my nostrils, filling them with love. And I vow to spend my whole life protecting her, keeping her safe from harm, safe from all the madness and the craziness and the badness.

'She's beautiful, Fi,' I say, laughing and crying at the same time. 'She's just so… so perfect.'

Fiona looks pale and exhausted and I kiss the top of her head.

'What are you going to call her?' the midwife asks. 'You have a name?'

'No… we…'

'Juno,' Fiona says. 'Juno Rachel Riley.' She looks up at me. 'That's OK, isn't it?' she says. 'We called her Junior throughout the pregnancy and so I thought Junior for a boy, and Juno for a girl… and,' she says, 'Rachel… for… well, for Rachel.'

The lump in my throat is like broken glass and I cannot see through the blurred tears.

'I love you, Fi.' There, I said it. 'Thank you.'

CHAPTER FORTY-EIGHT

Beth

February 2020

The iron door slams shut behind her and she hears the latch deadlock. It's a unique sound that she has not got used to during the past few weeks she's been a resident at HMP Longcroft – nor ever wants to.

She sits down on her stiff bunk and looks at the cream envelope, holds it between her fingers, runs them over the smooth surface and sharp edges. The paper looks – and feels – expensive, embossed, not your common or garden envelope you picked up at the corner shop, and this gives her a little frisson. She knows what it is. *And who it's from.*

'Got a letter, Beth?' Her new cellmate, Helen – a likeable but troubled young woman with a bad childhood and a worse temper as a result – stirs awake from the bunk above and pops her head over the rail.

'Is it from your girl? When's she coming to see you next? Did she have a nice Christmas? God, I love Christmas me, do you? Not in here though. It was shite, weren't it? Cold meat and lumpy gravy… tinsel older than me nan…' She lies back down on the bunk. 'What were your family Christmases like? Bet they were a bit special, eh? In that big house of yours… Did you used to do it all up, lights outside… those icicle ones that look like they're melting? And up round the bannisters, like ivy, all wrapped around… Ahh, lovely. In our house…'

Beth tunes her out. She's learned how. Needs must. Helen is young, and thankfully quite easy company. But she asks a lot of questions. No bad thing, Beth thinks. In hindsight, she only wished she'd asked more questions herself.

Six years – that's what he'd given her, the judge. Six years for manslaughter on the grounds of diminished responsibility. She knew it was a 'result' as they called it inside, and she also knew why.

Mercifully, she had been spared the ordeal of a trial, proving to her that it was less of 'it's not what you know but who you know' and more of 'it's what you know and who it's about'. They had accepted her plea of diminished responsibility, citing the death of her mother, the death of her lover and the estrangement from her daughter as grounds of her mental instability. In sentencing her, the judge had been more than lenient. Then again, he'd also been on the list.

The detective, Dan Riley, the one whose eyes had reminded her of Nick's, had been good to his word. They'd dug up the swimming pool at the house, discovered poor Marta's remains underneath, in the concrete foundations, just like Evan had said. Beth had cried when the news had reached her. Part of her had clung to the hope that Evan had been lying about how Marta met her end, saying he'd killed her just to scare her. At least now she would have a proper burial, one she was deserving of.

Evan had arrogantly believed right up until she'd shot him dead that he would get away with Marta's murder, and make her the fall guy in the process, and he'd secured a network of protection around him to make sure of it. But his arrogance had been his downfall in the end.

Marta's concrete coffin had helped to slow down the decaying process, leaving forensics much more to work with, and when it revealed she had probably, though inconclusively, been sexually abused before her death, those 'associates' of his had panicked and lifted the lid on Evan, so to speak.

He'd been exposed and vilified as a murdering, sexually depraved, vindictive control freak, hung out to dry by the very people whose help he had enlisted to assist in covering his tracks. The people he had used as a cloak of respectability had distanced themselves entirely, many of them giving interviews to the press feigning their 'total shock' of how their 'mild-mannered', 'amenable' and 'thoroughly likeable' friend had hidden such dark and ugly secrets and was capable of such evil. In a bid to keep their own dirty secrets from scrutiny – and therefore any accountability – they had thrown him under the bus – and reversed back over him a few times for good measure. After all, the dead can't object, can they?

The best part? The press interest in her case had been voracious and she had been able to speak the truth about Nick – how Evan had vindictively set out to destroy him, destroy his reputation and label him a monster; she had been able to tell them how Evan had used his own daughter as a vehicle with which to execute his revenge and the damage it had caused as a result, how her mother had dropped dead, how Nick had ended up dead too and she had ended up in a prison cell. In coming almost clean, she had become something of an anti-hero – at least that's what the hundreds of women who wrote to her after reading her story told her. Beth Lawler wasn't stupid. Not anymore.

Helen is still talking, something about Quality Street and green triangles or something, although it's more like white noise now as she rubs the cream embossed paper between her fingers once more. Cath.

In her mind Beth re-enacted the journey she had made on the 3.15 p.m. to Bristol that day when she had met Cath. She thought about chance, even though she was convinced it had been nothing of the sort. You don't meet your doppelganger for no reason.

Two and a half years she has in here at most. That's bearable, isn't it? The alternative would have been much more of a life sentence. Lily would be coming on for ten years old by the time she came out, her whole life ahead of her – the rest of their lives together. She was safe and happy now, with Joyce, another promise Dan Riley had kept. He'd made sure her baby had not been lost in the care system and placed with Nick's mum instead. Joyce had brought Lily for painfully anticipated visits and they had decided together that they would tell her the truth when they felt she was emotionally ready, if anyone ever could be. It was painful beyond comprehension to see her daughter, moreover to say goodbye, but those visits, they gave her strength, and whenever she faltered, broke down and wanted to tear every hair from her head, she thought of Cath instead.

Beth had never spoken about Cath, had never uttered her name or existence to anyone but Riley – and certainly not to the press. Riley had come good on that too and hadn't gone after Cath. Or at least she didn't think he had. He was a man of integrity after all. And integrity meant doing the right thing, even if somehow it made it the wrong thing at the same time.

Beth stares at the envelope for a little longer before she carefully turns it over, picking at the edges of the flap with her fingernails.

Gently, she peels it open, hoping to keep it intact. She wants to save it, *to savour it.* Her breathing is shallow and laboured as she slides the card inside upwards. It is a postcard with no picture, with just three words written in black ink on the back. She smiles as she reads them, relief and happiness washing through her:

'A fait accompli.'

EPILOGUE

Dan

February 2020

Juno is gurgling and cooing in her Moses basket next to me on the sofa. I look over at her and grin, pull a face. She stares at me with her big brown eyes, grips her toes with her tiny fingers – remarkably strong for their size – and pulls them up into her mouth, rolling to the side. She's smiling now, and I'm thinking it's not just wind like Fi tells me it is because she does it every time I show her Teddy, a pink fluffy thing with goggly eyes. She loves Teddy. I watch her as she contentedly eats her toes, making noises that bring me a strange new sense of happiness I never knew existed. I could watch her for hours. Stare at her all day. Sometimes I still can't believe she's really mine and that I made her. That Fiona and I made something so beautiful and perfect. But we did. We really did. I know that Rachel, wherever she is, would be proud of me. Of us all.

I'm on babysitting duty today while Fiona is working. She's been itching to get back to the *Gazette* now that she's done all the hard work of growing a small person and pushing her into the world. It's the least I can do.

So I've taken a couple of weeks off to be with my girl. Woods had been right about one thing – since Juno everything has changed. I look down at the piece of paper in front of me and read through the names once more. Davis, God bless her, had the foresight to make a copy of it before it went missing from my desk. It's why she's going to someday make a fantastic DI. Good old Davis. I knew I could rely on her. She's one of life's good eggs. The best even.

Beth Lawler got six years in the end. She'll be out in less than three. She spared herself the ordeal of a trial by pleading guilty on the grounds of diminished responsibility. It was a farce really because I've never known a murder so well planned and executed – certainly nothing diminished about it. She got a light sentence because she had an insurance policy, just like the one I'm looking at now. Do I think it's right that the judge was so lenient, that he bought her silence? No. I don't. But I can't say I'm not glad she's not going to spend the rest of her life behind bars and that she will soon be back with Lily again, where she belongs. A little girl needs her mother. And her father. I look at Juno next to me and can't comprehend how any father would ever want to cause their daughter any harm. It's not natural. But I guess not everyone thinks as I do. Evan Lawler certainly didn't – and look where he is now.

The Lawler case has stayed with me, lingered on my mind. I know I could've done what Woods asked and let it go, let Beth Lawler walk. Part of me wanted to, after all that had happened to her, but I couldn't do it. I did, however, do what Beth asked me to. I made sure her girl went to live with Joyce Wainwright and I didn't go after Cath Patterson. Some people, they've already paid enough. As it stands, Woods came out of it all quite well too. The list had disappeared from my desk and with it any evidence of his little boys' club, or so he thought. Scandal averted, he could now bow out gracefully – and he did. He retired soon after the case. I went to his leaving bash – thought I owed him that much at least.

'I never thought I'd ever say this, Riley,' he'd said to me, a little glassy-eyed with whiskey and emotion. 'But I actually think I'm going to miss you.'

'The feeling is entirely unmutual, sir,' I'd replied with a wry smile. But I think we both knew I didn't mean it, not really.

'Listen, Dan…' He'd moved in a little closer to my ear, dropped his tone down to clandestine. 'What you did, well, rather what you didn't do I suppose… it saved a lot of important people from a lot of… how can I put it… *embarrassment*. The names on that list… put it this way, I know they'll look favourably on you for keeping shtum. Destroying it will have stood you in very good stead.'

'What list, sir?' I'd said.

'That's a boy, Riley.' He'd slapped me on the back, toasted my glass. 'It's the right thing to do.'

Now, I pick up the list and fold it up, placing it inside the envelope.

'Shall we send this to Mummy, Peanut?' I say to her and she burps, spitting up a little of her milk. 'I will take that as a resounding yes,' I say.

Dear Miss Li,
    A riddle for you: What have Nick Wainwright and Angels and Demons got in common?
    All my best. X

I disguise my handwriting; she won't know it's from me. But I know Fiona – she will get to the bottom of that list. She will make the connection and she will blow the lid. And with a bit of luck, it will make her career in the process.

I bundle Juno up in her snowsuit – it's cold outside – and put her in her pram.

'Daddy's got to post an important letter,' I tell her as we make our way down the street. 'One that's going to upset a lot of people.'

We stop at the postbox with me still giving my daughter a running commentary, and I slide it inside, Woods' words echoing in my mind.

'That's a boy, Riley. It's the right thing to do.'

A LETTER FROM ANNA-LOU

Dearest Reader,

Thank you so very much for choosing *The Stranger's Wife* as the latest title in your reading list. This book was personally an important one for me to write. As well as developing Dan's character and story (I do hope you like him as much as I do), I wanted to focus, among other things, on the issue of domestic abuse (both physical and psychological) and how it can transcend all walks of life, class and gender.

If you want to keep up to date on my new releases, or view my past ones, just click the link below to sign up for my special newsletter.

www.bookouture.com/anna-lou-weatherley

You'll need to give your email but I will never share it with anyone and only contact you when I have a new release, promise.

I'd love to know what you thought of Beth and Cath's respective stories and characters and if you felt that, while they were contrasting in many ways, they were also similar in others. Over the years I have read about and experienced many women's (and men's) stories of both overt and covert domestic abuse, both physical and emotional, and the damage it can cause. As a subject close to my heart, I felt I needed to explore it in it's different (but no less equally damaging) forms. I am genuinely heartened that the government has now seen fit to criminalise abusive behaviour such as coercive control – long overdue in my opinion.

Did you like how Cath and Beth met? The idea of this, in fact, came from something I had read about someone who'd experienced the exact same thing (although she didn't murder anyone, I should add!). I've yet to meet my own, but I'd love to hear from anyone else who has ever met theirs and how they felt!

Revenge – particularly in divorce – is also another issue I felt important to cover, namely how (sadly) children can often be used as leverage and pawns between their warring parents. I hope I have touched upon these important subjects with understanding, empathy and compassion.

Your comments, feedback and reviews mean absolutely everything to me as an author, so I'd be delighted to know what you thought of *The Stranger's Wife*. If you enjoyed it, it would mean a lot to me if you would take the time to 'share the love' and leave a review letting me, and other readers, know why.

I often read titles by recommendation from friends and family and vice versa, so if your review encourages others to read one of my novels and enjoy them too then I cannot thank you enough.

Detective Dan Riley and the gang's work is never done, so watch this space. Until then…

Much love,
Anna-Lou x

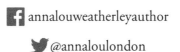

annalouweatherleyauthor

@annaloulondon

ACKNOWLEDGEMENTS

As always, I have so many people I would like to thank. Like a supporting cast, this book would not have been written without your inspiration, knowledge, love, support and encouragement. My family are – and always have been – my biggest champions and an essential source of support to me when I write, my mummy in particular, for all her wisdom, her ideas (which I sometimes pinch) and her rock-solid faith in me whenever I have a little wobble. If only I'd known as a teenager how you are always right!

My beautiful sister, Lisa-Jane, is a huge inspiration to me as a person. I'm in awe of her strength, kindness and resilience – and stylishness! The conversations we have always give me so many ideas for developing my characters and their emotions. I hope one day we can brainstorm together on Nikki Beach!

My boys, Lou and Flick, who inadvertently do the same and who I hope that when they're older will understand that it is largely for them that 'Mum is always glued to her flippin' laptop.'

Thanks also to Liz and Colin, Kelly, and a special mention to Ann-Marie and Vince.

My darling David, where to begin? Without you this book wouldn't have been written – or it certainly wouldn't have been as much of a joy to write. Being with you has changed so much for the better, and your belief in me and support on so many levels makes me believe that anything is possible. I'm so glad I got to write this in your spot on the 90-degree angle of chaos within the three floors of carnage. Thank you. You are my best friend, my love, my everything, and I love you to the moon and back. Next stop: the Del Duque!

I'd also like to thank my agent, Madeleine Milburn, and everyone at the Madeline Milburn Literary Agency. Thanks also to the ridiculously lovely Kim Nash (Mama Bear), Noelle Holten, Peta Nightingale, Oliver Rhodes – to everyone on the incredibly hard-working Bookouture team. It's such a privilege to be part of such a brilliant family.

Lastly, I want to express my heartfelt and deepest thanks to Claire Bord, my truly amazing editor and publisher at the phenomenal Bookouture. Your incredible support, guidance, advice, unwavering faith, knowledge, suggestions and friendship – I love our conversations – is absolutely invaluable to me and has helped me to become a better, happier and more confident writer over all the years we have worked together – and I hope the many more to come. You can't know just how much I value you both professionally and personally, so this one is for you.